Flashback

The Erin O'Reilly Mysteries
Book Nine

Steven Henry

Clickworks Press • Baltimore, MD

First publication: Clickworks Press, 2020
Release: CP-EOR9-INT-P.IS-1.0

Ebook ISBN: 1-943383-67-2
Paperback ISBN: 978-1-943383-68-9
Hardcover ISBN: 1-943383-69-6

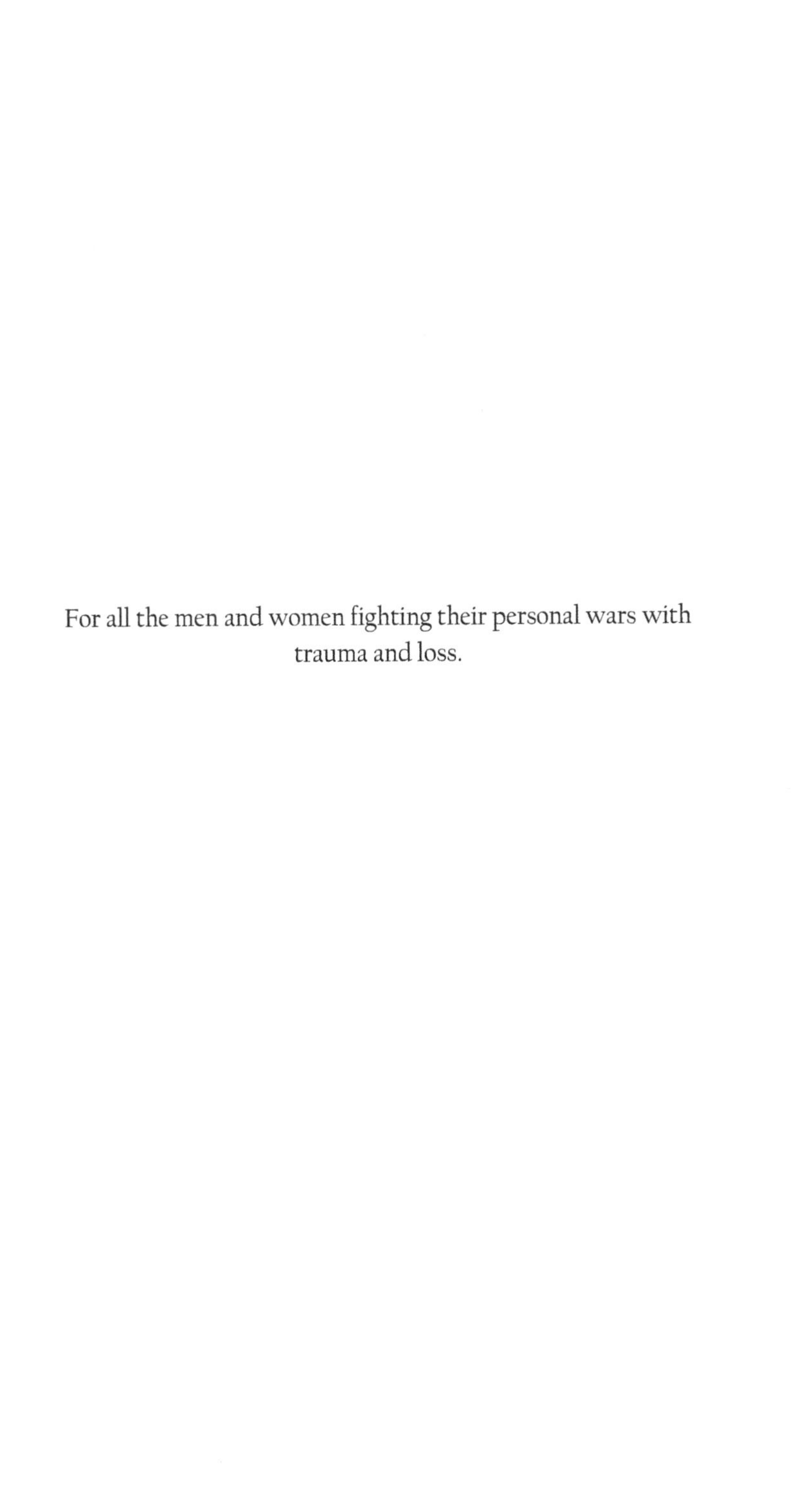

For all the men and women fighting their personal wars with trauma and loss.

We've got a bonus story for you!

We're so grateful for the love and support you've shown for Erin and Rolf. As a special thank you, we want to give you a free bonus story starring Ian Thompson, Carlyle's bodyguard.

Keep reading after Flashback to enjoy

Dehydration

An Ian Thompson Story

Ian doesn't like to talk about his time in the military. *Dehydration* is the story Ian doesn't tell.

Flashback

Pour 1 oz. ginger ale, 5 oz. Gatorade energy drink, 3 oz. vodka into a collins glass filled with ice cubes. Stir and serve.

Chapter 1

Erin reflexively punched her radio. "Dispatch! 10-13, shots fired, Brighton Beach Avenue and Seventh!" She rattled off the words as she tried to push the Charger's accelerator through the floor. She could see muzzle flashes in the dark under the train tracks.

"Erin!" Kira said, her voice pitched a little higher than usual.

"Not right now," Erin growled.

"Erin, I don't have my vest!"

Erin wasn't wearing hers, either. She hadn't taken the time to get it out before they started driving. Rolf, of course, wasn't wearing his. They'd been relaxing after work, for Christ's sake, not gearing up for World War III.

At least three shooters, large muzzle flashes. Those weren't handguns. They were using assault rifles.

"Get the rifle," Erin snapped at Kira. The bad guys were still shooting. Maybe Vic was still alive.

Then they were on scene and there was no more time to think. Everything was action, training, and reflexes.

Erin stood up on the brakes, bringing the Charger squealing to a stop. She hadn't turned off the flashers. Even as she reached for the buckle on her seatbelt and opened her door, she saw a flash of gunfire to her front. In a strange slow-motion daze, she saw a ragged line of bullet holes chew their way diagonally across her windshield. The first three tore through the car between the seats. The fourth, fifth, and sixth slammed into Kira's chest, slamming her back against the passenger seat. The woman slumped against her shoulder belt, eyes wide and staring.

Erin tried to scream, but no sound came out of her mouth. Then she had her door open. She slid sideways onto the asphalt, keeping the door panel between her and the shooter. It might stop a pistol round, but she knew an assault rifle would punch right through.

Another gunman zeroed in on the car. A burst of bullets tore into the front grille. The headlights shattered and went dark. Now the only light came from the blue-and-reds and the muzzle flashes of the guns. Broken moments of the scene burst across her eyes in lurid red and blue, like strobe lights in a disco from Hell.

Erin thrust her pistol just over the doorframe of the car and fired again and again. She had no idea if she'd hit anyone. Rolf, trapped in his compartment, was barking his head off.

Rolf. Erin reached behind her for the release on his compartment. She just turned him loose and hoped for the best.

The K-9 was out of the car so fast she hardly saw him move. The dark-pattern German Shepherd streaked forward, low and hard, toward the closest gunman. Erin let off four more shots over him. Somewhere to her left, somebody fired a pistol. She saw Vic, blood all over his face, stumble toward her. He fell to his knees, then collapsed on his face, unmoving.

Ahead, in the dark, an assault rifle rattled off a long burst. Rolf's snarl cut off in a strangled whimper.

* * *

Erin O'Reilly jerked awake, gasping for breath. She opened

her eyes and saw the dim, shadowy shapes of a bedroom that wasn't hers. The light was faint, the early morning blue that came just before sunrise. She groped instinctively for her gun on the nightstand.

It wasn't there.

Adrenaline burned through her like a heroin junkie's fix. She was wide awake, completely alert to every sound.

The man beside her stirred slightly but didn't wake. She remembered where she was, then, and let out a long breath.

The gunfight hadn't happened like that. Vic had been wounded, but not badly. Kira and Rolf hadn't been scratched. They'd gotten the bad guys, killed a couple and taken the rest in. They'd won.

But it could so easily have gone the other way. A couple of bullets a few inches to either side and none of them would have made it out.

There was no chance of getting back to sleep. Erin wondered whether she should wake up her sleeping companion. He'd want to know she'd had a nightmare. He'd hold her and take care of her.

Erin didn't want to be that woman. Her whole life she'd been tough and self-reliant. She wasn't about to start dissolving in tears into the arms of whatever man was handy. No way.

She eased out from under the blanket. Her boyfriend didn't stir. But Rolf was more attentive. The Shepherd had been sleeping at the foot of the bed. Now he was up on his paws, tail wagging.

Erin dressed in the dark, slowly and quietly, sweatpants and an NYPD sweatshirt. She pulled her hair back into a ponytail. Then she went out to the patio door and pulled on her sneakers. She clipped Rolf's leash to his collar and opened the sliding door. The eastern sky had turned pink. The sun would be coming up soon.

The house was in Water Mill, which she'd heard was the second most expensive village in the Hamptons. It had probably cost something like three million dollars. But it hadn't been her money. The house was nice enough, but most of the cost had gone to pay for the waterfront location. She crossed the well-kept grassy lawn down to the beach.

She ran. Rolf ran at her side in an easy, loping motion. She ran as if she could outrun the nightmare. The damp sand flew up behind her feet. She ran, hoping to find some peace of mind. The cold March air burned in her throat. She welcomed the burn, embraced it. She ran until her legs ached and her racing heart steadied into the hard, firm pounding that came with good exercise. Then, with her brain finally cleared, she came back to the house on the beach and stopped. Rolf was panting a little, but didn't even look tired.

Erin stood on the shore of Mecox Bay, looking out over the water, and just breathed. She tasted salt spray on the air and smelled the fresh sea breeze. For the first time in what seemed like years, she felt clean. No gasoline fumes, no smells of gunpowder or blood, none of the noise and confusion of downtown Manhattan. Why had that nightmare chosen now to come calling?

At her side, Rolf sniffed the air. He opened his mouth and let his tongue hang out in an unmistakable broad grin. The wind ruffled his hair. He looked at the water, then back at Erin.

"It's colder than it looks," she warned him. It was the off season in the Hamptons. Mecox Bay might be sheltered from storms, but it was still part of the North Atlantic.

Rolf thought the water looked fine.

"Seriously, kiddo," she said. "It's forty degrees. You'll be sorry."

Rolf nudged Erin's hand with his snout and wagged his tail. The German Shepherd wasn't going to take no for an answer.

"Okay, boy. You asked for it." It wouldn't hurt to give him a little training, even if they were supposed to be on vacation. Erin stooped for a piece of driftwood, cocked her arm, and hurled it into the water. She called the command in Rolf's native German, which in this case happened to be pretty much the same as it would be in English.

"Bring!"

Rolf exploded into motion, his powerful legs launching him through the air. He hit the water with an almighty splash. Paws churning, he forced his way to the floating piece of wood, snatched it in his jaws, and turned around, paddling back into shallow water.

"I believe that's entrapment, darling," said a voice behind her, speaking with a thick Belfast brogue.

"What're you talking about, Carlyle?" she retorted. She didn't turn, continuing to watch her K-9.

She felt Morton Carlyle come up behind her, slipping his arms around her waist. He kissed her cheek just below the ear, a gentle kiss that almost tickled. It was a spot only he knew about, one that never failed to send little tingles down her spine.

"You tell a lad he's doing something unwise, then get him to do it anyway?" he said. "Sounds to me like you're leading the poor lad astray."

Rolf scrambled up the embankment and dropped the stick triumphantly at Erin's feet. He didn't look the least bit cold. Tongue lolling, he braced his shoulders.

"Oh, no," Erin managed to say just before the dog vigorously shook himself, showering cold water onto his partner. Trapped in Carlyle's arms, she had no escape. She had to just stand and take what was coming to her. She couldn't help laughing, despite the icy water dripping down her face.

"I didn't mean to wake you," she said.

"Don't fret, darling. I find I'm a bit of a light sleeper these days myself. And there's no shame in wanting to see the sunrise. It's lovely here, aye? You're happy?"

"Yeah." She felt a twinge of guilt for letting him think something that wasn't quite true, but she told herself that wasn't the same as lying to him. God knew he'd told her enough half-truths of his own. And it really was a beautiful morning. The rising sun painted the eastern horizon in glorious shades of pink, red, and gold. Rolf ran down the beach and flung himself into the water again, oblivious to the cold.

Life wasn't perfect. Erin knew that better than most. But right here, right now, was about as good as it was likely to get. Why borrow trouble over a few bad dreams? None of the really bad stuff had happened. They'd won. That was what mattered.

Chapter 2

"I'm not very good at vacations," Erin admitted.

Carlyle smiled. "Are you telling me you didn't enjoy it? None of it?"

They were in Carlyle's car, on the way back to Manhattan from the Hamptons. He was letting her drive, for several reasons. First, he usually had his driver Ian to take him places, so he was out of practice. Second, Erin was accustomed to driving, and always felt a little twitchy when she wasn't the one behind the wheel. Third, his car was a brand-new Mercedes, and Erin wasn't about to pass up a chance to try one of those on the road. Finally, he'd grown up in Northern Ireland, and said he'd never gotten used to driving on what he called the wrong side of the road.

Erin returned his smile. "No, it was fun. Really. All of it. I think maybe I've forgotten how to relax. Or maybe I never learned it."

"When's the last time you took a trip that wasn't to see your family?"

She had to think about that. "I guess I'd have to say never. You?"

"Well, darling, as you know, I'm not precisely on the best of terms with my relations, so one could say my whole life's been one long vacation from them."

"It doesn't count as a vacation if you're working."

"That's a fair point. But I suppose the main question isn't whether you're good at it, but whether it's done you any good. Are you ready to go back?"

They'd been in the Hamptons for a week, by far the longest Erin had gone without working since she'd joined the NYPD twelve years earlier. She felt a little strange about it, almost like she'd been cutting class or cheating on a spouse. Maybe that was because she'd been making time with a gangster, a relationship she had absolutely not told Internal Affairs about.

Not that it was an Internal Affairs issue, she told herself. No, this was definitely an external affair, about as external as she could get from the police. She chuckled.

"Did I say something amusing, darling?"

"No, I just had a funny thought," she said. "I'm ready to go back. So is Rolf."

Carlyle glanced at the back seat, where Rolf was perched on a folded blanket. The K-9 was watching the world roll by, his ears perked to full attention.

"That lad will be working until his dying day," Carlyle said.

"As long as his body holds out," she said. "Most K-9s have to take medical retirement. Police work is hard on a dog. But they hate it when they can't work anymore."

"The both of you will have to take care of yourselves, then."

"You're one to talk. At least the NYPD has a pension fund. They expect most of their officers to make it to retirement."

"No pension for lads in the Life," he agreed. "I've lasted better than most. I can go a bit longer, I'm thinking."

They were coming up on a slow-moving pickup truck. Erin smoothly shifted into the passing lane and glided by. The

Mercedes hummed happily, eating up the road.

"This is a nice set of wheels you've got," she said. "I'm glad you were able to get a replacement so fast."

They didn't talk about why Carlyle had needed a new car. His old one had been totaled during a police raid a few days before they'd left for the Hamptons. Since Carlyle hadn't been charged with a crime, or even arrested or officially questioned, the NYPD would probably be paying for the replacement rather than risk a lawsuit... eventually. Fortunately for Carlyle, he had the cash on hand to shell out for a new Mercedes. Bureaucracies took a while to pay their bills. But then, cash flow wasn't usually a problem for a guy like him. Another thing they didn't talk about was where his money came from.

"You ever think about retiring?" she asked. "I mean, you sure aren't hurting for money. I'll bet you've got some laid away."

"In a secret Swiss account, you mean?" he laughed. "I've a tidy bit tucked away, aye. But I like running the Barley Corner, darling. Take that away, I'd not know what to do with myself."

"I meant, have you thought about leaving the Life?"

Carlyle stopped laughing. "I know what you meant. We've discussed it before. Some things, it's not so easy to leave behind."

She knew he was right. They said a cop never truly stopped being a cop, but it was even harder to stop being a mobster. He'd always have to have one eye over his shoulder, for fear that old enemies, or even old friends, might want to retire him more permanently. He'd probably have to go far away from New York City, and that would mean leaving not only his whole life, but also her. Erin knew she'd always want to live and work in New York. The city was a part of her.

She did what they always did when the subject came up. She let it drop. They had enough to worry about in the present.

"It's been a great trip," she said, giving him her best,

warmest smile. "And you've been a great guy to share it with. Sorry for bringing up that other crap."

* * *

They took 495 into Queens, passing Erin's old stomping grounds, then worked their way around north Brooklyn to the Williamsburg Bridge. That got them onto the Lower East Side. They'd long since caught up with the infamous New York traffic and slowed their pace accordingly. Erin considered how the increase in cars and tall buildings made her feel like the city was getting a hold on her again. She didn't mind. Cut open one of her veins, she'd bleed one part NYPD blue blood, one part asphalt.

By chance, just as their wheels touched pavement in Manhattan, Erin's phone rang. She glanced down at it and saw Lieutenant Webb's name on the caller ID.

"He didn't waste any time," she said. She swiped the phone screen with her thumb. "O'Reilly."

"I hope I didn't catch you at a bad time, Detective," Webb said.

"Just on my way home, sir."

"Did you have a good few days off?"

"Yes, sir." She'd told him she was going up to the Hamptons to stay at a friend's place, but had left out any mention of who exactly the host was.

"Good. Break's over. I know you technically aren't back on duty until tomorrow morning, but we've got a hot one that just landed in our laps. You good to jump right back in?"

"With both feet, sir."

"Excellent. We've got a double homicide, probable home invasion on Warren Street. Apartment building. I'll text you the address. Looks like someone shot a husband and wife. We've got uniforms on scene."

"Okay. I'll be there as quick as I can."

"I'll be on scene when you get there, with Neshenko."

"Got it. O'Reilly out."

She hung up and glanced at Carlyle. "Sorry. Vacation is definitely over."

He smiled. "Oh, it's no trouble, darling. I'm glad of the time we've had. We'll do it again sometime."

"I'll switch cars," she said. She'd left her Charger at a parking garage a couple of blocks from the Barley Corner, just in case anyone was sniffing around her or Carlyle.

"Grand. Shall I call you later?"

"Better let me call you. I never know how long these things will run."

Erin pulled into the garage and parked alongside her beloved black Charger. She and Carlyle got out. Always the gentleman, he took her bags from the trunk of the Mercedes and handed them to her. She put her arms around him and gave him a quick kiss.

"Thanks again," she said.

"I love you, darling," he said.

"Love you, too." It was so natural and easy to say what had once been an earthshaking admission. Erin was amazed at how completely things could change. But then she was back in her old police rhythm, loading Rolf into his quick-release compartment, clipping her gold shield to her belt, and adjusting her Glock in its holster at her side. The Charger's 24-valve V6 roared to life and Erin O'Reilly went back to work.

* * *

Erin arrived on scene to the familiar sight of a pair of police cruisers and an ambulance on the street in front of the apartment. A uniformed officer at the door directed her to the fourth floor. She passed the paramedics on their way out, never a good sign. If they weren't carrying anyone, it likely meant everyone inside was dead. The door of Apartment 423 was open, voices spilling into the hall. A burnt smell, like overcooked steak, caught her nostrils. Rolf sniffed the air with interest. At least it didn't smell like charred human flesh. Erin had smelled that before, and would be fine if she never came across it again.

She glanced at the door on the way in. Contrary to what Hollywood said, most burglars didn't bother learning how to pick locks. They just kicked in the door, or smashed their way in with a sledgehammer or crowbar. This door was completely intact, no signs of damage to lock, doorknob, or frame.

On her left was a small closet, everything hanging neatly in place. She saw coats, scarves, boots, and shoes lined up in tidy rows. On her right was the kitchen. Wisps of smoke trailed around the edges of the oven door. The smoke alarm was sitting on the counter, deactivated, batteries next to it. A police officer had probably done that to stop the beeping. Food and utensils were scattered haphazardly, like someone had been interrupted in the middle of making dinner. A broad-bladed knife lay on the cutting board beside some half-chopped carrots.

Erin kept going, following the voices. She pulled on a pair of disposable gloves from the roll she always kept on her. She came around the kitchen doorway and into the combination dining room/living room.

"There she is," Vic Neshenko said. "Welcome to the party." He, Lieutenant Webb, and Sarah Levine, the Medical Examiner, were standing around a pair of bodies, one sprawled on top of the other. The carpet was beige. Blood had pooled under the corpses, a dark maroon.

"Some party," Erin said. She saw a string of balloons that hung across the room with a "WELCOME HOME" banner in the middle. A sheet cake, like you'd buy at a grocery store, sat on the coffee table. Several liquor bottles surrounded the cake, accompanied by a package of red plastic cups. Erin saw vodka and whiskey, but also ginger ale and, for some reason, lemon-lime Gatorade. One of the bottles had spilled on the floor, making another stain on the carpet.

"We've got preliminary ID on the victims," Webb said. "Husband and wife, Frank and Helen Carson."

"Levine's been here a few minutes," Vic said. "Whaddaya say, Doc? What killed these two?"

Levine had been making some notes and hadn't acknowledged Erin's presence at all. She looked up at Vic with mild annoyance, like he was interrupting her in the middle of something more interesting.

"Both victims suffered multiple gunshot wounds," she said. "Preliminary forensics indicate a handgun, probably .45 caliber. It appears the male victim was struck first. As you can see, he was facing his shooter and fell on his back. From the angle of the bodies, the female victim was not standing when she was shot. I believe she was kneeling beside the male victim. She then fell forward across him. Death was instantaneous in both cases. The female was struck by three bullets: two in the torso, one in the cranium. The torso wounds would likely have proved fatal, as one transected the aorta and the other perforated the right lung. However, that is academic, as the third bullet destroyed the cranium. As you can see, the entrance wound is just above the right eye. The exit wound detached most of the back of the skull. Cause of death was destruction of the brain. This will complicate facial identification."

"Yeah, that'll do it," Vic muttered. "I've seen .45 slugs before. They do some damage."

Erin tried to retreat into the clinical detachment cops and doctors learned as a coping mechanism. She told herself these bodies weren't people anymore. They were just the shells people left behind when they died, shells the detectives could use to find out who'd killed them and why.

Levine was still talking. "I haven't been able to make a full examination of either body, due to their entangled posture, but I believe the male was also struck at least once in the torso, as well as a single bullet to the cranium. Cause of death is congruent with the other victim, with similar wound presentation."

"Brass?" Erin asked Vic.

He nodded and pointed to the hallway that led to the bathroom and bedroom. Little yellow plastic markers with black numbers had been placed next to each shell casing. Erin counted six.

"That's a little weird," she said.

"Just means it was an automatic, not a revolver," Vic said with a shrug. "Either one can be chambered in .45 caliber."

"I mean the location," she said. "It looks like the killer didn't come in through the front door."

"Right," Webb said. "It looks like he came from either the bathroom or the bedroom."

Erin walked carefully around the shell casings. Rolf sniffed at the familiar scent of gunpowder, but kept padding alongside her. The bathroom door was ajar. She poked it open the rest of the way. Like the rest of the apartment, there was no sign of robbery or ransacking. She caught a faint, sour smell that reminded her of dirty subway stations, or the back of her cruiser after a night of transporting drunks. The window was small and unopened. She went to it and peered through. She saw the street four floors below. The one thing that was out of place in the bathroom was a bottle of pills on the sink. She glanced at the label and saw it was oxycodone, the prescription made out to Frank Carson.

She came back into the hallway and, together with Rolf,

tried the bedroom. The bed was neatly made. Very neatly, in fact. The corners were perfectly squared, the sheet stretched so tight she figured she could bounce a quarter off it. The bedroom window also overlooked the street in front of the building.

"No fire escape," she reported, coming back to the living room. "And no sign of entry through either window. They latch from the inside. I don't think anyone could've climbed in."

"I guess our guy could be a ninja," Vic said.

"A ninja," Webb repeated, deadpan.

"Sure!" Vic said defensively. "You know, an assassin, in those black suits. He sneaks in while the couple's getting ready for their party..."

"Ninjas don't use .45s," Erin said.

"*That's* your problem with this theory?" Webb asked, raising an eyebrow.

"That was the first one I thought of," she said.

"Okay, probably not a ninja," Webb said. "What I want to know is, who else was supposed to be here?"

"For the party?" Erin asked.

"Yeah," Vic said. "Who was being welcomed home? And what about the rest of the guests?"

"Let's start by finding out who the Carsons were," Webb said. "We're just guessing this is who the victims are, since it's their apartment. Facial recognition... well, like Levine said, that's not going to be much help here, given the bullet damage. Doctor, check them for ID. I want a positive identification as quickly as possible. Then let's find out whether one of them was coming home, or if this cake was for someone else."

Erin was looking at the cake. Someone had decorated it with icing that spelled out "Welcome Home, Hero!" Beneath that was an American flag made of frosting, and little starbursts that might be intended to be fireworks.

"Hero," she said quietly. "I think maybe this party was for a soldier."

"Looks like a war followed our boy home," Vic said.

Chapter 3

The Crime Scene Unit techs arrived while the detectives were still going over the scene. The forensics guys were looking for anything that would identify the shooter: hair, fingerprints, clothing fibers, dirt, blood, sweat, and any number of things Erin didn't even know to look for.

"Check the toilet," she suggested to the CSU team leader.

"What am I looking for?" he asked.

"Vomit." Erin had identified the familiar smell.

"I bet they didn't tell you about this sort of thing when you went to school for this," Vic said to the guy.

He shrugged. "I've got an eight month old at home. This isn't the grossest thing I'll be cleaning up today."

"Now that's good police training," Vic said approvingly.

"You want to get one of your own?" Erin asked.

"A kid? Hell no!"

"Why not?"

"Are you kidding? Look at me! You think New York wants a bunch of little gremlins running around with my genes? I mean, I can see you'd want it for job security, but seriously?"

Erin frowned. "That's a really good point. Forget I asked. But how's things with your girl?"

"What girl?"

"You know, the blonde. Zofia."

Vic grinned. "She's all right. We got an understanding."

"Is that the same thing as a relationship?"

"No. It is not."

"As long as both of you are happy." Erin knew Vic had been spending time with Zofia Piekarski, a plainclothes officer with the Street Narcotics Enforcement Unit. Apparently Vic was glad to keep it a casual thing for the moment. Erin wasn't worried about either of them. Piekarski was small, but tough as nails. She could take care of herself. In a fight between Zofia and Vic, Erin would bet against the big Russian.

"How about you?" Vic asked, moving into the bedroom and looking in the closet. "You have a good vacation?"

"Pretty good, yeah."

"You seem more relaxed," he said. "You got a nice, healthy glow around you."

"What the hell is that supposed to mean?"

"You got laid."

"That's none of your business."

"Just like Zofia is none of yours," he said with a knowing smile. "But you still asked me about her, so I can turn it around on you."

"I'm a healthy adult woman," Erin said. "Draw your own conclusions."

"I'd rather not," Vic said. "Some things, I just don't want them in my brain."

"Then why ask questions you don't want answered?" she asked, coming to stand beside him. "Anything in the closet?"

"Clothes, some cardboard boxes. Hey, check this out." Vic pointed to a clear plastic garment sleeve. Inside it was a neatly pressed military dress uniform.

"Looks like one of our folks here was a soldier," Erin said. She pointed to the stripes on the sleeve. "US Army, sergeant."

Vic had turned his attention to the nightstand and bed. He opened the drawer, then closed it, dropped to his knees, and peered under the bed.

"What're you looking for?" Erin asked.

"Guns," Vic said. "A lot of veterans keep one handy. Bingo!"

"Found one?"

"Maybe. Found a gun safe." Vic tried the handle. "Locked. Sensible guy."

"Not so sensible," Erin said. "If his gun hadn't been locked up under the bed, maybe he and his wife wouldn't be dead in the living room."

"Having a gun in the house doesn't make you safer," Vic said. "You know that. If you've got an unsecured firearm, your odds of getting shot go up about four times."

"Accidental discharges and suicides, mostly," Erin said. "But I bet you keep yours handy at home."

"Of course I do," Vic said. "And so do you. But that's different. We're active duty. Some gangbanger asshole might kick down my door some night looking for payback. If all I got is my dick in my hand, it's not gonna be pretty."

Erin shook her head. "You're right. That's not pretty, for all kinds of reasons." She got down on the floor to look at the safe. Vic was right. It was locked down tight. "We need to look inside. If he's got a gun, and it's still there, at least we know he didn't get offed by his own piece."

Their preliminary search turned up some other military memorabilia. In a dresser drawer, Erin found a medal case with a set of military ribbons and decorations, along with a photo album. She flipped through it and saw page after page of pictures of soldiers in desert fatigues, standing in front of Humvees, posing with rifles, pointing to clouds of smoke on the horizon. The pictures were labeled IRAQ 10-11. It was impossible for her to tell any of the guys in the pictures apart. They all had the same haircuts, clothes, and physiques.

"Got a wedding picture here," Vic said. The couple, apparently Frank and Helen Carson, looked very happy. She was wearing a traditional white dress. He was in his military uniform. In the wedding party, the best man was also in military dress.

"You don't expect a soldier to go down like this," Erin commented.

"Training and experience don't matter if the other guy gets the drop on you," Vic said. "I don't care how much of a badass you are, it only takes one bullet. Remember, soldiers get shot. It's kind of their thing."

Webb came into the room. "Any signs of robbery?" he asked.

"No," Erin said. "Place is clean. Neatest crime scene I can remember."

"Gun safe under the bed," Vic added. "Unopened. Got the wife's jewelry box here, doesn't look too pricy, but a robber would've taken it. There's gotta be a few hundred in jewelry."

"She's still wearing her wedding ring," Erin said, remembering the body in the living room. "This wasn't a robbery, sir."

"A hit, then?" Webb asked.

"Looks pretty professional," Erin agreed.

"What were these folks into?" Webb wondered aloud. "CSU will take some time processing. You two get back to the Eightball and look into the Carsons. History and financials. This wasn't random, whatever it was. I want answers, and we need to start with the right questions."

* * *

"I have to say, this place feels more like home than my apartment does," Erin said, looking over the Major Crimes office.

"We spend more waking time here," Vic said. "Makes sense."

"My dad was a cop, too," she said. "This may sound kind of crazy, but the first time I showed up for work, at my old precinct in Queens, I recognized the smell. Dad had the same smell when he came home after a long shift. It wasn't a nice smell, but it was a familiar one, and it reminded me of my father. I felt right at home."

"I swear," Vic said, "you get more like that mutt of yours every day. Half of me wants to ask what I smell like to you, the other half doesn't want to know."

Erin called up Frank Carson's information on her computer. "We've got a couple of moving violations," she said. "And a drunk and disorderly. That's the worst of it. This guy's basically clean."

"How about the wife?" Vic asked.

Erin typed in Helen's info. "Public indecency."

"Really?" Vic was interested. "She looked like a typical housewife. What'd she do?"

Erin pulled up the arrest report. "Looks like she was picked up along with three other young women for lewd behavior. She said it was her bachelorette party. She blew a point one two on the breathalyzer and spent the night before her wedding in detox. You wouldn't know it from the wedding pic."

"Girls just want to have fun," Vic commented. "But none of that will get you shot."

Erin checked Frank Carson's military records. "Looks like he was with the First Infantry Division," she said. "He was a sergeant, just like his uniform indicated. He was on his second three-year hitch, but didn't complete it."

"Dishonorable discharge?" Vic asked hopefully. "Misconduct?"

"No," Erin said, working her way down his service history. "Wounded. IED explosion in Baghdad."

"The dead guy in the apartment still had all his parts," Vic said. "Not counting the ones that got shot off right there in the room."

"Looks like the blast tore up one of his legs," she said. "But the doctors were able to save the limb. It was enough to get him out of the service, on partial disability. Levine will probably be able to confirm his ID from the hardware the VA installed in his shin. He's been home since he got out of the hospital in June of '11."

"So the party wasn't for him," Vic said. "One of his buddies, maybe?"

"That's what I'm thinking," she said.

"So why isn't the buddy one of the bodies in the living room?"

"Maybe he hadn't shown up yet. What's the timeline?"

Vic went to the whiteboard and started writing. "Downstairs neighbor called 911 at 2:45, said she heard gunfire and someone screaming. Said at first she thought it was a TV, so she hesitated a few minutes before calling it in. Call it 2:40 or so when the shots were fired."

"Who's the neighbor?" Erin asked.

"Homebound retiree, older lady name of Lynch. She's in 323, right underneath. Of course she didn't see anything from there, just heard the noise."

"How many shots?"

"She thinks six, two groups of three. Bang bang bang, a woman screams, then three more."

"The scream, was it just a scream, or could she make out any words?"

Vic shook his head. "It's a solid old building. She could tell it was a female voice, that's all."

"Security camera?"

He shook his head again. "I checked when we first got there. The lobby has a mounting for a camera, but according to the super, the camera's been broken for months."

"Traffic cams?" Erin tried without much hope.

"Looking for what? It's Manhattan. Officers responded to the apartment at 2:53, so that's about a thirteen-minute window after we're guessing the shots were fired. How many cars and pedestrians go around a corner in this town every minute? Take that, times thirteen, and double it, since we don't know which direction the shooter went. Hopeless."

"I could take Rolf back, see if he can track the shooter from the apartment," Erin said doubtfully. "He'd have to have stayed on foot, and I don't know if we'll be able to pick up the right scent. Urban tracking is hard."

"If it was a professional hit, the shooter had a car waiting," Vic said.

"We can't solve this by following the guy from the scene," Erin decided. "We need to know who wanted the Carsons dead."

"That means talking to the families," Vic sighed. "I hate doing death notifications."

"We have to wait on the ID confirmation before we can do that," Erin reminded him.

"And we'll need ballistics on the gun," he said. "Plus bloodwork on the victims. Is there anything we're *not* waiting on?"

"Not really."

* * *

The evidence started to arrive from the crime scene. Levine had conclusive IDs on both victims. Frank had his wallet in his pocket, which included his driver's license and his old military ID, along with credit cards. Helen's purse had been in the apartment and had contained her own identification information.

That was enough for Erin to legally run their financials. She'd never been particularly good at this part of police work.

"When are they going to give us a forensic accountant?" she asked Vic. "Ever since we lost Kira, we've been weak on numbers."

He shrugged. "Budget bullshit. The bean counters down at One PP don't want to pay for more bean counters. Remember that old question, who watches the watchmen? I wanna know who audits the auditors."

"I guess once you go far enough in, it's CPAs all the way down," Erin said. "Maybe I should go back to school and get a business degree."

"You do that, you're gonna have to lock up your guns," he said. "Otherwise you'll get so sick of it, you'll blow your own brains out. If you had the stomach for that kind of work, you wouldn't be here with me."

"I'm not seeing anything unusual in Frank's records," she said. "No large cash withdrawals, no strange deposits. If he was moving lots of money, he wasn't doing it through his personal account."

"How about the wife?"

"They had a joint checking and savings account," she said. "Looks pretty typical. Not a large balance." Erin thought for a moment, then stood up. "The hell with this. I want to go back to the apartment, look over the place again."

"CSU will be all over it," he said.

"I don't care. I can't just sit here at this desk." Erin couldn't explain it. She felt twitchy, restless, impatient.

"You're the Detective Second Grade," Vic said. "I'm not the boss of you. But you're not hanging the family notifications on me. I'll come back with you."

"We'll talk to the Lieutenant about that," she said. "Come on, if you're coming."

Erin wasn't sure what was wrong with her. She felt scattered, disoriented. It was probably just having been away from the Job. She just needed to get back into her groove. She could tell Vic was watching her all the way to the crime scene, but he didn't ask her anything, and she didn't volunteer.

Back at the apartment, they saw the coroner's van leaving. That was good; she knew Levine would want to be getting to work on the bodies, and at least she'd missed running into Hank and Ernie. Those two guys had one of the worst jobs in New York, carting off fresh bodies, and they compensated for it by pitch-black humor. She was in no mood to deal with them.

Upstairs, they met Webb talking with a CSU guy.

"O'Reilly?" he said, surprised. "Neshenko? I wasn't expecting you back here. What'd you need?"

"I wanted to take a look around the place again," she said. "I feel like I rushed it."

Webb looked at the CSU man, who nodded.

"Sure thing, Detectives," the tech said. "Just don't contaminate the scene. And be careful with your K-9."

"We know the drill," she said. "Rolf? *Sitz. Bleib.*"

Rolf obediently sat and stayed.

"You were right about the toilet," the CSU guy said. "Somebody vomited in it."

"Could be the perp, could be one of the victims," Webb said.

"Levine will be able to check for a match with the victims," Erin said. She went toward the bathroom first, probably because of what they were talking about.

The evidence techs were photographing and cataloguing everything, a very time-consuming process. Oddly, the lack of ransacking and collateral damage made their job harder rather than easier. If the murderer had thrown things around, CSU would've known which items to check for fingerprints and fibers. In this case, they were going over the whole place with a fine-toothed comb.

Erin, like any cop, knew to check the medicine cabinet. It contained the usual aspirin, antacid, dental floss, razor blades, and a prescription bottle. She turned to the nearest tech.

"You guys do anything with this yet?" she asked him.

"Nope. Just getting to it."

Erin put on gloves and carefully rotated the bottle to see the prescription. It was made out to Frank Carson, and appeared to be Vicodin. Pain pills, strong ones. She copied down the prescription info, including the name of the doctor and the pharmacy. Both that bottle and the one she'd seen on the sink on her first visit still contained pills, which was yet more evidence this hadn't been a robbery. Opiates were a very popular target for thieves and junkies, and no junkie would've just taken some of the pills and left the rest.

She moved on to the bedroom. The gun safe had been pulled out from under the bed, its key in the lock. Vic was kneeling beside it.

"The husband had the key in his pocket," Webb commented from the doorway.

"You take a look inside?" she asked.

"Yeah. Have a peek. We haven't removed anything yet."

Erin opened the lid. "Whoa," she said.

It was a sizable safe, so she'd been expecting a long gun or two in addition to a handgun, but what she found was a veritable arsenal. Pistols, rifles, and even...

"Is that a *grenade*?" Vic said in disbelief.

"Looks like it," Webb said. "From what I can see, we've got five handguns, three rifles, a shotgun, a whole lot of ammo, and yes, a hand grenade."

"What the hell did he need a grenade for?" Erin wondered aloud.

"What the hell *don't* you need a grenade for?" Vic replied.

Erin studied the weapons. "That's a Beretta," she said, pointing to one of the automatic pistols.

"And a Smith and Wesson .357 Magnum," Vic said, indicating a revolver. He knew his guns. "USP .45 next to it, a Walther PPK, and a Beretta Nano. That's it for the little guns. The shotgun's a Mossberg. Then we got an AR-15, civilian configuration, a bolt-action Remington Model 33, and Jesus Christ, an honest-to-God AK-74."

"Russian gun," Webb said. "What's he doing with a Russian assault rifle under his bed?"

"Souvenir from Iraq, maybe," Erin guessed. "Took it off a dead guy or a prisoner and smuggled it back."

Vic whistled. "You know, if we found all this shit under a bed in a drug den, we'd arrest everybody in the place."

"We'd do that anywhere," Erin said. "This is military weaponry."

"It's legal to own hand grenades," Vic said.

"It's just suspicious as hell," Erin said.

The funny thing, Erin thought, was that the really scary weapons were the legal ones. You could own a semi-automatic rifle, or even a grenade, but the handguns were illegal without a permit. Even the AK-74 was legal as long as Carson had registered it with the state prior to January of 2013.

"I'd agree this is suspicious," Webb said.

"Suspicious?" Vic snorted. "There's enough hardware here to take Belgium. I'd say it's a little more than suspicious."

"Maybe he was dealing arms," Erin said. "On the black market."

"It's worth checking," Webb said. "Some former military guys get into that. We'll be sure to take down the serial numbers, see where all this came from."

Vic was still eyeing the grenade. "That's US military issue," he said. "I'm pretty sure it's an M67."

"How much damage can something like that do?" Webb asked.

"If you're within five meters when it goes off, you're toast," Vic said. "If you get unlucky, you could catch a splinter a lot further off than that. Rule of thumb is, you don't want to watch it blow up. It can throw shrapnel farther than you can throw it. It's best to chuck it and duck for cover."

"I don't think I'd sleep well on top of one of those," Webb said.

"They're perfectly safe," Vic said. "As high explosives go."

"Skip will love hearing about this," Erin said, thinking of Precinct 8's resident bomb-disposal expert.

"The weapons are the best lead we've got so far," Webb said. "Neshenko, you run the background on them. O'Reilly, I want you to look up next of kin."

Vic gave Erin a furtive but triumphant glance. He got to research guns, she had to talk to the families. That was a shit job, for sure.

"Yes, sir," she said with a sinking feeling. Then she had a thought. "I have a CI I can talk to about arms smuggling. Maybe he's got something on Carson."

"Good thought," Webb said. "Look up your guy after you talk to the families."

"Yes, sir," she said again. The sinking feeling was still there.

"See if they can tell you anything about potential smuggling," Webb added.

"You really think the family will know?"

"Won't hurt to try."

But Erin thought it might.

Chapter 4

It was getting on into the evening when Erin drove up to the Carson house. Frank's next of kin were his parents, Joseph and Hanh. They lived in Brooklyn, in a small house in a relatively quiet neighborhood. A telephone notification would've been easier than doing this in person. It would also have been heavily frowned on by the department, and earned Erin the disapproval of her own conscience. It was the worst job a cop had to do, but it should be done in person whenever possible.

Erin did have backup for this job. She'd dropped Rolf at home, but acquired Father Kelly, the Precinct 8 police chaplain. The priest had done this more than Erin had, for which she was grateful. He was in his mid-forties, stout around the middle, and had a quiet, calm presence.

"I hate doing these," she muttered as she made the last turn onto the Carsons' block. "I just keep imagining my mom and dad getting a call about me."

"You're performing a sacred duty," Kelly said. "Both to the living and the dead. It's good that you feel so much empathy with the victim's family."

Erin nodded and put the car in park. She took a deep breath and got out onto the street.

A man was sitting on the front porch, watching them approach. He had a tough, leathery face, steel-gray hair in a buzz cut, and a pockmarked pattern of scars on his cheek. He was on the porch swing with a glass of whiskey in his hand, a newspaper on his lap, and a black Labrador curled up next to him. In spite of the cold mid-March evening, he was wearing no coat, just a flannel shirt and jeans.

"Help you, ma'am?" he asked.

"Are you Joseph Carson?" she asked.

"Yes, ma'am." He folded the paper and stood up. He was a few inches taller than Erin, muscular and barrel-chested.

"Sir, my name is Erin O'Reilly. I'm a detective with the NYPD. This is Father Kelly. He works with my precinct. Sir... we've come to talk to you about your son, Frank. Is your wife home?"

"Yes," he said. "She's in the kitchen, getting dinner ready."

"We need to speak with both of you," Erin said. "May we come in?"

He nodded. He went to the door and opened it, ushering them into a small, neat, well-kept living room. The dog followed them and immediately curled up on the rug.

"Sit down," Joseph said. "Make yourselves at home. I'll go get Hanh." He went out of the room.

With a pang, Erin saw a photo of Frank and Helen in a place of honor on the mantel. Beside it was another shot of Frank in his military uniform. She also saw other photos, from an earlier generation and a previous war. She was sure these were Joseph, carrying an M-16 and wearing jungle fatigues. The background in those snapshots looked like Vietnam. Frank had been a legacy soldier, just like Erin was a legacy cop.

Mr. and Mrs. Carson came into the living room. Hanh was, as her name suggested, Vietnamese. She looked younger than Joseph, but Erin was always bad at guessing the ages of other ethnic groups than her own. Hanh was petite, quiet, and polite. She smiled a little shyly at Erin.

"I think we should all sit down," Father Kelly said. The Carsons did so, Joseph in his armchair, Hanh bringing a chair from the dining room, while Kelly and Erin sat on the couch.

Mr. Carson sighed. "So, Frank's in trouble, I suppose," he said. "He's always been a good boy, so I hope it's nothing serious."

"No, sir," Erin said. "I'm afraid I have some bad news. We received a call today from your son's apartment. It appears he and his wife were attacked in their home this afternoon. They were shot and killed."

She'd found there was no easy way to break that kind of news. The best thing to do was just say it and get the worst of it out in the open.

Hanh put her hand on her husband's arm and said something to him in Vietnamese. He replied in the same language. Her eyes went wide.

"I don't understand," Joseph said. "He was shot? At home?"

"Yes," Erin said. "Both him and Helen."

"They're both dead?"

"Yes, I'm afraid so."

Mr. Carson shook his head. He held his wife's hand. "Damn," he said softly. "You just... you never expect it. Not like this. When he got his orders, sure, we knew there was a chance he wouldn't come home. I know what war's like."

"I see you were in the service, too," Erin said, glancing at the photos on the wall.

"Central Highlands, Vietnam, '68 through '70," he said, and she heard the pride in his voice. "I volunteered for a second tour.

Four generations of Carsons have all worn the uniform. My dad was in Korea and Big Two, his dad fought under Pershing in the Argonne."

"Thank you for your service," Erin said. It was the cheap, trite thing, but she didn't know what else to say.

"But Frank came back," Mr. Carson said. "After he got blown up. We knew he was wounded, but he came back alive. I saw some guys in Nam who left pieces of themselves over there, and they were never quite right afterward. But Frank came back strong. It was supposed to be over."

He looked at Erin with a hard light in his eyes. "Who did this? Who cheated my boy?"

"Sir, we're going to do everything we can to find the person who did it," she said. *Promise effort, don't promise results*, her dad had always advised her. "Do you know anyone who might have had a reason to want to hurt him or Helen?"

"Plenty," Joseph said. "He was a soldier, and a damned good one. America's got plenty of enemies, so Frank does, too."

"I meant in a more personal way," she said. "When we got here, you asked whether Frank was in trouble. Why would you say that?"

Joseph's eyes went even harder. He stared at Erin as if he was testing her willpower, seeing how tough she was. She returned the look, not giving in, but trying not to be confrontational. This wasn't a staredown with some street tough; this was a grieving father.

His eyes softened a little. "Frank's a good kid. But he was in a lot of pain, with the wound and all the operations. He got these prescriptions. When I was overseas, it was the Sixties. You could get all kinds of stuff in Saigon, for cheap. We had weed, heroin, LSD. Now these kids got their pills. But it's always the same. You start taking 'em for the pain, maybe you keep taking 'em so you sleep better."

"Mr. Carson," Erin said. "Do you think Frank had an opiate problem?"

He nodded. "I had a monkey on my back for a while myself. I had some bad years when I got back to the World. Hanh straightened me out. I was hoping maybe Helen would do the same for Frank." He shook his head. "Helen's a fine woman. She's dead, too? This crazy goddamn world. She was so good for him, wrote him letters practically every day when he was overseas. Old-fashioned letters, pen and paper. She'd squirt a dash of her perfume on them, so he'd be able to smell they were from her."

Erin felt a lump in her throat. This was why she hated this kind of assignment.

"Frank was getting help," Joseph went on. "One of those anonymous programs. He was doing okay. He had less pain, and he told me he was sleeping better lately. I guess he still had some pills in the house, but he was trying to cut down on them."

"He had a lot of guns in his apartment," Erin said. "Was he afraid of someone?"

"You ever been to war, Detective?" Mr. Carson asked.

"No, sir," she said. "But I've been shot at."

"You keep a gun at home?"

She nodded.

He nodded, too, as if the issue had been explained sufficiently. She decided to try another angle.

"Sir, Frank was hosting a welcome-home party for someone today. We think it may have been one of his military buddies. Do you know who he might have been expecting?"

He shook his head. "No, ma'am. But you can look up his unit. It really tore Frank up to be sent home while his guys were still over there, getting shot at. He had guilt like you wouldn't believe about that. You know, I got hit out in the bush, summer of '69." He touched the scars on his face. "Shrapnel from a

Chinese-made RPG. I was in the hospital two weeks. They wanted to fly me to Japan. I couldn't stand it. I went AWOL from the hospital and hitched a ride on a medevac Huey back to my platoon. They couldn't believe it, but there was no way I was gonna lie around in Japan while my brothers were taking incoming.

"Frank was the same way. He would've died for his guys. They were his brothers, all of them. You better believe, if one of 'em was coming home, Frank would've put on a party for him."

Erin nodded. "I understand. Sir, Father Kelly will talk to you about what you can do, and what the NYPD can do for you. But if there's anything you need to discuss, or if you think of anything that may help us with our investigation, here's my card. You can call me any time, day or night. We'll let you know of any major developments."

Joseph Carson leaned toward her. "You find the man who killed my boy," he said. "You find the damned coward who didn't have the balls to fight him on the battlefield, and you take him down. You hear me?"

"Yes, sir," she said. "I hear you. We'll do everything we can."

"Don't come up my front walk with an excuse," he said, pointing his finger at her like the barrel of a pistol. "And don't tell me you couldn't do it. We always found a way. You find a way."

Hanh spoke for the first time in English. Her voice was low and almost musical, heavily accented.

"My son. May I see him?"

"Ma'am," Erin began.

Mr. Carson nodded to Erin. He said something to his wife in her native language. She flinched, but nodded in return. Then she abruptly stood up and left the room.

"I'm sorry," he said. "This is... a shock. To both of us. But she grew up in war. She'll understand. Her family came here after

Saigon fell in '75. She was very young at the time. She's got some difficult memories, from when she was a girl."

"No need to apologize," Erin said. "I'm sorry."

"I guess we all are," he said. "You think you're ready, but then... my boy. Why my boy? Why let him come home, just so this could happen? It should've been me." He clasped his hands between his knees and looked down at them. "It should've been me."

* * *

By the time Erin and Father Kelly got done at Helen's mother's house, it was after ten and Erin was emotionally exhausted. That had been even worse than talking with Frank's parents. Helen's mother, a stout, middle-aged woman named Louise Decker, was all alone in the world. Helen's dad had died in a construction accident three years earlier, Helen had no siblings, and they'd left Louise howling her grief. There really wasn't another word for the sound the woman had made. They hadn't been able to get anything meaningful out of her, and finally Erin had given up, left her card by the door, and beaten a retreat.

She dropped the priest back at the precinct. He paused when he got out of the Charger.

"Are you okay, Erin?" he asked.

"What do you mean?"

"This work takes an emotional toll. If you need to talk to someone, I'm ready to listen."

"Thanks, Father, but I'm fine. Good night."

There wasn't a lot more she could do that night. She figured she'd go home, have a drink, and hit the case fresh in the morning. In the meantime, she owed her boyfriend a call, and needed to talk to her mob informant about arms smuggling. Fortunately, those two people were in fact the same person.

"Evening, darling," Carlyle said, picking up the call on the second ring.

"Miss me?" she asked.

"I started the moment I lost sight of you."

"That's sweet of you. I just figured out what you can do with the rest of your life. You can sell the bar and write greeting card slogans."

"Is something the matter, darling?"

"I just had some tough stuff to deal with at the end of the day. Are you hungry?"

"I can make myself available for a late dinner, if that's what you're suggesting."

"Get something Italian and bring it to my place. I'm on my way home now. I could use some comfort food."

"I'll be there."

Police and gangsters both tended to keep late hours. To have supper after ten was hardly unusual. Erin had time to give Rolf a quick walk around the neighborhood, then change into comfy clothes. She reflected that she and Carlyle had seen one another at their worst, so it was nice not to have to always spruce herself up for him. Erin wasn't the vainest woman, but she knew she was nearer forty than thirty and did use makeup to hide some of the telltales of age. But he'd seen her just out of bed, unkempt and natural, and still loved her. She wasn't about to put on an evening gown and jewelry at the end of a long day.

When Carlyle showed up at her door, of course, he was wearing a suit and tie. But that was his personal style. Even on vacation, he kept himself clean-shaven and impeccably dressed. He could make a white T-shirt look like the height of fashion. Erin was wearing sweat pants and her NYPD sweatshirt. That was just the way of it.

He'd brought tortellini in marinara sauce, a loaf of garlic bread, a salad, and a bottle of red wine. Erin was more a whiskey girl, but she appreciated the wine with the pasta. The food was fresh and hot, from a restaurant just up the street. She kissed Carlyle and helped lay out the meal. Then they sat down together. He poured the wine and clinked glasses.

"*Slainte*," he said, the traditional Irish toast. "I hope you weren't overwhelmed on your return to duty."

"Same old, same old," she said. "A couple got shot in their apartment. Probable home invasion, but might've been a professional job."

He raised an eyebrow. "Most professionals won't hit a lad in his home," he observed. "It's more likely they'll take him on the street. Though I've known it to happen the other way."

Erin saw the old pain behind his eyes and felt a jab of remorse. She'd momentarily forgotten that Carlyle's wife had been murdered in a home invasion, probably by anti-IRA paramilitary guys looking for him.

"Sorry," she said quickly.

He raised one hand. "It's nothing, darling. You were saying?"

"The shooter knew his business," she said. "We know one of the victims had a narcotics problem, and he had a lot of firepower at his place. I'm thinking maybe he was running guns, or drugs, or both."

"And you're wondering what I might know on the subject?" Carlyle asked with a slight twinkle in his eye.

"Yeah."

"I trust he's unaffiliated with Evan O'Malley?"

"As far as we know. He's got basically no record. The guy's former military. Does the name Frank Carson ring any bells?"

Carlyle shook his head. "Nay. But remember, I'm not well connected on the subject of narcotics."

"But you know who moves guns," she said. "Can you check around, see if any of your associates know the guy?"

"I can ask," he said doubtfully. "But I don't think I'll have much to give you. You might talk to my driver."

"Ian?" Erin was surprised. "You told me he wasn't part of the Life."

"He's not. But he's a veteran, and he knows how those lads operate. He's also interested in firearms. He might be helpful if you're looking for former military lads who might be moving guns about."

"Okay. When would he be available?"

"There's something you have to understand about Ian," Carlyle said. "He doesn't open up easily. You can't simply go at him with your questions. He'll just clam up, like a polite piece of stone, and once he does there's no moving him. You're lucky he likes you. I think he'll talk to you, but you'll need the proper approach. The lad likes to take an early-morning run in Central Park. If you don't mind making the drive up past Midtown, you can find him there."

"What time?"

"About five o' clock. Go in on Center Drive at the south end and get on the Avenue of the Americas by the bronze statue of that Cuban lad."

"Jose Julian Marti?" Erin guessed. She knew some of the Central Park landmarks.

"Aye, that's the one."

"You think this is necessary?"

"Ian doesn't talk much about his time in the service. If you want him to talk about it, you'll have to earn it."

"By running?"

"You're a runner, so is he. I thought it might be the best way for the two of you to connect. It's a mite easier to understand someone when you're moving in rhythm with him."

"Okay, I'll give it a shot. I'm an early riser."

"Aye, so I've noticed. I fear I'm not."

"You stay up too late. Plus, you're getting older. You need your sleep."

He gave her a wounded look. "I can still keep up with you, lass."

"Not on the running trail, you can't."

"I wasn't talking about that."

Erin smiled at him. "I don't have any complaints."

"Well, that's a relief," he said. "I'll tell Ian to expect you. But if you're needing to be up early, perhaps I shouldn't be keeping you awake."

He was teasing, getting back at her for calling him old. "And I don't want to wear you out," she replied. "After all, we just got back from a vacation together. You telling me you haven't had enough of me yet?"

"Never."

Chapter 5

Central Park was generally safe, and most crooks were asleep at five in the morning. Muggers were also sensible enough to leave a woman alone when she had a ninety-pound German Shepherd for a running companion. But Erin still tucked her backup pistol into a fanny pack, just in case. Then, clad in sweats and sneakers, she leashed Rolf, loaded him into the Charger, and headed north.

The sun wouldn't be up for a couple of hours yet. The air had a sharp edge to it, reminding her it wasn't quite spring. Erin parked her car and jogged into the park, taking it easy, not wanting to strain a muscle in the cold.

She found the statue of Jose Marti, looking serious and brave, and like his horse was about to fall over sideways. Erin remembered one of her teachers telling her that a statue with a rearing horse meant the rider had been killed in battle. From what she could see, Marti was in more danger from his horse than from his enemies.

The park was quiet and almost deserted. Erin started doing some stretches. Rolf sniffed a few things while they waited.

"Ma'am."

Erin's heart jumped into her mouth. Ian was behind her, less than ten feet away. He was wearing dark gray sweats and a fanny pack of his own. Erin would bet he had a gun in there, too. That was okay. Ian was licensed to carry a firearm, though God only knew how he'd managed that. New York City had some of the most restrictive gun laws in the country.

"You move pretty quiet, you know that?" she said. "Not many guys can sneak up on me."

"Didn't mean to be sneaking, ma'am. No excuse. Just habit."

"Carlyle talk to you?"

"He told me you might be here, ma'am. Something you need?"

"I like to run in the mornings too. I thought it'd be nice to have someone to run with for a change. Someone human, I mean." She scratched Rolf's head.

Rolf looked up at her, his tail moving in slow, expectant sweeps. He'd come to run, not stand around talking.

"No problem, ma'am. How far do you want to go?"

"You lead," she said. "I haven't run much in this park. Don't worry, I can keep up."

Ian took her at her word and started running.

It took a few minutes for her to fall into rhythm with him. He was younger than Erin, and in peak physical condition. He set a higher pace than she was accustomed to. She didn't complain. She just kept her muscles loose and fluid, kept her breathing slow and regular, and stayed with him. Their breath misted in the air. The only sounds were the clink and jingle of Rolf's leash, the thudding of their shoes on the trail, and their breathing.

For the first mile, she didn't try to say anything. She did glance at him from time to time. He was looking straight ahead, no expression on his face. Ian was a paradox to her. She'd spent a little time around him and knew he was always alert, always on duty. She wondered if she'd ever seen him completely calm, or if that was an emotion he'd lost the ability to feel. But his self-control was so extreme, she'd also never seen him lose his outward cool. Not even in a gunfight.

Midway through the second mile, she was starting to feel pretty good. She and Rolf were breathing easy, moving in tandem. Rolf made running look absurdly simple. She'd once had a buddy back in Queens clock him with a radar gun. His top speed was 31 miles per hour. Ian had set a pace of about seven. That barely counted as running to the K-9.

"You do this every day?" she asked Ian.

"Pretty much. You?"

"I try. Never know when I might need to run. For the Job."

Ian nodded.

"What do you have to do for Marine PT?" she asked.

"For the fitness test, three miles under twenty-eight minutes. Thirty-one if you're a woman. Plus pull-ups and crunches."

Erin didn't like the differing requirements for different sexes. "That's it?"

"For combat fitness there's Movement to Contact, Ammunition Lift, and Maneuver Under Fire."

"What're those?"

"Movement to Contact is a sprint, 880 yards," he said, timing his sentences to coincide with his breathing. "Ammo Lift is hoisting a thirty-pound ammo can, as many times as you can. Maneuver is an obstacle course, three hundred yards."

"Do that and they make you a Marine?"

"There's some other stuff, too."

"Like what?"

"Weapons. Equipment training. Discipline."

"Do you miss it?"

Ian was silent for a while, for such a long time she was afraid she'd offended him with the question.

"Yeah," he said at last.

"You could've stayed in the Corps."

"They sent me home."

The admission startled her. She knew some things about his last mission. She'd read his file as part of a previous investigation. He'd been in a chopper crash in Afghanistan. He and one other Marine had been the only survivors. The other guy had been badly hurt. Ian had basically carried his injured buddy on his own back for five days through hostile country. He'd finally been picked up, exhausted, dehydrated, and wounded. The Marine Corps had given him the Silver Star.

"Because you'd been hit?" she asked.

"That's what they said."

Her interrogator's ear caught the distinction between what she'd asked and his answer. "Why'd they really do it?"

"I only had a few weeks left on deployment."

That wasn't an answer either.

"You could've re-upped," she said.

"It was a psych thing," he said.

Erin said nothing and waited.

"I heard about your thing in Queens," Ian said, unexpectedly.

"What thing in Queens?"

"The cop who got shot. At the museum."

Erin stumbled, losing her stride. He'd caught her totally off guard. She gasped in a quick breath of cold air and windmilled her arms to keep from falling. Ian paused, waiting for her to recover. Erin stopped running and put her hands on her knees, bent over to catch her breath.

"What's that got to do with anything?" she asked sharply, once she could speak.

Ian wasn't even breathing hard. He was in fantastic condition. "You know what it's like," he said.

"What?"

"Losing a brother."

He wasn't talking about blood relations. The flash of memory hit Erin like a fist to the stomach. Brunanski, the fat old Polish cop, lying on the pavement. How warm his blood had felt on her hands, trying to hold the life in him, feeling it run out onto the ground. The gritty feel of asphalt under her nylon stockings. She'd kicked off her heels so she could run faster. She still hadn't been fast enough.

"Yeah," Erin said. "I do."

"My team was gone," Ian said quietly. "All of them. Only Robbins got out, and he lost his leg. So they sent him home. They didn't know what to do with me, and they were worried. Thought I'd snap, maybe. I wasn't hurt that bad. I was a psych casualty. They wouldn't let me re-up, ma'am."

"They told you that?"

"They didn't have to."

She waved a hand to indicate they could start running again. Ian did, setting the same pace as before. Erin fell into the rhythm more easily this time.

"So you came home and went to work for Carlyle?" she asked.

"Yes, ma'am."

"You like working for him?"

"Yes, ma'am."

"You don't have to call me ma'am all the time. Makes me feel like my mom."

"Old habit from training, ma'am."

"Have to be polite on the battlefield, huh?"

"It's not about being polite. It's about respect, ma'am."

"Isn't that the same thing?"

That got his attention. He slowed his pace a little and looked at her. "Of course not. Polite is for everybody. Respect is for people who deserve it."

"Like other soldiers?"

He worked a shrug into his running motion. "Most of them."

"You can call me Erin."

"Thank you, ma'am."

"Or not."

Ian didn't say anything.

"You were one hell of a good Marine," she said.

"I did my job."

"Ian, I've read your citation. You did more than your job."

"Oh. That."

"You don't like talking about it?"

"Don't even like thinking about it, ma'am."

"How come?"

"Wasn't a good week."

"I heard once that if a situation needs a hero, it means someone's screwed up pretty bad," she said.

Ian gave the closest thing to a smile she'd ever seen on his face. "Oorah, ma'am."

"How long have you been back?"

"Back?"

"From Afghanistan."

"That's the thing," he said.

"What is?"

"Not sure I came back."

Erin wanted to ask Ian about guns, about veterans and how they connected. That was what she needed for the case. But Ian's last answer had a tone of finality to it, and she didn't want to push him.

They finished their run in silence, looping back to the statue. Erin figured they'd done about six miles. The sun still wasn't up, but the sky was looking a little lighter to the east.

"You want to do this again sometime?" Erin asked.

"Sure," Ian said.

"See you around."

"Oorah, ma'am."

* * *

One theory making the rounds of Precinct 8 was that Sarah Levine was a vampire. She pretty much lived underground in the morgue, she had an unhealthy fascination with blood, her complexion was pale, and she often seemed to be trying to mimic human interaction like someone who'd heard how it was done but didn't quite understand it.

Erin didn't believe it. For one thing, she'd seen Levine outdoors in sunlight, and the doc hadn't burst into flames. For another, vampires slept in coffins. Levine didn't seem to sleep at all.

The Medical Examiner's report was waiting for her when she got to the office. Fortunately, Levine could run the bloodwork herself, so they didn't have to wait on those lab results. DNA took longer, but the tox screens were done in-house. Erin immediately updated the Major Crimes whiteboard with the relevant details.

Frank and Helen Carson had each been killed by three .45 caliber bullets, fired from reasonably close range, but far enough not to leave powder tattooing around the wounds. The bodies had not been moved; they'd died in the apartment, right where they'd been found. Bloodwork showed that both had been intoxicated at time of death, with blood-alcohol readings of .14 for Frank and .11 for Helen.

Neither body showed defensive wounds, though Frank had slight scratches on his face. These matched Helen's fingernails, under which Levine had found some of his skin cells. She'd probably grabbed at him, either trying to help him or just clutching him in fear or grief.

Time of death matched their timeline for the shots that'd been heard. The cartridge casings were a match for the wound caliber, so had almost certainly come from the murder weapon. All this suggested a single shooter.

Very little of it was useful in pointing them toward their killer. But Erin had learned to be patient with murder cases. Every piece of the crime they could reconstruct would ultimately help them.

She looked on her computer for any further updates. CSU was still sifting through the potential evidence from the apartment. The guns under the Carsons' bed had probably not been used during the shooting. None of them had been fired since their last cleaning. That didn't mean they hadn't been fired recently. They could've been shot off two hours before the CSU guys checked them, as long as the shooter had cleaned them afterward. But it seemed unlikely the shooter had pulled Frank's .45 out from under his bed, shot the two of them, cleaned the gun, and put it away again.

Still, it was possible. Erin filled out the request for a test firing of the USP .45 so they could match its ballistics against the rounds recovered from the scene. The other guns were all the wrong caliber, so they didn't need to do anything with those. She ran their serial numbers while waiting for the rest of the squad to arrive. Vic might have already done that, but she didn't see the harm.

Vic beat Webb in by a few minutes, an unusual occurrence. He actually seemed pretty chipper, which was even more unusual before nine o' clock. He favored Erin with a nod and a grunt, which was his version of a pleasant good morning.

"Piekarski's being a good influence on you," she said.

"You kidding?" he retorted. "She was out all night doing buy-and-busts with her team. She gets all amped up on the action. You got any idea what it's like seeing a girl who wants her booty call when she gets off-duty at five in the morning? That woman's wearing me out."

Erin grinned. "You telling me you never worked the dog watch? I used to do it all the time."

"Yeah, but I need my sleep."

"Wait a second. Did you just refer to yourself as a booty call?"

"You got a problem with my ass, O'Reilly? I've got gym-sculpted glutes."

"No problem whatsoever, Mr. Universe. I'm just glad to see some gender equality in your objectification."

"I think that's the most politically correct thing I've ever heard you say."

"Thanks."

"That wasn't a compliment."

"Okay, you're still a Neanderthal caveman."

"That's better. Let's talk about guns."

"I was just looking up the weapons we recovered," she said. "The AR-15 was legally purchased upstate at a gun show for hunters."

"Yeah, those automatic rifles are awful handy," Vic said. "Suppose you're out in the woods and run into a deer wearing a Kevlar vest who cheated you on a drug deal? A 5.56 round doesn't have the stopping power for big game, and it's overkill on rabbits and squirrels. Plus, no hunter on Earth needs a thirty-round magazine. Seriously, how many shots you gonna fire at that deer before it figures it better go somewhere else?"

"I thought you supported the Second Amendment," she said.

"I do. But let's not pretend that gun's for anything but shooting people. It's the hypocrisy that bugs me."

"Moving on," Erin said. "The Mossberg 12-gauge came from a Cabela's, and actually is a hunting gun. My dad's got one just like it. The Remington is a museum piece, an old gun. This serial number dates back to a 1934 manufacture. I don't know where he got it. It was last registered to a guy in freaking California. Neither of those are military guns."

"True," Vic said. "That Remington was in great condition. It's worth a lot of money to the right guy. But a bolt-action .22 isn't something you use for home defense or for shooting gangbangers. I guess maybe our boy did do some hunting after all."

"The handguns all came from gun stores in New Jersey," Erin said. "All legally purchased. The AK-74 isn't registered in the US."

"No surprise there," Vic said. "I'm telling you, he picked that one up in Iraq off some dead militant."

"And the grenade isn't in our system either," she concluded. "I think I'll ask Skip about that. So the only really illegal gun was the AK. You find anything different?"

"Nope. I got the same as you."

"Maybe he's been smuggling assault rifles in?"

Vic snorted. "There's so many Kalashnikovs out there, you practically trip over them in Third World countries. You ever seen that movie, *Lord of War*? With Nic Cage?"

"No."

"It's about a gun smuggler. There's this one scene, they've got a room full of AKs. According to the director, their prop guys couldn't find enough prop guns for the scene, so they just went out and bought real assault rifles. It was easier and cheaper. Yeah, maybe our boy was smuggling them, but if he was, he sure wasn't getting rich off it, and having one under the bed doesn't prove a thing."

"That's depressing."

"Not if you want a cheap, reliable assault rifle."

"I really don't."

"Your loss. It's a great gun."

"You ever fire one?"

"Oh, yeah. You oughta try it sometime. So, you gonna go play grenade catch with Skip?"

"He's the best guy to ask about it." Skip Taylor was the Bomb Squad guy at Precinct 8, and was also a veteran Army EOD technician.

"Okay," Vic said. "I'll see what else turned up on scene and look at the autopsy reports."

"They're on my desk," she said, leading Rolf to the elevators.

Skip's office was in the basement, festooned with warning signs and a coil of decorative razorwire. Some of the signs were comical, some dead serious. All warned of explosives. She hit the doorbell and waited, hoping he wasn't working on anything too unstable.

Skip opened the door. His boyish face broke into a big smile when he saw her. She knew he was in his mid-twenties, but he looked and acted more like a friendly teenager.

"Erin! And Rolf! How's it going? Sniff out any bombs for your partner?"

Rolf permitted Skip to scratch him behind the ears.

"We found something yesterday that I wanted to ask you about," Erin said. She produced the sealed evidence bag with the grenade in it.

"Well, hello there, old buddy," Skip said. He took a second to look it over before taking it from Erin. Bomb technicians learned to restrain their grabbing reflex, if they wanted to keep being able to count to ten on their hands.

"What can you tell me about this?" she asked.

"C'mon in," he said. "It makes some of the other folks nervous if they see me juggling high explosives in the hallway."

Skip's office had a perpetual burnt, chemical smell to it. He was always working on something, usually arson cases. There really weren't many criminals who used bombs these days, so Skip's primary job was investigating fires that might have been deliberately set. As a result, his desk was usually covered with bits of whatever crime scene he'd been most recently working.

"It's an M67 fragmentation grenade," he said. "They were first put in service back in 1968, as a replacement for the old M33, which replaced the M26, which came after the good old Mark 2 pineapple you might've seen in World War II movies."

"Okay," Erin said. Skip was a regular database of bomb knowledge. She tried to look interested.

"Standard usage," he went on. "Put your finger in the ring and pull it out while holding down the safety lever. Use your hand, not your teeth. Seriously, I don't care what Schwarzenegger does, you try to bite the pin out of a grenade, you can lose teeth. As soon as the lever is released, the fuse initiates. The fuse is a pyrotechnic delay element."

"Meaning what?"

"It's something that takes a couple of seconds to burn, a chemical fuse. It's initiated by a striker cap, a lot like in a cap gun, only bigger. The fuse runs about five seconds and then the device detonates with a lethal radius of five meters and an injury radius of fifteen. It's a reasonably reliable weapon, but the fuse length can be variable. That's why it's good to throw it as soon as you pull the pin."

He casually tossed the evidence bag from one hand to the other. Erin flinched.

"It's useless for demolition work," he said. "It only has a hundred and eighty grams of comp B explosive in it. All the work gets done by the shrapnel. You know, shrapnel is named after a British guy who invented a new kind of explosive shell back in the Napoleonic Wars."

"That's nice, Skip."

"You don't care, do you."

"About Napoleon? Not right now. But I bet knowing that stuff gets you plenty of girls."

"You'd be surprised. Chicks dig bomb technicians. They know we've got those clever fingers."

"Too much information, Skip. So tell me, where would you get one of these?"

"In New York? Nowhere. Leastwise, not legally. They're banned here, along with California and Delaware."

"So, Jersey?"

"Jersey," he agreed. "You'd have to know the right people. But this here is an official US Army grenade. See the markings? To get this, as a private citizen, you'd have to steal it."

"You sure?"

"The US Army doesn't sell its grenades to private citizens. We mostly ship them to places like Israel and Saudi Arabia. Then they throw them at one another. We gave a bunch to the Taliban back in the Eighties. Then they threw the ones they had left over at us. Hell, maybe this is one of those, went overseas and came right back like a long-range boomerang."

"How hard are they to get your hands on?"

He shrugged. "Pretty easy if you know a guy, like I said. Hey, you guys need this grenade for anything, or do we get to dispose of it?"

"It's evidence in a Major Crimes case."

"Bummer. Otherwise we could take it out of town and toss it at something. You ever thrown a grenade?"

"No. They don't even let us use flashbangs anymore."

"Just as well. Those things will mess up your eardrums."

"That's the idea."

"Well, hey, if they do decide to get rid of it, give me a holler. I got an old gravel pit where we dispose of ordnance."

"Skip, you're a veteran."

He gave her an odd look. "Yeah?"

"Do you still practice with guns and stuff?"

"Well, yeah. I have to keep qualified on the range. I'm a cop, Erin. Just 'cause I'm a bomb guy doesn't mean anything. I still carry a sidearm."

"Would you anyway? If you weren't a cop?"

He thought about it. "Maybe. The way they train us, we get to depend on our guns. If I didn't have one handy, I probably wouldn't feel safe."

"What was it like, Skip?"

"What, the war?"

"No. Coming back from it."

He gave her a long, hard look, very different from his usual demeanor. "It was weird. I can't really describe it. Not to someone who hasn't been there."

"Skip, I've been shot at."

"It's different. There's nothing, no way I can tell you. And that's the thing. You can't tell someone about war. You have to be in the shit yourself, and not just for a day or two. I mean, months at a time. And then get dropped right back in the world and people expect you to go on like it didn't happen. Because they don't want to know, you know? They don't want you to tell them what it was really like. They just want to get this thrill, like in the movies, or a video game. They're fine if you tell them about wasting bad guys, but they don't want to know about that time you were cleaning up after a bomb in a marketplace and the Iraqi Army guys, they were just trying to help, but they were putting body parts in these cardboard boxes. And the blood soaked through the cardboard, so when I picked one of them up, the bottom just fell right out of it and all these... these pieces fell out. And one of them, it was this hand, and it looked just like a doll, this tiny plastic hand, except it wasn't plastic. It was from a little kid, and I couldn't even tell boy or girl, because that hand was all we found."

"Jesus," Erin said.

"That's what I mean," Skip said. "You didn't want me to tell you that. I got a hundred stories no one wants to hear."

"So what do you do?"

He shrugged. "Some of us talk to someone, a shrink, or maybe just our buddies. Most of us drink. Like, a lot. Drugs. High-risk lifestyle. Because the really dirty secret is that it's *fun*, Erin. You ride around in tanks, you blow shit up, it really is like a video game, right up until one of your guys gets hit, or you do. Then it fucking sucks, but the rest of the time, it's fun. And people don't get that, either. Try telling a civvie you blew a guy's head off and enjoyed it. Then they look at you like you're a psycho."

"You seem like you've got it together pretty well," Erin said. "But maybe you just hide it better than some."

Skip shrugged again. "It's a thing that happened. I hope it's the worst thing I'll ever do or see. But it's in the past. I've always been pretty good at doing the job that's in front of me. I did talk to a doc when I first got back from the Sandbox, for a while. But I was able to stay off the booze, mostly, and I guess I was lucky. It affects everyone differently. Put three guys in the same situation, they'll remember it three different ways. Maybe four."

"Just like eyewitnesses," she said, smiling.

"My experience isn't the veteran experience," he said. "It's just mine. Talk to the guys I rode with, they'll all tell you different stories, even though we lived together, shot the shit together, did everything together."

“Thanks, Skip,” she said. “I’ll let you know about the grenade.”

“Thanks.” He grinned. “I do still like to blow shit up.”

Chapter 6

Webb had arrived while Erin was downstairs. He was staring morosely at the whiteboard and sipping coffee when she got back to the office.

"Good morning, sir," she said.

"Prescription drugs," he said. "Lawfully prescribed to an injured soldier. Legally obtained weapons."

"Except the grenade and the assault rifle," she said.

"That's not enough," Webb said. "I talked to Levine. She's confident the vomit in the bathroom was not from either of the two victims, so there's a reasonable chance it belongs to our suspect."

"We can get DNA from it," Vic said.

"What's the current backlog at the lab?" Erin asked.

"Five months, I think," Webb said. "But if we catch our guy, a match will put him at the scene."

"Well, that's useless," Vic grumbled.

"Not completely," Erin said. "It means our guy threw up at the scene."

"I know that," Vic said with exaggerated patience. "But lots of guys toss their cookies after killing someone. Most people find murder upsetting. Thank God."

"Levine's got the sample, if she was looking at it," Erin said. "Did she check it for drugs and alcohol?"

"Probably," Webb said, picking up Levine's report and paging through it. "Yeah. High concentration of alcohol, and looks like some oxy, too. The oxy wasn't fully absorbed."

"That's interesting," Erin said. "That means the person in the bathroom took in the booze and the drugs pretty recently."

"So we're looking for a hopped-up junkie," Vic said.

"We're looking for a guy who was at the party," Erin corrected him. "I think he got drunk and popped some pills right there in the apartment. And he wasn't a robber, or he'd have taken the whole pill bottle."

"It wasn't much of a party," Vic said. "We don't have any evidence that more than three people were there."

"I'm guessing either the shooter was the first guest to arrive, or the guest of honor at a small get-together," she said. "I think we're looking for a soldier who just came home."

"Makes sense," Webb said thoughtfully. "Except there's no motive. Why would a guy mow down a couple that's welcoming him home?"

"I have no idea," she said. "But he'd have the skills to make those shots, access to weapons, and opportunity. Frank's dad said he was close to his unit. I'd like to find out who might've come home from a tour recently."

"Time to call the Pentagon," Webb said.

"Good luck breaking through the perimeter of petty bureaucrats," Vic added. "You better hold onto that hand grenade; you might need it."

* * *

Erin didn't have as much trouble as Vic predicted. To her surprise, she actually got a pleasant and helpful secretary, who was perfectly willing to look up Sergeant Carson's unit. Erin wasn't accustomed to navigating the organizational layout of the United States Army, so when the secretary asked what level of unit roster she was looking for, she had no idea what to say.

"Corps, Division, Brigade, Regiment, Company, or Platoon?" the secretary asked.

"Um... Platoon," Erin guessed, on the strength of having seen a movie with that name a few years ago and vaguely remembering a platoon was about thirty guys. That sounded about right.

"Okay, I've got the roster here. You want the list of all active personnel?"

"Actually, no. I need a list of soldiers who came home recently. Say, in the past month."

"Casualties or completion of rotation?"

"Both."

"Copy that. Looks like three soldiers rotated stateside, along with two casualties."

"Okay, can you e-mail me the list?"

"Can do."

Sure enough, a few minutes later Erin had a list of five names, along with ranks, serial numbers, and contact information. She put them up on the whiteboard, listed as persons of interest.

The two wounded men were Christopher Monson and Delray Freeman, both listed as patients at Walter Reed Army Medical Center. It was unlikely either of them had snuck out of the hospital and traveled from DC to Manhattan to shoot up an apartment, but they still went on the list. The other three, Toby Randolph, Jamal Smith, and Warren Forster, were more likely.

Of those, Forster's address was San Francisco, but it was possible he might've stopped off in New York before heading home. Smith and Randolph were both New Yorkers. Smith lived in Harlem, Randolph in Queens.

"That looks promising," Webb said, looking over the list. "Two local boys. Let's go have a talk with them."

"We gonna split up, or do this as one happy family?" Vic asked.

"Let's stick together," Webb said. "We've only got two names to check here in town, and I don't want anyone going off on their own on this one. Our shooter's already proved he knows what he's doing with a gun. I don't want us taking any stupid chances. We'll hit Smith first. Harlem's a little closer than Queens, and at least we can stay on this side of the East River. Neshenko, I'll ride with you. O'Reilly, you and the pooch can follow in your car."

* * *

Erin hadn't gone into Harlem very often during her police career. She always felt a little funny when she did. She tried not to think about the color of her skin when she was on the Job; she'd heard a fellow officer once say that if you arrested people who looked like you, you were a race traitor, and if you arrested people who didn't look like you, you were a racist. You couldn't win. It was better to just get on with what needed to be done. But she was very aware, walking up to an apartment in Harlem, that she was a white woman wearing a shield and a gun in a predominantly black neighborhood. The looks she, Vic, Webb, and Rolf got weren't exactly hostile, but they were definitely wary. She wondered whether they were the same looks Jamal Smith had gotten in the streets of Iraq, wearing a US Army uniform and carrying a gun. Even the civilians who were friendly were still aware you didn't quite belong there.

The helpful Pentagon secretary had listed immediate relatives of each soldier along with their addresses. Jamal Smith was twenty-one years old and lived with his mother and two sisters in a three-bedroom apartment on Lenox Avenue. The neighborhood was attractive, but not affluent. Erin liked the blue-collar feel of it better than the swanky Manhattan downtown. Make the names Irish and the skin of the inhabitants white and it would look a lot like where she'd grown up.

The Smiths' apartment was on the third floor of a four-story brick building. The structure was old but clean and well-kept. Webb stopped at the door. Then he gave Vic a look.

"Why don't you stand back a little?"

"Why?" Vic asked.

"Because you're scary looking," Erin said.

Vic looked offended. Erin tried again.

"If I saw a guy who looked like you outside my door, I wouldn't open it."

He took a couple of steps back, letting Webb and Erin take the lead. Webb rang the doorbell.

After a few moments, the door opened. A young man stood in the doorway, looking them over with curiosity but no apparent unease. He was a tough-looking kid, all wiry muscle, still sporting the military buzz-cut he'd had in the service.

"Help you?" he asked. "I think maybe you're looking for somebody else."

"Sir, are you Jamal Smith?" Webb asked.

"Yeah, that's me. Who're you?"

"My name is Lieutenant Webb. I'm with the NYPD. These are Detectives O'Reilly and Neshenko."

Smith said, "Ma'am," politely to Erin and nodded an acknowledgment of Vic. He saw Rolf and his eyebrows rose slightly, but he didn't comment on the K-9.

"We'd just like to ask you a few questions," Webb said. "May we come in for a moment?"

Smith thought about it, and in that pause Erin saw all the decades of mistrust between minority communities and the police.

"Sure," he said, stepping back from the door. "Come on in. If you wouldn't mind wiping your feet, I'd appreciate it. Ma doesn't like it when people track in dirt."

They obediently scuffed their shoes on the doormat. Erin made sure Rolf's paws were clean as well. They were in a living room, extremely neat and clean. Erin saw photos of the family on the walls, the mom plus Jamal and his sisters. Mom was a very tall, elegant woman, strikingly attractive. The sisters looked to be in their mid-teens in the most recent pictures, with bright smiles. She didn't see any pictures of Jamal's dad, or any other man.

"You all want to take a seat?" Smith asked.

"Thank you," Webb said, selecting a spot on the floral-print couch. "Is anyone else home right now?"

"Nah. Ma's at work, Leticia and Robin are in school. What's this about, sir?"

"You just got back from a tour in Iraq last week," Webb said.

"That's right."

"You were with the First Infantry Division?"

"Yes, sir." Erin saw a flash of pride in Jamal's face.

"What was your job there?"

"Rifleman, sir. Private First Class. Ran the fifty on the Humvee sometimes."

"Thank you for your service," Webb said.

Smith made no reply to that most worn-out of platitudes.

"Can you describe your relationship with Frank Carson?" Webb asked.

Smith blinked. "Sarge? He was in charge of my section, till he got blown up. Roadside bomb. Messed up his leg pretty good, and they sent him home. I ain't seen him since."

"Was he a good sergeant?"

"Hell yes," Smith said. Then he flinched and looked sidelong at Erin. "Sorry, ma'am. I mean, yeah, he was good. Looked after his guys."

"Was he your friend?"

"Well... no. I mean, yeah. He was my sergeant. You can't be friends with your sarge, not really. But he was a good guy. A real good guy. I mean, he'd kick your ass if you screwed up, but he always had your six. Why? He in some kinda trouble?"

Webb ignored the question. "Have you heard from Sergeant Carson since his discharge?"

"Yeah, he heard me and some of the other guys was getting out. He sent me a letter, asked if I'd get together with him and the others. That thing was yesterday."

"So you went to this gathering?" Webb asked.

Smith shook his head. "Couldn't make it. I had a job interview, already had it set up."

"With whom?"

"Delivery service. They wanted a guy with my experience, said military guys was reliable. And I guess they'd had some stickups, so they wanted a guy could look after himself."

"What's the name of this delivery service?" Webb asked. "Who was your interview with?"

"Wait a second," Smith said. "Why's that matter?"

"We need to establish your whereabouts," Webb said. "Where were you yesterday, between two and three o'clock in the afternoon?"

"That's just when the interview was," Smith said. "Two o' clock. I was there till almost three. Then I picked up my sisters from school and we got a hot chocolate at this place just down the block."

"We're going to need the name of the person you interviewed with, and their contact information," Webb said.

Now Smith definitely looked suspicious. "Sure," he said. "I can get that for you, but why you keep asking me where I been, what I been doing? I ain't done nothing bad. And I need this job. You call this guy up, like you from the NYPD and you checking up on me, then he'll think I'm into some sort of shady shit, and he ain't gonna hire me. It's hard enough finding a good job."

Erin had to admit Smith had a point. A recruiter wouldn't look kindly on a job applicant when police called him to verify an alibi. But there was no getting around it.

"Mr. Smith," she said quietly, "I apologize for any trouble. We'll try to avoid causing any difficulties for you. But it's good you have someone who can vouch for you during that time period. It may save you a lot more serious trouble."

"What happened at Sergeant Carson's place, ma'am?" he asked sharply. The kid was no idiot.

"Carson and his wife were shot," Vic said bluntly.

"Shot?" Smith echoed. "By who?"

"That's what we're working on determining," Webb said.

"They gonna be okay?"

"They were killed," Webb said.

Smith looked like he'd taken a bullet to his own chest. "Sarge? Ah, hell no. Not at home! That ain't how it's supposed to go!"

"Mr. Smith," Erin said. "Do you know who else was invited to that gathering?"

"I don't know, ma'am. I guess Randolph... that's Toby Randolph. He was in our section, too, and he came back on the same flight I did."

"Did Toby have any reason to want to hurt the Carsons?" Erin asked.

"Hell no, ma'am! He loved Sarge. More than I did!"

Webb stood up. "Thanks for your time, Mr. Smith. If you can just give me that name and phone number, we'll get out of your way."

"Someone really shot Sarge? And his wife?"

"I'm afraid so," Webb said.

"That's some heavy shit, man. I mean, that... that sucks."

Erin thought that was a pretty good description of what had happened.

* * *

After that, it was down to Queens, a long drive to Erin's old neighborhood. Toby Randolph's address was listed as being only three blocks from Erin's former apartment. According to the Pentagon, he lived alone. It was a new address for Randolph, only added to their database within the last day or so. The detectives pulled up to the plain brick building and got out of their cars. The place looked ordinary enough, like the buildings on either side. Its façade was crumbling a little. The sidewalk was cracked, and weeds were sprouting wherever concrete or pavement gave them an opening.

"What a shithole," Vic said.

"I used to live around here," Erin said, bristling.

"Oh," he said. "Sorry."

"Thanks."

"Sorry you used to live in a shithole, I mean."

"Look who's talking. As I recall, when we went to your old stomping grounds, people tried to kill us. With assault rifles."

"I didn't say my home was any better than yours," he said, smiling.

"Queens is not a shithole," she insisted.

"Knock it off, both of you," Webb said. "I'm from Los Angeles. Neither of you gets to talk about lousy hometowns."

"He's got a point," Vic said.

"Have you ever been to LA?" Erin asked him.

"Nope."

"Then how would you know?"

"I've never been to Baghdad, either, but I've got a pretty good idea what it's like."

"You take the lead, O'Reilly," Webb said. "This being your turf, as you so kindly reminded us. And be careful."

Toby's apartment was on the ground floor, with a door that led directly outside. Erin approached, remembering Webb's warning. But she didn't see any sign of trouble. She pushed the doorbell and waited.

Nothing happened.

She did it again, waited a few seconds, and tried a third time. Then she tried knocking.

"Hey, Randolph!" she called. "NYPD! We need to talk to you!"

"O'Reilly," Webb said quietly. She glanced at him. He nudged a newspaper with his foot. It was the Times.

"So he didn't bring in his paper yet," she said.

"I don't think he's home," Webb said.

"Great," Vic muttered. "We don't have a warrant."

That meant they couldn't break down the door. In fact, even if Toby Randolph had been stupid enough to leave his door unlocked, they couldn't legally enter the apartment without probable cause. There were various dodges they could use, but all of them might endanger their case when it came to trial, and most were unethical.

Webb sighed. "I guess we came all this way for nothing." He turned and started back to Vic's car. Vic, grumbling, followed.

Erin hesitated. She took a moment to open the trash can sitting by the corner of the building. Garbage cans could be freely searched, as there was no expectation of privacy regarding discarded items. She pulled on a pair of disposable gloves and dove in. A fellow cop had once told Erin it wasn't a true investigation until you'd been up to your elbows in trash. She wished that wasn't true.

She found a black plastic bag, pulled it out of the can, and ripped it open. Inside were a few takeout containers with traces of Chinese food, some used tissues, some broken pieces of Styrofoam packing material, and a couple of empty plastic bottles. She picked up one of the bottles and looked at the label.

"What've you got there?" Vic asked. He'd come back to stand behind her, looking over her shoulder.

"I think we better get that warrant," Erin said softly. She had a nasty, fluttery feeling in the pit of her stomach.

"Benzene," he said. "That stuff will give you cancer."

"Everything gives you cancer," she said. "Put in for a search warrant for this apartment, Vic. Now."

"On what grounds?"

"Didn't they give you basic explosives training in ESU?" she asked. She'd taken a brief course when she'd been assigned Rolf. He was an explosive-sniffing dog, and the NYPD had thought it was a good idea for his handler to know a little on the subject.

"Yeah. Benzene's flammable, sure, but it's no worse than gasoline."

She pointed to the chunks of packing foam. "And when you combine it with low-octane gas and Styrofoam, you get...?"

"Napalm. Shit."

"Unless you think he's drinking benzene by the bottle, we better get inside that apartment as quick as we can. And we better get Skip Taylor down here."

Chapter 7

Erin and her colleagues waited curbside for the Bomb Squad. They were squeezed into Vic's Taurus, Webb and Vic in the front seat, Erin in back with Rolf, so they'd all be together if they needed to coordinate quick action. There was a chance Randolph was home, or that he might return, and they wanted to be able to scoop him up if he showed. While they waited, Erin tried to make sense of things.

What the hell was Randolph doing making napalm at home? And why would he shoot his sergeant, a guy everyone seemed to love and who'd invited him to a party? She was missing something, something important. And that was bad. If she didn't understand what he was doing, she had no way of guessing what he'd do next.

"How bad is napalm, anyway?" she asked Vic and Webb.

Vic shrugged. "I know it sticks to kids."

She stared at him. "What the hell is wrong with you?"

"Okay, not funny," he admitted. "That's just an old song I heard once. I dunno. It's a firebomb, like those jokers used on that restaurant in Little Italy a couple weeks ago. You were there. What'd you think?"

"It was nasty stuff," she said. "You could do some damage with it, but it's not exactly the Oklahoma City bomb. Whatever this guy's planning, it's not big."

"Doesn't need to be big to rack up a body count," Webb said morosely. "It's just a question of picking the right target."

"We may want some uniforms here," Erin said.

"No," Webb said. "We don't want to spook him. And if he's booby-trapped the place, more officers just mean more potential casualties. Let's keep it low-key."

They kept waiting. Webb fiddled with an unlit cigarette, clearly wanting to smoke it. Vic had a toothpick in the corner of his mouth and was meditatively chewing it. Rolf was the only one who was relaxed: He'd laid his chin on Erin's leg and was having a late-morning snooze.

A Chevy Suburban, unmarked, rolled up in front of the apartment. All three detectives suddenly stiffened. Rolf, feeling the change in the energy in the car, opened his eyes and lifted his head. The driver's side door of the SUV opened and Skip Taylor got out. Erin was glad he'd gone low-profile for this job. The NYPD's Bomb Squad truck was a massive blue-and-white beast that would definitely have attracted all kinds of attention. Then they'd have had bystanders and reporters to deal with along with whatever was in Randolph's apartment, which would mean more delay while they got Patrol officers on scene for crowd control.

Erin and her comrades got out of the Taurus. She waved to Skip, who had the back of the Suburban open and was taking out a heavy-looking duffel bag.

"Hey, Erin," he said. "Miss me already?"

"I wasn't expecting to call you so soon," she said.

"What've we got?" he asked.

"Ground-floor apartment, single occupant," she said. "Either he's not home or he's laying low. I found benzene containers and scrap polystyrene in his trash. He's got military training, so I was thinking—"

"Homemade napalm," Skip finished for her. "Good call. Our guy, is he a combat engineer?"

"No, just an infantryman, I think."

"Small mercies. But he must have experience with IEDs. He a veteran?"

"Just back from Iraq."

Skip grimaced. "Okay, so we assume he knows how to be a sneaky bastard. Does he hate cops? Anti-government? Right-wing militia?"

"Not that we know of."

"Didn't you run his name for political affiliations?"

Erin cursed inwardly. They hadn't. It seemed like an obvious thing in hindsight.

"I'll do that," Webb said, going back to Vic's Taurus to access the on-board computer.

"I want the building evacuated," Skip said. "Everybody out."

"Napalm doesn't blow big, does it?" Vic said. "I mean, worst-case scenario, he sets his place on fire."

Skip gave him a look. "Worst-case scenario is he's got half a ton of fertilizer stacked floor to ceiling in his kitchen and takes out the whole block. Unless you're volunteering to go in there with me, don't talk to me about worst-case scenarios."

"You think that's likely?" Erin asked.

"How am I supposed to know that?" Skip retorted. "You're the detectives here. You're supposed to know who this guy is. I just take care of the bombs."

While he was talking, Skip was looking over his tools. He had a remote-control robot in the back of his vehicle, but didn't appear to be using it.

Erin jogged back to Vic's car and knocked on the window. Webb rolled it down.

"Sir, Skip wants the building evacuated. Maybe tell them there might be a gas leak?"

"Good idea," Webb said. "That'll get them moving. You and Neshenko take care of it."

Erin and Vic accordingly started knocking on the other doors of the apartment. Fortunately, it wasn't a very large building, and most of the inhabitants were at work. They routed out six irritable and worried New Yorkers, but were able to do it without too much fuss. Vic herded them to the other side of the street, where they stood in the cold and gossiped.

Skip approached Randolph's door. He got down on one knee and snaked a fiber-optic cable under the door. Then he looked at a laptop screen and slowly moved it around, taking in the room.

"How's it look?" Webb called from a respectful distance.

"I think we're good," Skip said. "I don't see any... oh. Wait a second. No, that's nothing. Got a gas can by the door, but it doesn't seem to be attached to anything. No sign of anybody here, no booby traps."

"I've got the warrant," Webb said. "You can make entry."

"We've got a key," Erin offered. She'd gotten it from the building's super.

"No thanks," Skip said. "I'd rather not make metal-to-metal contact in this door, if that's okay with you. The city good with paying for a new door if we're wrong?"

Webb sighed and nodded.

"Okay," Skip said. He got a short-handled, heavy hammer out of his bag and stood up. "The guy's not in his kitchen or living room, but he might be in the bedroom or bath. So if one of you wants to back me up?"

"I've got you," Erin said, coming up along the wall with Rolf in hand. "You might want my K-9 to sniff out bombs."

"I might," he agreed. "Okay, let's do this."

He swung the hammer and smashed open the door. The wood molding on the inside of the doorframe splintered and the door swung inward. Skip stepped quickly into the room and off to one side, drawing his pistol. Erin was right behind him, Glock in hand.

"Clear!" she called, moving through the living room to check the bathroom and bedroom. It was definitely a bachelor pad. She saw clothes strewn around, empty takeout containers in the kitchen. She caught a whiff of a strong chemical smell, a reek like a gas station. She saw some things on the kitchen table, but her primary concern was verifying Randolph's presence or absence.

She finished clearing the apartment. It was unoccupied. She came back to the kitchen, holstering her gun, to find Skip studying the table.

"You were right," he said. "Our boy was making napalm. Looks like he was mixing it in this big Tupperware here. You can see the residue."

Rolf definitely noticed. He leaned in, nostrils twitching, and assumed his "alert" posture, sitting bolt upright and staring at the table.

"How much of the stuff?" she asked, tossing Rolf his reward chew-toy. The Shepherd happily dropped to his belly and started gnawing.

"Hard to say. You found the benzene bottles in the trash?"

"Yeah. Two liters."

"Not too much, then. This is a retail operation, not wholesale."

Erin nodded. But she was looking around the apartment while Skip examined the table, and what she saw wasn't encouraging. In the living room was a gun-cleaning kit, and the coffee table had a couple of cardboard ammunition boxes on it.

".45 caliber," she announced. "And the other one is 5.56 millimeter. Both of them are mostly empty. Our guy's got a pistol and a rifle, and probably a couple of extra clips of ammo."

"And some homemade firebombs," Skip added.

"Looks like he's planning one hell of a night out on the town," Erin said. "I just wish we knew where he is. And where he's going."

* * *

They drove back to Precinct 8, leaving Skip and a CSU team at Randolph's apartment. Vic exercised some logistical foresight and ordered pizza before they left Queens, so it arrived at the station about the same time they did. It was a late lunch, but no one complained.

"I need everything we've got on Toby Randolph," Webb said. "Service history, legal records, political activities, friends, family, associates. We do not need Oklahoma City happening here."

"Damn," Vic said. "Didn't we just stop one of these assholes last year? I'm getting a little déjà vu."

"Neshenko, you work the political angle," Webb went on. "Get on Randolph's machine and find out what he's looking at online." They'd retrieved the soldier's computer from his apartment.

"It's gonna be porn," Vic predicted.

"What makes you say that?" Erin asked.

"He's a guy living alone. There's always porn."

"You're starting to sound like Sergeant Brown from Vice."

"O'Reilly, you need to talk to his army buddies," Webb said. "You'll want to hit Smith in Harlem again, and those two at Walter Reed. We'll also need to look up his family, find out what we can from them."

Erin obediently looked up the phone number for the military hospital and spent the next half hour being bounced from one automated menu to another, with a few live people thrown in for good measure. She finally ended up talking to a nurse in charge of one of the convalescent wards.

Erin identified herself and explained, "I need to talk to Christopher Monson and Delray Freeman. It's about an ongoing investigation in New York."

"I don't understand," the nurse said. "These men came straight here from Rammstein in Germany. Before that they were on deployment in Iraq. They can't have been in New York in over a year."

"I need to talk to them about someone they know," Erin said.

"These young men were seriously injured in the service of their country," the nurse said severely. "I don't want them being badgered. They need peace and rest after what they've been through, and frankly, they deserve it."

"I know, and I apologize. This won't take long. I promise, they're not in any trouble."

The nurse let out a slow breath through her teeth. "All right, I'll ask them if they feel up for a short, calm telephone conversation. But if they say no, I'm going to hang up."

"Fair enough."

The nurse put Erin on hold. Erin twiddled her thumbs at her desk and looked up Toby Randolph's police record while she waited. It was nonexistent. The kid was in the city's database, having graduated Townsend Harris High School two years ago and gotten his driver's license a year and a half before that. She found both his yearbook photo and his driver's license picture. Both showed a pleasant-faced kid with light brown hair, freckles, and a sparkle in his eye.

She kept poking around online and found his Facebook page. It hadn't been updated in a while. Apparently he'd had other things on his mind on deployment. She skimmed his page history. It looked like he was a big movie fan, with a particular interest in animation. He was also big into science. It looked like he'd been hoping to use his veterans' benefits to enroll in college when he got back stateside, with the idea of becoming a chemical engineer.

"Hello, Detective?"

Erin shook herself out of cyberspace. "Yes?"

"I have Corporal Monson here. Try to keep the call as short as possible, and don't upset him."

"Thank you."

There was a short pause. Then Erin heard a male voice on the line.

"Hello?"

"Hello. Mr. Monson?"

"That's me, ma'am. The nurse said you're a cop?"

"That's right. My name is Erin O'Reilly. I'm a detective with the New York Police Department. I'm sorry for disturbing you."

"No, it's fine. Really. Nurse, I'm okay. Why don't you check on Marmaduke down there? I think he's having some trouble breathing. Okay, Detective. She's gone. Jesus, this is like having a babysitter again. Seriously, I'm bored out of my skull here. I dunno why a cop's calling me, but I would love to talk to you. You're a lady cop, huh?"

"That's right," she said again.

"How long you been a cop?"

"Twelve years."

"So you'd be, what, mid-thirties?"

"Yeah," she said, wondering where he was going with this and afraid she knew.

"Okay, that's cool," he said. "So, what're you wearing right now?"

"Mr. Monson," she said in a deadpan, "I'm a police detective, not a phone-sex operator."

He laughed. "Okay, okay. Sorry. Like I said, I'm bored. And with this leg, it's not like I'm getting laid anytime soon. You can't blame a guy for trying."

"Nonsense," Erin said. "Lots of girls think scars are cool. You'll get plenty of play once you're out of the hospital. When did you get back to the States?"

"Two weeks ago. I was at Rammstein for three weeks before that. They did the main surgery there. Now it's all follow-up stuff."

"How'd you get hit?"

"Roadside bomb. Least, that's what they tell me. I was driving, just a normal patrol. Next thing I know, I'm thirty meters from the Humvee, still holding the steering wheel. You believe that? Whole thing just came off in my hands. Messed up my leg pretty good."

"Did you know Sergeant Carson?"

"Yeah, he was in my platoon. Not my section, though. That'd be Sergeant Vellner. V-man, we call him. Carson rotated home a while ago, after he caught one, but he was solid."

"How about Private Randolph?"

"Yeah, I know him. He could get all these bootleg flicks. We had this big, white-painted cinderblock wall in the compound and he set up a projector so we'd play 'em just like in the theater back home. He got these big speakers rigged up and everything." Monson paused. "Crap, you're a cop. I shouldn't have said that. I mean, I'm sure he legally obtained all the movies he showed us. When I said bootleg, I meant—"

"Mr. Monson, I don't care about bootleg movies. That's an FBI matter."

"I like the way you call me Mr. Monson," he said. "Sounds hot the way you say it."

"You've been in the Sandbox a while, haven't you," she said, using the nickname for Iraq she'd heard from Ian and Skip. Jargon was a great way to build rapport.

"You've got no idea. The women there, they all have those things on their faces, you can't see them." He lowered his voice a little. "And Nurse Joplin, she's the one you talked to, well, she ain't winning any Miss America pageants, you know? I miss American women."

"Are you friends with Toby Randolph?" she asked, trying to steer the conversation back to relevant subjects.

"Yeah, I'm tight with him. You get close to the guys in your platoon. He's a damn good soldier. He should be coming home right about now. He's from New York, so you could probably talk to him yourself." There was a short pause.

Erin knew the penny had just dropped in Monson's head. He'd started to wonder why a New York detective would be calling about a soldier from New York.

"Hey, is Randolph okay?" Monson asked.

"Do you know why he'd be in any trouble?" she asked, using Carlyle's favorite trick of avoiding a question by asking one of her own.

"Well, I mean, I felt like things were getting to him a little bit. There was this time, it was the night before I got hit, he was running the movie. And I had to get up and take care of business, and as I went past him, he had this look on his face. He was just staring, the thousand-yard thing. I said something to him, and I don't think he even heard me. I just wanted to make sure he hadn't, you know, hurt himself."

"You think maybe he was suicidal?" she asked bluntly.

"No!" Monson exclaimed, too quickly and too defensively. "I just mean, the shit we deal with over there, it gets to you sometimes. I just figured it was about time he went home."

"Was he upset with anybody in particular?" she asked.

"Yeah. Osama Bin Laden."

"Bin Laden's dead."

"Yeah. Navy boys got him in Pakistan. Don't care much for the Navy, but those SEALs are hardcore. Fuckin' hooah. Sorry, ma'am. But if it wasn't for him, we wouldn't have been sucking sand in the desert, and I wouldn't be lying here with half a hardware store holding my shin together. So yeah, not Bin Laden's biggest fans. None of us."

"Did he have any trouble with anyone in your platoon?"

"Nah, not Randolph. He's a good kid. Real badass in a fight, too. Good shot. I think he got more kills than anyone else in the company. Real good with a rifle, great eye. Nice guy on the base, but you flip that switch, and man, he's a machine."

"How do you mean, flip that switch?"

"I mean, just like that, it's game time. The training kicks in and you're ready to get it on. Ready to get some. You ever see Randolph in a fight, he's friggin' unstoppable. Some guys, they get scared when there's incoming. Randolph just turns into one of those guys, you know, those Vikings who'd go nuts and bite their shields and start, like, chewing on guys?"

"Berserkers?" Erin guessed.

"Yeah. Like them."

"Great," she said dryly.

"Oh, shit," Monson said quietly. "I'm busted."

There was the sound of a brief altercation, after which Nurse Joplin's voice came back on the line.

"Detective, I'm afraid this conversation is disturbing the other patients. I'm going to have to insist you discontinue the call. Thank you."

"Thank you for—" Erin began and was cut off by the dial tone. She looked at her handset for a moment and hung up.

"Got anything?" Vic called from his desk.

"Just that apparently our guy is a quiet, friendly boy who likes to show movies to his friends. And he turns into the Incredible Hulk in a fight."

"Really? Green muscles and everything?"

"Something like that. How's it going on your side?"

"I got nothing on his politics. It looks like he may have been interested in drugs, though."

"Weed? Heroin? Coke?"

"No. Antidepressants, hallucinogens, that sort of thing. And he was looking at all these conspiracy-theory websites about the US Army experimenting on soldiers."

"What sort of experiments?"

"LSD in their drinking water, that sort of thing." Vic looked disgusted. "Far-out bullshit theories. They'd never get away with that these days. Maybe back in Vietnam, but that was a long time ago."

"Randolph thought he was being experimented on?" Erin wondered aloud.

Vic shrugged. "Maybe. Or maybe he was just curious."

"That could lead to anger at authority figures in the military," she said. "Maybe including his sergeant?"

"Best theory I've heard today," he said. "But that's not saying much."

"If that's the case, then he might lash out at other authority figures," she guessed.

"And now you're an FBI profiler," Vic said.

"Don't even joke about that. I'm never joining the Feebies."

Chapter 8

Vic sat back from his computer and rubbed his eyes. Erin thought he looked more tired than he had after being shot by Russian gangsters. She reluctantly looked at the clock. They'd been in the office all afternoon. Now the sun had gone down and they were no closer to finding Toby Randolph.

"No anti-government websites," Vic said. "No loony right-wing militia groups. No jihadists. His e-mails are harmless. Hell, even the porn sites are vanilla."

"So there was porn?"

"I told you there would be."

Erin had called Jamal Smith again, but he hadn't been any help. All he'd been able, or willing, to say was that yeah, Randolph had been a little weird toward the end of his tour, but wasn't everyone? She had the feeling he had more on his mind, but he wasn't ready to talk trash about a fellow soldier.

It was like dealing with dirty cops. The members of any organization reflexively drew together against outsiders, but when that organization was made of armed men and women, who risked their lives for one another, the defensive barrier was even stronger. Cops called it the Blue Wall. She wondered what the Army term for it was. Maybe Skip would know. If he'd even tell her.

They'd put out a BOLO on Toby Randolph, putting his face and description on every police computer and radio set. They'd debated notifying Homeland Security, but Erin had recommended against it.

"Why not?" Webb asked.

Erin hadn't had a good answer to that. The truth was that she didn't completely trust Agent Johnson, their Homeland liaison. He'd proved a little shifty on their previous case together, and she wasn't a hundred percent sure he wasn't feeding information to the Mafia. But she'd spun something for Webb about Randolph being a little fish that they could handle. Besides, they had no proof Randolph was planning to hit anything.

"I'd feel better if we could find his firebombs," Webb muttered, but let it go for the moment.

Now Erin hoped she'd been right. No one had reported any sign of Randolph. Either he wasn't in New York, he'd gone to ground, or he was just damned lucky. He didn't seem to have much of a support network in the area. Jamal Smith claimed to have no knowledge of his whereabouts. Frank Carson was dead.

That left Randolph's family. It had taken Webb most of the rest of the afternoon to track down their information. He was an only child, his parents divorced. His dad's last known address was in Miami, but his mom was in Rego Park, in the western part of Queens. Unfortunately, she didn't have a phone number listed.

"I think I should go back to Queens," Erin said. "I'll try to find Mrs. Randolph. If anyone knows where her kid is, she might."

"I'll come with you," Vic said.

"Better not. Anybody might spot Randolph anytime and call it in. We need someone ready to move if that happens."

"We're too shorthanded," he grumbled. "When the hell are they giving us another detective?"

"Feeling overworked?" she said with mock sympathy.

"And underappreciated," he said.

"Tell you what. I'll get you some Mallomars. That'll cheer you up. They're only available for another month or so."

"You're a New Yorker, all right," Vic said with a grin. "I bet your mom kept those in the fridge for you over the summer when you were a kid."

"Guilty as charged," she said. "Don't worry, if I find any sign he's at his mom's, I'll pull back and call for backup. I've seen how our killer can shoot."

* * *

As Erin crossed the East River for the third time that day, she wondered why she'd bothered moving to Manhattan. Though she had gotten a fantastic deal on her apartment. She had her suspicions about that. She thought Carlyle probably had something to do with it. The landlord had been just a little too eager to bring his price down for her, and she'd gotten the place on the recommendation of a cop who'd turned out to be working for the O'Malleys.

Regardless, the Manhattan place was hers now, and she liked it, but she did seem to spend a lot of time on Long Island. She hoped Mrs. Randolph would be home so the trip wouldn't be wasted.

The house in Rego Park was a nice little two-story place, brick on the ground floor and wood siding upstairs. It was a lot of space for a woman living alone. Erin guessed it was the family home. Why had Toby taken a separate apartment?

She saw lights in the window as she and Rolf went up the sidewalk and climbed the front stairs. She rang the doorbell.

A short, round woman peered out at her through the window in the door. Erin held up her shield so the woman could see it. After a moment, the locks clicked and the door opened. The woman's hair was wet, like she'd just gotten out of the shower, and she was wearing a blue bathrobe and fuzzy slippers.

"Officer?" the woman said.

"Ma'am, I'm Erin O'Reilly. I'm a detective with the NYPD. This is my K-9. I was hoping I could talk to you for a few minutes. Are you Mrs. Randolph?"

"That's right. What's this about?"

"When was the last time you saw your son Toby?"

Erin was watching Mrs. Randolph as she asked the question, looking for tells. She saw no evasiveness, no guilt. What she saw was a slight flinch, as if the woman had been expecting a blow but still felt the pain from it. Mrs. Randolph's face went just a little paler and she took a half-step back.

Then she recovered. "I saw Toby three days ago," she said quietly. "We... fought. He moved out. Detective... please tell me. Is my son alive?"

"As far as we know," Erin said, wondering why she'd jumped to that conclusion. "But it's important that we find him as quickly as possible. May I come in?"

"Yes, of course." Mrs. Randolph stepped aside. Then, looking at Erin's K-9, she added, "I have a cat."

"That won't be a problem," Erin assured her. "Rolf is very well trained."

Erin saw no signs of Toby's possible presence. She automatically looked for men's shoes, extra clothing, anything that would suggest another occupant, but saw nothing. She did notice an orange and white cat watching her and Rolf from the landing with enormous green eyes.

"I'm sorry about this," Mrs. Randolph said, gesturing to her clothing. "I wasn't expecting company. Please, sit down. Can I get you a cup of coffee? I already have the machine going. Decaf, I'm afraid, because it's so late. Otherwise I'm up all night."

"Coffee would be great, ma'am," Erin said, taking a seat on an old but comfortable faux-leather couch.

Mrs. Randolph went to the kitchen. While she was gone, Erin took in the furnishings. The first thing she noticed was a big photograph of Toby Randolph in a nice frame. It hung above the fireplace in the place of honor. It looked like the same picture she'd seen from his high school, his senior portrait. He was such an ordinary-looking kid, a *nice*-looking kid. Maybe she spent too much time looking at mug shots. She expected people to scowl at the camera, so when they smiled it was a surprise.

A meow near her feet attracted her attention. The cat had ventured down to see the visitors. Rolf was watching it with interest.

"Rolf," she said, "*sitz. Bleib.*"

Rolf sat and stayed. The cat sniffed at the Shepherd, mewed, and rubbed its cheek against his chest, to the K-9's evident confusion. Rolf gave Erin a plaintive look, as if to ask what he was supposed to do with this small furry thing that wasn't afraid of him.

"Oh, you've met Jonesy," Mrs. Randolph said from the doorway. "He's not afraid of anything, in spite of his name."

Erin gave her a questioning look.

The other woman came in with a tray on which were two coffee cups, a little cream pitcher, a sugar bowl, and a plate of shortbread cookies. "He's named after the cat in *Alien*," she explained. "I didn't much care for that movie. Toby named him."

Erin extended a hand. Jonesy rubbed against it. She stroked his head and he arched into her touch and purred.

"I know Toby's big on movies," she said. "One of his Army buddies told me he'd put on shows for his unit at their base."

Mrs. Randolph nodded. "Yes, he's always loved films. Cream or sugar?"

"Cream, no sugar, thanks."

Erin took the offered cup and sipped. It was good coffee, despite the lack of caffeine.

"Detective... O'Reilly, was it?"

"Yes, ma'am."

"You're from around here, aren't you?"

Erin smiled. "Yes, ma'am. I grew up in Queens."

"I could tell by your accent." Mrs. Randolph tried to take a sip from her own cup. Her hand was shaking. She set the cup down on the end table. "Detective, why are you asking about my son? Is he missing?"

Erin knew it was best to be as honest as possible. She looked Mrs. Randolph in the eye. "Yes. Do you know where he is?"

"No."

"Please think carefully, ma'am. Toby may be in danger."

"I... I know." Mrs. Randolph looked down at her trembling hands. "I'm sorry, Detective. I really am. But I don't know what I can do to help. You've been to his apartment, I'm sure."

"Yes. Does he have a job?"

"No."

"A girlfriend, maybe? Or one of his old friends, from the Army or from school, that he might have crashed with?"

"No. He... he only came home a week ago. He was staying in his old room, but then we... fought. And he left." The woman began to cry silently, big round tears overflowing her eyes and rolling down her cheeks.

Erin put a hand on Mrs. Randolph's wrist. She'd learned the power a comforting gesture had to establish rapport. Knowing it was a calculated thing made her feel a little guilty, but only a little. She had a job to do, and if she did it right, she'd be helping both of them.

"What happened when Toby came home?" she asked gently.

"After his father and I divorced, we didn't have a whole lot of money," Mrs. Randolph said. "I'd always told Toby he could do anything, be anything, but he was such a responsible boy. He knew I couldn't really afford to send him to a fancy college. He wanted to go to MIT, to be an engineer. Do you know how much the tuition is? And he's such a bright boy. We talked it over, and he told me he'd decided to go into the Army. They told him he'd get training that would be useful to him in civilian life, that he'd be in an engineer program, and he'd get government aid for his education once he served his time."

Mrs. Randolph gave a shaky, bitter laugh. "They put him in the infantry. Carrying a rifle. No engineer school for him. And they sent him to Iraq. I was so afraid he'd be killed. On the news I'd see reports of roadside bombs, snipers, helicopter crashes, and I kept waiting for that knock on the door. It would be just like in those movies he loves, there'd be an officer and a priest standing there with a telegram. I don't even know if they use telegrams anymore. Do you know?"

Erin didn't. She shook her head, thinking that she'd been the officer on the Carsons' doorstep the previous night.

"And I prayed, Detective," Mrs. Randolph went on. "I prayed harder than I've ever prayed for anything in my life. 'Oh God,' I said, 'just let my boy come home to me alive. Don't let him die out there, so far away from home. Keep him safe.' Every morning and every night, I prayed until I thought my heart would break.

"Then he came home. When I saw him at the door in his uniform, with his bag on his shoulder, I was so happy I couldn't believe it. I just threw myself at him. Do you have children, Detective?"

"No, ma'am. But I've got a mother."

Mrs. Randolph tried to smile and couldn't quite manage it. "I hugged him, and he felt different. Rigid. As if something in him had hardened. I looked up at him, and he looked at me, and there was no light in his eyes. It was as if... as if he was already dead and what had come back was just his shell.

"He didn't smile or laugh all the time he was here. Not once. I tried to talk to him about it, after the first few days, and he blew up at me. He said some very hurtful things. Then he got his Army bag and left. He put a message on my voicemail the next day saying that he'd gotten an apartment, and he told me the address. He also told me to leave him alone."

Erin nodded. "Did he say why he was leaving?"

"He said this wasn't home anymore. He said... he wasn't my son anymore. But he is, Detective O'Reilly. He is! Something happened to him over there, but he's still my boy. He'll always be my son! Why is he missing? What's happening to him?"

Erin thought how to answer. What she said was, "A man who was in his unit was killed. We need to find Toby because we believe he has information that will lead to the killer."

She handed Mrs. Randolph one of her cards. "If he contacts you, or if he comes here, please let me know immediately. He may be in danger himself."

"I know," Mrs. Randolph said. She swallowed. "I thought, when I saw you there, and you asked about him, that you were going to tell me he had... that he had..." She couldn't finish.

"We'll do our best to keep him alive and well," Erin said. "Will you help us, if you can?"

"Of course." The woman wiped her eyes. "The wife of one of the other soldiers, at one of our gatherings, said I should... that I should think of him as dead. She said he would die over there, whether he came back with his body intact or not. That his spirit would be dead. I didn't believe her. But then, when I saw that look in my baby's eyes..." She started crying again.

"I'll do everything I can for him," Erin promised. "Where do you think he would go?"

"I... I don't know. I always thought he would feel safest here, with... with me. But maybe he doesn't know how to feel safe anymore."

Chapter 9

"Dispatch, we've got a 10-33 at the City Hall Loop," one of the Patrol cops said into his radio. "We need the Bomb Squad to—"

"Get down!" Vic shouted, an instant before Erin saw the men. There were two of them, dressed in black, in the stairwell halfway down the platform.

Erin reflexively dropped to her stomach. A split second later, muzzle flashes lit up the subway like a golden strobe light. The man fired so fast she couldn't distinguish individual gunshots. The sound was like tearing canvas.

The patrolman on Erin's right pitched over backward, his words cut off mid-sentence. Blood sprayed her in the face from the exit wound. She distinctly heard the crack of his head against the floor. The other uniform dove toward the wall. Bullets chewed into the concrete and brickwork.

Erin brought her Glock in line. As she did, the flat, hard crack of Vic's rifle cut through the rattle of the automatic weapon. He fired three quick shots, then two more. Erin braced her arms on the station floor and squeezed off a shot in the direction of the gunfire.

Vic grunted, like he'd been punched below the belt, and went down clutching his stomach. Blood gushed through his fingers. A liver shot, Erin thought, just like Brunanski back in Queens. He'd be dead in minutes if they didn't get a trauma team there.

More muzzle flashes flared in the stairwell. One bullet hit the ground just in front of Erin, stinging her face with chips of concrete. Dust blinded her. She fired four times, with no idea what she was aiming at. Spent cartridges, still smoking, skittered over the edge of the platform.

The remaining Patrol officer was shouting into his radio, repeating "10-13! Officer down! 10-13!" over and over. Erin wished he'd shut up.

She blinked frantically, clearing her vision as well as possible. She couldn't see Vic. He'd fallen on the subway tracks. She didn't have a clear shot at the bad guys. She gathered her legs under herself. "Rolf!" she shouted. "Fass!"

Hearing the "bite" command, the K-9 snarled and rushed the stairwell. Rolf was fast and hard to see in the dark. If the gunman had only had a pistol, the Shepherd might have made it.

The submachine-gun rattled again. At least three bullets, maybe four, caught Rolf mid-stride. The vest stopped most of them, but one punched into the dog's skull. His momentum carried him a few yards farther down the platform, his legs splaying out, limbs twitching in a last spastic motion.

Erin screamed.

* * *

Erin had her gun in her hand, heart pounding, finger on the trigger. The room was dark, like the subway tunnel. She saw movement and aimed. A pair of eyes caught a sliver of light, reflecting greenish-white. Her finger tightened on the trigger.

She let out her breath in a sudden exhalation as she recognized her partner. Rolf was watching her anxiously from the foot of the bed, tail wagging uncertainly. She was aiming her Glock right between his eyes.

"Jesus," she whispered, realizing what she'd very nearly done. "No."

She clawed for the light switch and flicked on the reading lamp next to her bed. She ejected the magazine from the Glock's grip. Then she pulled back the slide. A bright brass nine-millimeter bullet spun out of the firing chamber. She batted it away. It bounced off the nightstand with a little tinkling sound and landed in the corner.

Rolf came alongside the bed and nosed at Erin's hand. She stared at him with wide, horrified eyes. Mechanically, she rubbed his head. He licked her hand. He didn't understand. How could he? But he knew his partner was upset. His eyes asked her a question.

"It's okay, kiddo," she said, but her voice sounded dry and cracked. "Everything's okay."

Her alarm clock read 4:13. Erin set the pistol and magazine on the night table, lay back, and put her hands over her eyes. *Good luck getting back to sleep again*, she thought. *You almost shot your dog, O'Reilly. Because of a nightmare.*

Why was she having these dreams all of a sudden? She'd been fine, perfectly fine. Why now? What had changed?

"Everything's okay," she repeated. She got out of bed and went to the kitchen. The linoleum was cold under her bare feet. She poured a glass of water. As she drank it, her eyes strayed to her liquor cabinet. She knew she had three bottles of Glen D whiskey in there, Carlyle's best top-shelf brand, two unopened, the third nearly full. That'd help her sleep.

She felt eyes on her and saw Rolf in the kitchen doorway. He wagged his tail again.

"You're right," she muttered, leaving the cabinet closed. What would it mean if she started drinking at four in the morning? It'd mean she was a drunk, that was what.

She pulled on a sweatshirt and a pair of socks, went into the living room, and tried to think. As long as she was awake, she might as well get some work done.

Toby Randolph had gone away to war fine, and he'd come back wrong. That was the simple version. Then... what? He'd gone berserk and mowed down his sergeant and the poor guy's wife? Why? What possible reason did he have to kill Frank and Helen Carson? And why make a bunch of bombs? Where was he now? What was he going to do?

She couldn't organize her thoughts. She was too jumpy, too tense. She thought of the whiskey bottle again. Maybe just one shot, to steady her.

The couch was shaking slightly. She looked down and saw her leg moving like the needle on her mom's sewing machine, up and down with incredible speed.

Erin was suddenly scared. Was she cracking up? Going nuts?

"Oh, Jesus," she said once more. She didn't even know whether it was a curse or a prayer. She looked around the familiar furnishings of her home and knew she couldn't stay there. The walls crowded her.

She went into the bedroom and put on her running clothes. Rolf's worry disintegrated. He began wagging more excitedly. He knew perfectly well what it meant when Erin put on her sweats and sneakers. It meant a run, and Rolf was always ready for that, no matter what time it was.

She buckled on the fanny pack and put her backup pistol in it. Maybe she'd almost shot the wrong target when she was waking up, but she wasn't about to go out unarmed. That wouldn't help her state of mind at all.

Erin hesitated at the door. Maybe she shouldn't go out alone. And that thought shook her worse than almost anything.

When had Erin O'Reilly ever been afraid to go it alone?

"It's okay," she said to Rolf. "We're just going for backup."

She loaded him into her Charger and drove to Central Park. As she drove, she tried not to think about what she'd do if her backup didn't show.

* * *

"Good morning, ma'am."

She was ready for him this time, and instead of being startled she felt relieved. "Morning," she replied, taking a quick look at Ian. Those dark gray sweats made it very hard to see him, harder than if he'd been wearing black. People who worked by night, and who had to spot other people in the dark, knew that true black wasn't the best color for nighttime camouflage. In a city, dark gray was much better at blending into the background.

That was why he wore it, of course. Ian wasn't worried about what he should've been worried about, like being hit by a car that couldn't see him. No, he was worried about getting picked off by a sniper.

"Let's do this," she said.

"Yes, ma'am."

They started running. She set the pace this time, and he let her, but she ran at least as fast as they had on their last outing. They ran through the pre-dawn darkness in the park, through the woods and around The Pond. That was its name; just "The Pond." They saw a few other early-morning fitness freaks and a few dog walkers, but the park was mostly empty. It was too cold for the casual runners, too early for most New Yorkers and too late for the rest.

"Thanks," she said to Ian around the end of the first mile.

"For what, ma'am?"

"Being here. I wasn't sure you would be."

"I like routine, ma'am."

"Ian, can I ask you something?"

"If you want."

"I know you saw some shit. Over there."

Ian didn't say anything.

"Did you have any trouble when you got back? Dreams, flashbacks, that kind of thing?"

"Why?"

"I've been having bad dreams," she said, and as she said it, she wondered why the hell she was telling it to this ex-soldier she barely knew. She could've talked to Vic, or to Doctor Evans, the police psychiatrist. But she was too close to Vic, and she was reluctant to take this to the departmental psych guy. He might pull her off duty, or report her to Internal Affairs.

"About what?" Ian asked.

"Shootouts," she said. "Ones I've been in. But they're different. They go worse than they did. People get killed. Rolf... Rolf always gets hit."

"Yeah, I get those too."

"From fights you've been in?"

"Yeah. It's never me that gets hit. It's always the other guys."

"What do you think that's about?" she asked.

"Don't know, ma'am. Maybe it's like fear, except after the fact. Combat's not so bad. Thinking about it is worse, before and after."

"What do you do?"

"Just keep moving. When it gets hard, you dig deep, find more, keep going."

"That easy, huh?"

"Not easy, ma'am. Just simple. Not easy at all. Nothing worth doing is easy."

That silenced Erin for a few moments.

"We think a soldier killed a couple of people," she said after the pause had gone on long enough.

Ian didn't comment.

"What we don't know is why," she went on. "Or where he is now."

"You sure it was him?"

"Pretty sure."

"But you don't know why?"

"No idea."

"There have to be a reason?"

Erin opened her mouth and found she didn't have an answer to that. She had to think.

"There's always a reason," she said. It didn't even sound convincing to her, but it was the best she had.

"Okay," Ian agreed. "He had a reason."

"So what was it?"

"Don't know. I'm not him. Neither are you."

"What's that supposed to mean?"

"You want his reason, you have to be in his head. And you're not."

"Okay, put me there."

"Can't, ma'am."

"The hell you can't. You're a veteran. Help me understand."

This time Ian was the one who stopped running. He didn't look tired, but he wanted her full attention. Erin gave it to him.

"Your problem is you haven't been there, ma'am," he said. He didn't say it in a judgmental way. He said it like he was stating a fact. "You talk about 'the war,' and you think there's just the one."

"No, I know, there's Iraq and Afghanistan—" she began.

"That's not what I mean," he said. "That's all one thing, the political thing, and that's not the point. The point is, there's as many different wars as there are soldiers. Everybody's got their own. This guy's war isn't mine. People think war isn't personal. They're wrong. It's the most personal thing there is. It's so personal, I can't give you mine, or even show it to you. You have to fight your own. Take a Marine squad, thirteen guys, that's a squad leader and three fireteams. Put them under fire, that's thirteen firefights happening. Everyone fights their own war and brings it home with them. We trade a piece of us for the war. We leave that piece over there and bring the war home, inside us where that piece was. It's like a scar. I can't give you my scar."

"But you can show it to me."

Ian nodded. "But you don't know how I got it. Even if I tell you that, you still don't know how it felt."

"What's your point?"

"My point is, I can't put you in this other guy's head, ma'am. I don't even know what's going on in mine half the time. You think he wanted to kill those people?"

"I don't know."

"Maybe he didn't mean to."

"He shot both of them."

"How many times?"

"Three times each. Two in the body, one in the head. With a handgun."

"Mozambique Drill," Ian said, nodding. Erin knew the term. It was a pistol exercise they taught soldiers, along with some cops. The first two shots went into the target's body, injuring and hopefully killing them. The third shot, an aimed shot into the head, was to make sure, or to take the target down if the victim was wearing body armor.

"Yeah, that's one of the things that tells us it was a guy with military training," she said.

"Who got shot?"

"One of his comrades and that guy's wife."

"He treated them both like combatants," Ian said.

"Okay," Erin said, not sure where he was going with this.

"Was she?"

"Was she what?"

"A combatant?"

"No. The wife had no training. Both of them were unarmed."

"But he thought they were."

"I don't understand," Erin said.

"He was in combat, ma'am," Ian said. "Right then."

"No, he wasn't. These were executions."

"You're not listening, ma'am."

If he'd said it less politely, Erin would've gotten mad. She still felt a prickle of irritation. She wasn't stupid and didn't like having it suggested she might be.

"Explain," she said, "please."

"He was in combat," Ian said. "Whether or not the other two were, *he was.* That's his war. The brass talk about this thing they call battlespace. They're talking about the terrain, the airspace over it, the comms network, all that. But they're full of shit, ma'am. The only battlespace that matters to a foot soldier is the one in his own head. This guy was having a firefight in his mind and it spilled out."

Erin thought about herself, waking up out of a nightmare and pulling a gun on her own dog, and then she did understand.

"Thanks," she said.

"Don't mention it, ma'am. Want to finish the run?"

"Yeah."

So they did. And Erin felt better. Not completely. She looked at Rolf and wondered why the hell she'd taken aim at her K-9, her partner. And she still wondered whether she was going a little crazy. But at least she had some idea what to do next.

* * *

Doctor Evans was in his office at the precinct when Erin knocked on his door just before eight AM. His posted hours were nine to five, and by appointment, so she hadn't known if he'd be in yet.

"Come in," he said. She opened the door and found the police psychiatrist reading a file and making notes. He took off his reading glasses and tucked them into the breast pocket of his shirt.

"Hey, Doc," she said. "Got a minute?"

"Of course, Erin. My first appointment isn't for an hour and a half. If you want to get the door and have a seat, I'll be right with you."

He made it a point to know the names of every cop in the precinct, and to address them by first name. Erin had only spoken with him a couple of times, but he'd been pretty approachable. She sat down on his couch, so much comfier than the one in the Major Crimes break room. Rolf sat at one end of the couch, upright and alert.

Evans put away his paperwork and came around his desk, sitting in the armchair opposite her. He was a very everyday sort of guy, gray-haired, long-faced, pleasant but serious. He nodded toward Rolf.

"I see you've still got your K-9 with you. How's the partnership going?"

"Great," she said. "Rolf's great. Best partner I ever had."

Rolf gave Evans a look that suggested he might, indeed, be the best partner in the whole NYPD.

"You're in early," Evans said. "What's on your mind?"

"I had some questions about PTSD."

"Fire away."

"It's not about me," she said quickly. "It's about a suspect in a case."

"Okay," Evans said evenly. "You know, Erin, I'm not a profiler. I'm not one of those guys who can magically describe the guy you're looking for, based solely on his psychoses."

She smiled. "That's not what I need. I just need to understand how his mind might be working."

"Okay," he said again. "I'll do what I can to help."

"How does PTSD work?"

He laughed. "That's a question that would take more time than we've got. It's a complicated condition, and manifests differently in different cases. Each case is more or less unique, and it's very common and widespread. In fact, some people say they shouldn't call it a disorder at all. They say we should rename it Post-Traumatic Stress Syndrome."

She nodded, thinking of what Ian had said about everyone fighting their own separate war. "Right. But what are the usual indicators?"

"Anxiety, nightmares, and flashbacks are common," Evans said. "The effects can start soon after the triggering event, or may not show up for months, or even years. There's a whole encyclopedia of potential effects."

"Is someone with PTSD dangerous?"

"To whom?"

"To other people."

"They can be. But they're more likely to be a danger to themselves. Self-destructive behavior is very common, particularly substance abuse and suicidal thoughts or actions. When we experience a serious trauma, something outside our normal frame of reference, our brains have trouble processing it. We often feel guilty for having witnessed something bad happening, because we feel we should have somehow been able to prevent it. That feeling is even worse when the trauma results in the injury or death of a loved one, which leads to survivor guilt. We have trouble sleeping or concentrating. We often feel distanced from those we love, even when they try to help us."

Erin's interrogator's ear caught the change in Evans's pronouns, his use of the word "we." He was an experienced trauma counselor and, either intentionally or reflexively, was trying to build rapport with her in their conversation by placing them on the same team and the same plane of experience. She did the same thing in interrogations.

"You said something about substance abuse. You mean drinking? Drugs?"

"Both. A lot of trauma survivors turn to narcotics and alcohol to try to numb their senses. Hyperawareness is exhausting and nerve-wracking."

She thought of Ian and nodded. It could be tiring just being around someone like that. "Would those drugs cause the user to see something that wasn't there?"

"Hallucinations?" Evans nodded. "Certainly. Opiates can lead some users to hallucinate even with normal prescribed usage."

"And if the user was drinking and doing drugs at the same time?"

"That's always a risky thing to do. Combining substances can create extreme effects." Evans leaned forward. "Erin, this... suspect. What sort of hallucinations are they experiencing?"

Oh God, Erin realized. He thought she was talking about herself, using the classic "It's for a friend" dodge.

"Doc," she said, "I'm not talking about me. I really do have a guy I'm trying to figure out. He's a combat veteran."

"I see," Evans said, with no change in his expression or body language. "Well, it's difficult to predict the effects of a drug cocktail on anyone, particularly someone who's already experiencing an unusual cognitive event. How do you know your guy's been mixing drugs and booze?"

"Vomit sample at the crime scene."

"Ah. Nausea is certainly a symptom."

"I mostly need to know whether drug use might trigger a flashback."

Evans clasped his hands on his knee. "It might. I think it's more likely it would exacerbate an episode that would occur in any case. Unfortunately, if we try to numb ourselves with multiple substances, sometimes we create the opposite effect. The user might suffer an extremely vivid flashback. On the other hand, they might pass out, or even die. Let me say again, mixing drugs is an extremely bad idea."

"Right," Erin said. "So let's suppose a guy took a bunch of stuff and flashed back to his combat experience. Would he attack someone close to him? A friend, or even family member?"

"He might," Evans said. "But that wouldn't be what he thought he was doing. He wouldn't accurately perceive what was happening. Unfortunately, there have been cases of trauma victims attacking and even killing family members during episodes. It's terribly tragic, though thankfully rare."

"What would he do afterward?"

"That depends on the duration of the episode. As long as he was operating in a combat mentality, I expect he'd work within the fabric of his delusion. He'd follow his training, most likely. Hallucinations have their own internal logic. He'd do what made sense to him based on his perception of the world. If he realized what he'd done, there'd be a high probability for self-harm."

"I need to find this guy, Doc. We think he's already killed two people, and we found evidence he's been making homemade firebombs. Anything you can tell me about him would help."

Evans spread his hands. "I don't know the man, Erin. I'd need to study him, personally and at length, to make any sort of accurate prediction. Sorry I can't be more help."

Erin stood up. “Thanks, Doc.”

“Erin?”

“Yeah?”

“How are you sleeping these days?”

She felt a cold twist in her gut as she remembered sighting down the barrel of her Glock and seeing Rolf’s face at the other end of the gun. “I’m fine,” she said, knowing it was a straight-up lie but also knowing she didn’t have time to fall apart. Not now, not while she was chasing a man who might be planning something terrible.

Evans nodded. “Well, if there’s anything you do want to talk about, you can always make an appointment and I’ll be glad to listen. It’s my job, but I really do want to help my officers. You’ve been under a great deal of stress lately. There’s no shame in needing to let some of that out. We’re not built to be pressure cookers.”

“I’ll keep that in mind,” she said.

“I’m glad you have your partner,” he said. “Pets are a proven aid for dealing with traumatic stress.”

“Rolf’s not a pet,” she said.

Rolf, hearing his name, looked at Erin, then at Evans. He certainly didn’t consider himself a pet.

“Soldiers have collected mascots as long as there have been battles,” Evans said with a smile. “Military units with a working dog attached to them have lower PTSD rates than units without them. You take care of that boy, Erin, and he’ll try to take care of you.”

“Always do,” she said. “I have to get to work, Doc. See you around.”

“I’ll be here,” Evans said. He watched her go, and Erin thought from the look in his eyes that he’d guessed she was full of crap.

Chapter 10

"Randolph's our guy," Erin said.

"I believe you," Webb said. "Now you just need to convince the jury."

"This case won't ever go to trial," she said. "If we can bring him in, he'll plead out."

"You sound pretty confident," Vic said. "Want to put ten on it?"

"Twenty," she offered.

"Before you start counting your winnings, tell us what you've got," Webb suggested.

"Randolph's one of Carson's old military buddies," she said. "From Smith, we know Carson was inviting his veterans to come over. That suggests Randolph was at the scene. If he's the one who threw up in the bathroom, DNA can place him there. The victims were killed by someone trained in close-quarters handgun use."

"Could be a soldier, could be a cop," Vic said.

"They teach you the Mozambique Drill in ESU?"

"Actually, yeah, they did. After the North Hollywood shootout back in '97, they figured ESU might have to nail bad guys who were wearing vests. We qualified if we could do it in five seconds at seven yards. I can do three seconds at ten."

Erin didn't have a comeback for that. She knew the technique herself, and there were NYPD instructors who taught it. Standard police training, when they needed to fire their weapons, was to aim for center mass and shoot until the target went down. But when that didn't work, they were prepared to aim for the head.

"Okay, so he could have law-enforcement training," she allowed. "But what's more likely? We've got no evidence Carson knew any cops, and we know he was tight with soldiers."

"Go on," Webb said.

"I talked to Randolph's mom last night. According to her, he was psychologically unstable. She said he wasn't the same as he'd been when he left home. He moved out of the house after fighting with her. He'd only been at his apartment a few days. Monson, the guy from his platoon, said Randolph went berserk in firefights."

"This wasn't a firefight," Webb said.

"I think for Randolph it was," she said. "I think he had a flashback to combat in Iraq. I just talked to Doc Evans downstairs, and he confirmed that drug and alcohol use can make flashbacks worse, and can contribute to hallucinations."

"So you're saying he shot these folks because he thought he was back in Iraq?" Vic asked. He looked skeptical.

"You've been in gunfights," she said. "You telling me you've never had a flashback or a nightmare?"

"Well, not like that. I guess maybe I've had some funky dreams, but no, I'm good."

"How much vodka does it take for you to sleep after a nightmare?"

He bristled. "Just what the hell are you suggesting?"

"Calm down, both of you," Webb said. "We're not talking about Neshenko's personal habits. As long as he's sober on duty, and doesn't pick up DUIs in his off hours, what he does there is between him and his liver. This is a high-stress job. We've all got some unhealthy coping mechanisms." He looked down at his trademark unlit cigarette and sighed. "We're all cruising for heart attacks and kidney failure by the time we're sixty."

"You're not sixty yet?" Vic asked, the picture of innocence.

Webb gave him a weary look. "I'm young enough to plant my shoe up your backside, Detective First Grade Neshenko. Please, Detective Second Grade O'Reilly, continue to enlighten us."

"Randolph was looking up the effects of psychoactive substances on his computer," she said. "I think he knew taking drugs screwed with his head. But suppose he went to see his old sergeant. They had liquor, so they got drunk. Why not? It's just a good time with friends. But one way or another, he got his hands on the oxy in the Carsons' bathroom. He popped a couple of pills. Maybe he felt an episode coming on and tried to knock himself out, or just go numb. He went into the bathroom in New York, and came out in Baghdad."

"So he comes out of the bathroom," Vic said, "sees this guy he thinks is an enemy, and shoots him. The wife goes to her dead husband, grabs him, probably starts screaming..."

"Which doesn't help," Erin agreed. "He probably got used to that kind of thing over there. Hell, maybe he shot people in the same circumstances."

"Shooting noncombatants is a war crime," Webb observed.

"So I'm sure it never happens," Vic said, his voice loaded with sarcasm. "Where'd he get the gun?"

"He had it with him," Erin said.

"How do you know?" Webb asked.

"I don't. But I'll bet we can match the shell casings to that box of ammo we found at Randolph's apartment. That's good enough for me."

"Okay," Webb said. "So, he's gone nuts and killed two of his friends. What does he do next?"

"He's not nuts," Erin said. "I think Doc Evans might call it something like a psychotic break."

"Sounds pretty nuts to me," Vic muttered.

"According to the doc, his perceptions are just different than they should be," she said. "If he thought he was still in Iraq, he'd probably try to get back to his base, to safety."

"But we've been to his apartment," Webb said. "He wasn't there."

"He was only living there a couple of days," she said. "He probably didn't think of it as home yet. I think he went back there to collect more weapons and ammo. Given the ammunition boxes we found, he's almost certainly got a rifle, either an M4 or an AR-15. He also made some homemade firebombs, which tells me he was still pretty screwed up while he was there."

"All great news," Webb said heavily. "So he loaded for bear and left the apartment. Where'd he go next?"

"You were at his mom's house," Vic said. "You think she's hiding him?"

"No. She was too worried about him, too genuine. She doesn't know where he is. The question is, where would he feel safe?"

"You're assuming he wants to feel safe," Vic said. "What if he decides to go on the attack instead?"

"I think we'd already know if he'd done that," she said. "He'd have blown up a car, or shot some more people."

"Let's make sure he didn't," Webb said. "Neshenko, look at the violent crimes that've been reported in the last forty-eight hours. Pay particular attention to Queens and Brooklyn, but he could be just about anywhere. Does he have a car?"

"He's got a Nissan Stanza in his name," Vic said. "I checked the vehicle registry yesterday evening. POS from the mid-'80s. Red in color. License plate's on the board there. Not too many of those still on the road, so it'll stand out."

"I assume that information's on the BOLO?" Webb asked.

Vic nodded.

"Traffic cams will pick him up if he drives through them," Webb said. He didn't add that they'd have to get lucky for that to happen. There were about a hundred and fifty traffic cameras set up in New York City, with most of them covering Manhattan, not Queens.

"We'll have better luck with Patrol officers," Erin said. "We've got a lot more of them on the street than there are cameras."

"Okay, but we can't count on that," Webb said. "Come on, people. There's got to be somewhere he'd go."

"The guy's been deployed for, like, a year," Vic said. "He doesn't exactly have this huge support network."

"He's one guy, on his own," Webb said. "Find him."

"Does CSU have some of his clothes from his apartment?" Erin asked.

"They should be able to get you something," Webb said. "For Rolf?"

"Yeah. I want a scent sample handy, just in case."

"I'll start checking the crime reports," Vic said. His tone of voice suggested he wasn't optimistic.

"I'll get on the phone with some of the other precincts," Webb said. "See if I can put some pressure on them to help locate this guy. I don't think he's in Manhattan."

"Can we hand it off to the Homicide boys in Queens?" Vic asked.

"Because they're so good at their job," Erin said, matching Vic's earlier sarcastic tone. She'd had bad experiences with some of the detectives from her old precinct.

"I suggest we close the case we've been assigned," Webb said. "O'Reilly, what do you want to look into?"

"I want to get in Randolph's head," she said. "I can't talk to him, so I want to talk to his comrades again. If I can understand him, maybe I can tell what he's thinking right now. He's not crazy, just broken. What he's doing makes sense to him. I need to see the pattern."

"Smith's the only local guy," Webb said. "I hope you're not planning to ask me to fly you down to DC on the department's dime."

"No, sir. I figure Harlem's easier."

"Okay, get up there," Webb said. "Let me know what you find. And remember, there's a chance Randolph may have gone to his buddy for help. If you see any sign at all he's there, or that he's been there, get out and call in reinforcements."

"Our taxpayers gave us thirty-five thousand officers," Vic said. "It'd be a shame not to give them their money's worth."

* * *

Erin wondered how many times she'd driven the length of New York, from Harlem to Long Island and back again, since coming back from vacation. It was a big damn city. She opened the sliding panel between the seats that connected to Rolf's compartment. He stuck his head through, tongue hanging out.

"You don't care, do you, kiddo?" she said. "You love car rides."

Rolf's opinion appeared to be that he was the best dog, working the best job, with the best partner in the entire world.

But Erin wasn't feeling good. Usually, at this point in a case, she could feel her own prey drive kick into gear. Just like her K-9, when she had a strong scent to follow, she would run until she dropped. She normally liked chasing down the bad guys. There was no feeling quite like slapping the cuffs on a perp in a righteous bust. Even little kids understood. Cops and Robbers was a nearly-universal playground game. She'd always wanted to be a cop, from the moment she'd understood what her dad did for a living.

But now? This was a case she wasn't sure she wanted to see all the way to the end. This bad guy, from what she knew about him, wasn't bad at all. He was desperate, frightened, in need of help. But he was also armed and extremely dangerous. Her duty was absolutely clear. She had to bring him in before anyone else got hurt. But arresting Toby Randolph wasn't going to give her any sort of a rush. The best she could hope for was relief when it was all over.

And what if he didn't come quietly? What if he made her shoot him? In the end, what if they were pointing guns at each other and only one of them got to walk out? Could she do it? Kill a man she couldn't hate?

The worst of it was, Erin was pretty sure she could and she would. It was no different than what Randolph had been doing. For all the politicians' talk of fighting the "axis of evil," she knew most of the guys shooting up American soldiers were young men who'd been told, by people they trusted, that the Americans were the bad guys. That was how war worked. Kids on both sides got guns in their hands, went out, and killed the kids on the other side.

Erin respected soldiers, but she didn't want to be one of them. She only hoped Randolph wouldn't force her into that situation. If she gunned him down, she'd have nightmares about it for sure.

"You don't think I'm going crazy, do you, Rolf?" she asked.

He nosed her ear and panted.

"Lots of perfectly sane people talk to their dogs," she argued. "And have nightmares. I'm okay."

Rolf didn't disagree.

"I've got this," she said firmly. "I'm going to run this guy down, put him away, and then I'll get my shit together."

Rolf was completely on board with her plan. He just hoped she'd bring him along.

"Sorry about this morning," she said. "I don't know what happened. You don't get it. You think you're invincible, you big fuzzball. I'm not sure you've ever been afraid of anything in your life. But then, if I had your teeth, I wouldn't be scared of much either. You got my back, kiddo?"

He nosed her ear again.

"Thanks."

* * *

Erin parked outside the same building in Harlem they'd been to before. She and Rolf went upstairs to Jamal Smith's apartment. The time was about noon. She knocked on the door, which opened almost immediately, so fast she reflexively fell back a step and dropped a hand to her gun.

Smith was as surprised as she was. He jerked back from the doorway and ducked, like he expected to get hit. Rolf, seeing the sudden movement, tensed and prepared to spring.

There was a brief, awkward pause. Erin took her hand away from her Glock. Smith straightened up.

"Shit, lady, you scared the hell out of me," he said.

"Sorry," Erin said. But she was confused. "I knocked."

"Yeah. I thought you were the pizza guy."

"What pizza guy?"

"I ordered a pizza half an hour ago. He should be showing up, like, any second."

"Oh." That explained why he'd gotten to the door so fast. He'd been expecting a delivery.

"You that detective that was here yesterday?"

"One of them, yeah."

"There a problem? I thought we was good. I told you on the phone, I got nothing more to give you."

"No, we're fine. I just had a few more questions."

"About Sarge?"

"About your platoon. Can I come in?"

"Sure, I guess."

Erin and Rolf entered, Erin remembering to wipe her feet. She looked quickly around the room, searching for any sign of Randolph's presence. If he was there, he hadn't left anything lying around. She still made sure to sit where she could see all the entrances to the living room.

"Anyone else here?" she asked as casually as she could.

"Nah, this is a school day. I guess cops are like soldiers, huh? You don't keep track of the weekends, 'cause the enemy don't take Saturdays off, right?"

"Jamal... is it okay if I call you Jamal?"

"No problem, ma'am."

"I'm hoping we can just talk a little about your unit in Iraq. What it was like, what was going through your head, that sort of thing."

He looked perplexed. "Okay," he said cautiously.

"What did it feel like, going out on a mission?"

He thought about it. "I dunno. I mean, it was weird, but after a while we got used to it. It was hot, mostly."

"Hot?"

"Yeah, hot. I mean, you're wearing, like, a hundred pounds of shit, right? You got your BDUs, your body armor, your helmet, spare ammo, a couple canteens, boots, weapon, pistol, spare pistol mags, emergency rations, plus whatever else you gotta carry for the mission. And it's, like, a thousand degrees out there. You got AC in the Humvee, but only if it's working right, and if you got the turret open that heat comes right in on you. Plus, you can't just sit in the Humvee all the time. So you're out in those crowded streets, there's people all over the place. It's hot. Smelly, too."

"Did you get scared?"

He looked at her like it was the dumbest question he'd ever heard. "You ever been shot at, ma'am?"

"Yeah, I have."

"Were *you* scared?"

"Yeah. When I had time to be."

"Then you know what it feels like. Except you don't. 'Cause you're in a city that mostly don't want to kill you. Over there, you never know who's gonna try to pop you when you're not looking. You start feeling like everyone's the enemy, and every guy who looks at you funny is a guy you maybe need to kill."

"It gets to be a habit," Erin guessed. "So everyone you meet, even when you come back, you look at them the same way?"

"Yeah, I guess."

"Is that why veterans aren't comfortable talking to anyone but other veterans?"

He shrugged. "Nah, I don't think so. I think that's mostly just wanting to hang with people who understand you. I mean, you hang out at cop bars after work, right?"

Erin chuckled, though he'd guessed wrong in her particular case. "Yeah, I see what you mean."

"Hey, ma'am, I don't wanna get in any trouble, you know? You call the guy about the job interview?"

"No, we didn't want to jam you up," Erin said. Vic had looked the man up and verified that he existed, but hadn't asked about Jamal Smith. He'd figured, and she'd agreed, that they didn't need to screw up Smith's prospects if they didn't have to, and at this point, Smith wasn't suspicious enough to be a suspect.

"Thanks. I appreciate that."

There was a knock at the door. Erin jumped.

"Pizza guy," Jamal guessed. He stood up and went to the door. Erin stood and watched him, staying alert. What if it was Randolph?

But it was the pizza delivery. Smith handed over some bills and took custody of a pizza. Its size told her he was telling the truth about being alone. Two young soldiers would eat more than one medium pizza.

"That smells good," she said.

"Yeah. We didn't get real pizza in Iraq," he said. "Man, there were times I'd have volunteered for two weeks of latrine duty for one hot slice. Hey, you want some? Spicy salami, from the Harlem Pizza Company. Best you gonna find."

Erin almost said no, but she knew eating together was a great way to establish a connection. "Sure, thanks," she said. "Just one slice."

"Let's go in the dining room. Mom will kill me if I get tomato stains on her carpet."

He fetched a couple of plates and napkins, along with two cans of Coke from the fridge.

"It's weird," he said. "You think getting shot at is the worst part, but when you're there, you miss stuff like this. Just sitting at the table at home with a pizza and a can of Coke, where the air don't stink and there's no flies. You wouldn't believe the flies they got in the Sandbox. Billions of 'em, and they get everywhere, I mean everywhere."

"You seem like you're doing okay, Jamal."

"Yeah, I get by."

"I've talked to some other guys who were there," she said. "Some of them have had trouble leaving it behind."

He nodded. "I feel you. I guess we all got some weight on us. There was this book we read in high school, about Vietnam. My ninth grade English class. I didn't really get it back then. It was these short stories, all about the war. *The Things They Carried*, that's the name. The first chapter, it was all about the shit the soldiers carried with them. The writer, he listed all the normal stuff, like can openers and cigarette lighters and equipment, but then he talked about hopes and dreams and letters and shit. Everybody carried some of the same stuff, and everybody carried their own."

"Everybody fights their own war," Erin said, thinking of Ian. "And everyone's war is a little different."

"Yeah," Jamal said. "That's what I mean. You know, everybody I knew over there brought back souvenirs. Little things, mostly. Cheap shit you buy in the market, little trophies from guys you took out, good-luck charms. So you bring some stuff back with you. Maybe so you know you're still alive. Live soldiers carry things. Dead guys get carried."

"Do you know Toby Randolph?" she asked.

"Yeah. Some."

"What do you think he brought back with him?"

Jamal was silent for a moment, buying time by chewing a big bite of pizza. Erin took the opportunity to try her own slice. It was good, really good. She could see how a guy in the Sandbox could miss it.

"Randolph was okay," he said at last. "He was a good kid. But he got dinged up a little, from an IED. He spent a few days in Germany, in the hospital there, but they sent him back to the Box. They gave him some pills for the pain, and... I dunno. Mom always told me, be careful of pills. She said, 'Jamal, I ever hear you touch those things, I'll tan your hide.' I got hit once, the medic tried to give me a shot, I wouldn't let him. The rest of my squad thought I was some kinda hardass, but I told them I was more scared of my mom than the bad guys."

Erin laughed. "But Randolph got hooked on the pills?"

"I think so, yeah. Lotta guys got problems with that, I hear. And he'd see some weird shit and say some weird shit when he was on them. Sarge would take his gun away when he popped a pill. I think Sarge tried to get him some help, but I dunno what happened with that. Then Sarge got hit and they sent him home."

"What made Randolph feel safe, when he was on the pills?" Erin asked. "What calmed him down?"

Jamal shrugged again. "Movies, I guess."

"Yeah, I heard about the movies," she said. "He'd show them on the wall of a building."

"Yeah, that was cool," Jamal said, remembering. "It worked, too. I mean, for all of us. We could just about forget we was hanging in Iraq. He said he used to like war movies, but now he was in a war, he didn't see the point. He said if we wanted a war movie, we could just go out on mission. He'd show cartoons and shit, kid movies, you know. And we'd all just pretend we was in a movie theater back home. Of course, some of the guys would make jokes, talk to the screen, throw shit. But that was all part of the fun."

Erin thought she had it. The answer was right there in front of her. "Jamal," she said slowly. "Did Randolph ever say anything about a special place, where he'd go to watch movies, here in New York?"

"Yeah, I guess so," he said. "There was this theater, he said, near his house. He took his first date there, when he was fifteen, and he tried to make out with her and she screamed and threw her drink on him and they got thrown out by the manager."

Erin laughed again. "Do you remember the name of the theater?"

Jamal shook his head. "Nope. Sorry."

She finished her piece of pizza and stood up. "Thanks for the help, Jamal," she said. "And for the food. You're right, that's some fantastic pizza."

"It sure is. But I don't think I helped you any, ma'am."

"You did."

Jamal thought for a second. Erin was almost at the door when he said, "It's Randolph, isn't it?"

She paused with her hand on the doorknob. "What?"

"He's the guy who shot Sarge."

"I can't tell you anything about that," she said. "Sorry. It's the rules. Ongoing investigation."

"Ma'am, he wouldn't have hurt Sarge. He loved Sarge."

"I know."

"But you still think he did it." He paused. "Shit. It was the drugs, wasn't it?"

"Jamal," she said, "if that job you applied for doesn't work out, you might want to think about the Police Academy. I think you might make a pretty good detective one of these days."

That was the closest she could come to telling him the truth.

Chapter 11

Erin was glad of Jamal Smith's generosity. That slice of pizza was all the lunch she was getting. She'd wasted too much time already, chasing her tail all over New York, and she still had a lot of driving to do. She called Webb from her car.

"O'Reilly here," she said when he answered.

"Give me good news," Webb said. "We've got uniforms all over Long Island and no trace of this guy. Tell me he's not going to blow up a subway or something."

"I'm thinking movie theater."

"Oh, no," Webb groaned. "Like that shooting in Colorado?"

"I don't know," she said. "It's just a hunch. But I think he might be hiding at a theater."

"What's this hunch based on?"

"Something Smith said about Randolph. He said Randolph relaxed after missions by playing movies for the guys. Monson, at Walter Reed, told me the same thing. And Smith said he remembered Randolph telling him about hanging out at a theater in Queens back in high school."

"That's a little thin," Webb said, using his favorite word for evidence.

"It's more than we had."

"True. Which theater is it?"

"I don't know."

"O'Reilly, there's got to be a dozen theaters in Queens."

"I know. But we can check them, right?"

"That's a lot of ground to cover. I'll get word to the Queens precincts and have them start checking."

"We can't be obvious about it, sir. If he's planning something, or if he's still in combat mode, he's likely to fight if uniforms corner him."

"Well, which is it, O'Reilly? Do you want to check the theaters or not?"

"Yes, but let's try to keep it low-key."

"Where are you right now?"

"On my way south from Harlem. I'm going to stop at the Eightball and collect some of Randolph's clothes. Then I'll take Rolf across the river and start tracking, see if we can pick up a scent."

"You can only be in one place at a time."

"But I can still be there, sir."

"True. I'll liaise with the precinct captains and get the search organized. I'll send Neshenko with you. You may need him." Webb paused. "I hope your hunch is right."

"Me too. O'Reilly out."

* * *

"I don't think your definition of low-key is the same as mine," Erin said.

"What's the problem?" Vic asked. He was wearing body armor with ceramic inserts, the word POLICE emblazoned in white on the front and back. He had a tactical helmet on his head and an M4 assault rifle in his hands.

"We're trying not to spook him."

"I don't know if you've noticed, Erin, but I'm not the world's most inconspicuous guy. If he sees me, he's gonna make me as a cop whatever I'm wearing. I don't want to get in a gunfight with a combat infantryman unless my gun's as big as his."

Erin snickered.

"That's not what I meant and you know it," he growled. "And for your information, there's times and places size does matter."

"I'm just wondering what Piekarski would say."

"None of your damn business, is what she'd say. Get in the car."

"I like it when a man with a big gun gives me orders," she said, grinning.

"Shut up."

"It turns me on. I'm getting hot right now."

"I said, shut up."

They were taking Erin's Charger, since Vic's Taurus didn't have the special compartment for Rolf. Vic buttoned his jacket over his vest, with some difficulty. He pitched the helmet onto the floor of the passenger side.

"There. You happy?"

"You still look like a cop."

"My point exactly. If he shoots me in the head, I'm blaming you."

"Oh come on, we both know it'd just ricochet off your thick skull." Erin put the car in gear and started rolling. "You really think it'll help if you look like a Stormtrooper? He's more likely to shoot you, not less. Now you want to get on the computer and find out which theater we're starting at?"

"I'll know once the Queens Patrol guys get on the horn with us," Vic said. "The boss was talking to some guy down there name of Murphy."

"Oh, I know him. He was my old lieutenant, back at Precinct 116. He's good police."

"Glad to hear it. You got Randolph's clothes?"

"Socks," Erin confirmed. She'd grabbed a pair of used socks from Randolph's bedroom, which were now in a paper bag under her seat. It wasn't the body odor of the man they needed; it was his dead skin cells. That, so Erin had been told, was what Rolf would track. Interestingly, that meant a wet target was at least as easy to track as a dry one, since a bath would just wash more cells off the target's body, leaving an even more obvious trail.

"It won't be enough just going in the front door," Vic said gloomily. "He might've used a side exit and drafted in behind someone who was leaving."

"We'll need to check all the hallways," Erin agreed.

"There's fifteen movie theaters," he said. "This is gonna take all night."

"Maybe. You have something better to do?"

"I was looking forward to my five AM booty call."

"Maybe we'll get lucky and find him quick, and then you can get lucky again."

"I'm telling Zofia this is all your fault. You're betraying the sisterhood."

"Vic, I'm betraying the sisterhood by not telling her to stay the hell away from you."

"Where's your sense of romance?"

"You're the one who calls it a booty call."

"Those can be romantic."

"Speaking of romance," Erin said after a moment.

"Uh oh." Vic braced himself.

"Have you and that Russian girl, Tatiana, kept in touch?"

"Uh, yeah. A little. She's doing okay. Natalie Markov is looking after her, helping her through the whole citizenship thing."

"That's good. So, you and she aren't a couple?"

Vic shook his head. "No. Too much baggage."

"Baggage?"

"She did try to kill me that one time."

"She was coerced into it," Erin reminded him.

"That still puts a kink in things. Gives a guy like me trust issues."

"Does that still bother you?"

"What, that the Russian Mafia tried to whack me, and used my girlfriend to do it? Yeah, it bothers me."

"That's not what I meant. I mean, all the gunfights."

"You're on about that again? Jesus, Erin, give it a rest already. I don't like getting shot, but I don't sit up all night worrying about it either. You want my therapist's phone number? I don't have one. You wanna report me to Internal Affairs as a psych case?"

"Whoa, Vic. Take it easy." Erin had meant to open up to him a little, tell him about her own bad dreams, but his response was anything but inviting. "I didn't mean anything. You can be super sensitive, you know that?"

"That's me," he said. "A sensitive twenty-first century guy."

* * *

They finally made it back to Queens. They started at the Fair Theatre in East Elmhurst, not because it was very likely, but because it was on their way in. Webb had been communicating with the Queens precincts, as promised, and two squad cars were loitering in the parking lot.

"Subtle," Vic observed.

"Low-key," Erin agreed, rolling her eyes. At least theaters didn't have many windows, so if Randolph was inside he might not have seen the police. The detectives dismounted. Rolf was ready, eager, and willing.

A pair of uniformed officers got out of their car and approached. Erin flashed her shield.

"O'Reilly?" the one on the left said.

"Paulson!" she exclaimed, recognizing him. She'd worked with Paulson when she'd been at the 116. He was generally agreed to be the scariest man in the precinct. He was small, wiry, and unassuming. He was also a former Army Ranger who'd probably saved Erin's life on the case that had made her a detective.

Erin offered her hand, which Paulson clasped in a quick, tight shake. "What're you doing here?"

"Murphy told us some hotshot detectives from downtown were coming, so I volunteered to babysit. Figured they could use some adult supervision. If I'd known one of them was you, I wouldn't have bothered." He gave her a rare half-smile. "The LT said something about a potential active shooter."

"That's some trick," Vic said. "Either a guy's an active shooter, or he isn't. A potential active shooter's just a guy with a gun, ammo, and personal issues."

"In other words, you," Erin said. "Vic, this is Oscar Paulson. Paulson, Vic Neshenko."

The two men gave each other the standard tough-guy stare-down. It was a draw, even though Vic was twice Paulson's size.

"They told us not to go in," Paulson said. "I guess we were waiting on you."

"We're here now," Erin said. "It'd be great to have ESU for this, but we've got a bunch of theaters in the area and we don't know which one our guy's in."

"Or if he's in one at all," Vic added.

"Your K-9 found the last guy you and I looked for," Paulson said. "You got a scent for him?"

She held up the bag of socks.

"Copy that," Paulson said. "Let's do this."

They left one of the Patrol units outside to cover the exits, in case Randolph made a run for it. Paulson and his partner accompanied Erin, Vic, and Rolf inside. It was afternoon on a Friday during the school year, so the building wasn't too crowded. Erin showed her shield to the woman at the ticket counter, who summoned her manager. They explained the situation.

"We don't want to cause a disruption or a panic," Erin said. "We just need to do a walkthrough of the building. We won't even go into any of the screening rooms unless my dog tells us our guy's inside."

"Okay," the manager said. "But go back to the part where you think there might be a gunman." He looked very nervous.

"He's probably not here," she assured him. "This is just an elimination search."

"I can just wait out here. You go on back."

"We'll do that," Vic said, giving the man a less respectful look than the one he'd given Paulson.

Erin opened her bag. "Rolf!" she said.

The K-9 snapped to attention, tail wagging, ears perked.

She held the bag open in front of his snout. "*Such!*"

Rolf took a good sniff. One of the trainers in K-9 school had told Erin that for a dog, the smell of a human was like a fingerprint. It was completely distinct from every other human on Earth. Bloodhounds, the trainer said, remembered every smell of every person they'd ever encountered. Erin found that hard to believe, but a dog like Rolf could convince a doubter.

The Shepherd snuffled his way across the lobby, past the turnstile, and into the back hallways. A K-9 building search was very systematic. Erin had Rolf on a long leash. The dog went to each door in turn, sniffed at it, and moved on. To be really thorough they should have entered every room, but they had a lot of ground to cover, so unless Rolf gave a positive alert, they weren't going to open the doors.

At the start of the search, all four officers were as tense and keyed-up as the dog. But as time wore on, and they found nothing, some of the energy drained out of them.

"He's not here," Vic said at last.

Rolf whined low in his throat. He knew he'd been supposed to find his target and he hadn't done it. He wasn't a happy dog.

"We'll try again," Erin said. "Next one."

"We've got orders to stay here," Paulson said. "Until further notice. Just in case the guy turns up. Good luck."

* * *

The next theater, the Regal UA Midway on Queens Boulevard, was another time-consuming washout. Rolf went up and down the hallways, attracting some attention from moviegoers heading into matinee screenings. Erin, Vic, and the two officers who accompanied them into the Midway played it off as a drug search. To Vic's amusement, this led to two teenagers abruptly turning and running for the exit.

"Want to chase them?" he asked.

Erin was tempted. Like her K-9, seeing a target running made her want to run after them. But she shook her head. "Let 'em go. We've got bigger fish to fry than a couple half-ass misdemeanor possession busts."

"How much volume, you figure?" Vic asked the two uniforms.

"Unless they were planning on dealing in the theater, just a dime bag or two," one of them said. "And if it's just weed, it wouldn't even be worth hauling them downtown."

"Do you guys arrest anybody for pot anymore?" Vic asked.

The Patrol cop shrugged. "If we find, like, a garbage bag full of it in their trunk, then sure. Or if it's collateral at a crime scene. Otherwise, the DA doesn't even wanna hear about it, so why bother? I got enough paperwork."

"Real credit to the force," Vic said.

"What's that supposed to mean?" snapped the other uniform. "Just 'cause we don't bring down fancy cases like you downtown boys—"

"Knock it off, both of you," Erin said. "Vic doesn't care about pot, either. Nobody cares."

"I wish they'd just legalize it," muttered the first uniform. "That way at least I wouldn't have to feel guilty when I don't run these kids down. It's like speeders. You pull one over and he gets all pissed, 'cause everybody does it, so why'd we have to stop him?"

"And his wife's on the way to the hospital, and his grandma's dying," Vic added. "Hey, we all worked Patrol once upon a time."

"I liked it," Erin said. "Except for the drunks throwing up on me."

"Now that, we can agree on," the second cop said.

* * *

After that, it was on to the Regal Atlas Park Theater. They'd spent so long clearing the previous two, it was getting dark. Vic was turning surly and Rolf was a little dispirited by lack of success. Erin diverted just short of the theater and pulled over.

"Vic, give me one of your gloves or something."

"What for?"

"Morale boost."

He raised his eyebrows but handed over a glove.

"Now get out and hide in that parking lot."

"We got time for games, Erin?"

"It helps. Trust me."

He shrugged. "You're the hotshot Detective Second Grade." He got out of the car and jogged into the lot that stood next to the theater. He was quickly out of sight in the gathering dusk.

Erin gave him a couple minutes' start, then held up his glove to Rolf.

"Rolf! *Such!*"

The K-9 was off. He was very familiar with Vic's scent and the trail was fresh. The Shepherd moved fast, threading his way through the parked cars, Erin hurrying behind him. Less than ninety seconds later, he rounded the back end of a Ford F150 pickup and barked sharply. He stood up on his back paws and thrust his snout over the tailgate.

"Okay," Vic said, sitting up. "You got me." He'd been lying in the bed of the truck.

"Good boy, Rolf," Erin said. "*Sei brav. Sei brav.*" She'd never been a hundred percent clear on what those German words meant, but she'd been told they were what his original trainer had said when he'd done a good job.

Rolf sat proudly beside Erin, looking as pleased with himself as a German Shepherd ever did. Erin handed him his Kong chew-toy and let him gnaw it for a minute or two.

"It'll keep him fresh," she explained to Vic. "Search dogs lose their edge if they keep looking and never find anyone. After 9/11, when they were checking the Trade Center for survivors, they had volunteers hide for the rescue dogs between searches, so they'd feel like they were doing some good. Dogs have feelings too, you know."

"Maybe they should issue the rest of us those rubber things," Vic said, pointing to Rolf's toy. "Looks pretty satisfying. Or maybe you need to give him some vodka. Maybe he'd do an even better job."

"Now there's a thought," Erin said. "What do you think, Rolf? Want to try some Stoli?"

Rolf was fine with the chew-toy.

"We ready to get on with the job now?" Vic asked.

They went the rest of the way to the theater. This one was shorthanded, with just two officers in the lobby. Erin decided to leave them there, to block any escape, while she, Vic, and Rolf conducted the search.

"You ever notice, modern theaters are just like motels?" Vic asked as they made their way down the main hallway.

"Overpriced, bad food?" Erin guessed.

"No. Well, yes, but no."

"Unidentifiable stains on the upholstery?"

Vic snorted. "Good point, but not what I was thinking."

"Okay, I give up."

"They all look pretty much the same."

"I guess the theater isn't the point," she said.

"Oh, right," he said. "If you're taking your girl to a motel, you don't care what the wallpaper looks like. That's not what you're there for."

"You don't take Piekarski to motels, do you?"

"No! The nice ones are too expensive and the cheap ones are too sleazy. Besides, her roommate works nights and doesn't come home till after eight. We get plenty of privacy at her place."

"You've got your own place."

"Yeah, but I'm not letting her see it. I want her to like me."

Rolf paused at the door to one of the screening rooms. He snuffled uncertainly at it, whined, and moved on. Erin let out the breath she'd been holding.

"How many more places we gonna hit tonight?" Vic asked.

"There's one more in Rego Park, just down the road," she said. "The Cinemart. Then we'll see how we're doing. I guess we could try the neighborhood Randolph moved to. I just figured it made sense to look close to where he grew up."

"Nostalgia," he agreed. "What makes a guy feel better than going back to where he grew up? Only problem with your theory is he grew up in Queens."

"You're still on about that? Little Odessa is worse."

"I'm just saying, I'm not sure I'd consider anywhere in Long Island to be exactly the Garden of Eden."

"It's funny," Erin said. "I think I heard back in Sunday School that the Garden of Eden was between these two rivers in the Middle East. The Tigris and... something else."

"Yeah, I think you're right," Vic said. "What's your point?"

"Those two rivers make the borders of Iraq."

"Where he just was," Vic said. He snorted. "You're right. That is a little funny. So that's what happened to Paradise. It turned into a desert and got taken over by militant fanatics. Figures."

They got to the end of the last hallway and stood looking at the red-glowing exit sign.

"Nothing," Erin sighed.

Rolf wagged his tail anxiously. He wanted his partner to know he'd tried. Erin scratched him behind the ears.

“One left,” Vic said. He looked at his watch. “Seven thirty. You know, the after-dinner movies are in full swing. If this guy is in a theater, and if he decides to do some damage, we’ll hear about it from Dispatch any second, and we’ll have dozens of casualties.”

“Let’s get going, then,” Erin said. “Maybe we’ve still got time.”

Chapter 12

Erin pulled onto a side street and stopped next to a darkened building. It was concrete, with marble facing on the bottom couple of feet. A corrugated metal service door was in front of them, tagged with the graffiti of three or four local artists. She saw no sign of police, or of any other activity.

"Is this the right place?" she asked.

Vic double-checked the Charger's on-board computer. "Yeah. The main entrance should be around the corner."

Erin unloaded Rolf. She walked the K-9 to the corner, Vic right behind. The theater marquee advertised birthday greetings for somebody named Julia, alongside movie announcements for last year's summer films. The lobby was dark.

She saw a small sign behind the glass in one of the doors. In the dim light it was impossible to read. She thought she saw something about renovation.

"Closed?" Vic asked.

"I guess. That must be why the Patrol boys aren't here."

"Yeah. They must've come by, seen nobody was here, and moved on."

Erin nodded and kept studying the front of the building.

"C'mon," Vic said. "Let's bounce. There's other theaters to check."

"Just a second," she said. She tried the handles on each of the doors. All of them were locked. She held open the bag of socks for Rolf again.

"*Such!*" she ordered.

Rolf dutifully took another sniff of Randolph's scent. He cast around the doors but gave no sign of smelling anything interesting. He went back and forth on the sidewalk, tail waving uncertainly.

"City streets are hard," Erin explained to Vic. "So much foot traffic. There's got to be hundreds of people leaving trails, all crisscrossing."

"Erin, he's not here," Vic said. "We can't break down the door without a warrant, and I don't exactly see the landlord hanging around to let us in. Let's go."

At that moment, Rolf abruptly swerved and started walking down the sidewalk. He was on a trail, but he didn't go toward the front doors. He went back the way Erin and Vic had come. However, he wasn't pulling as hard as he usually did on the scent.

"It's a weak trail," Erin said. But she gave the Shepherd his head and let him lead.

"He's just retracing our steps," Vic grumbled. "Maybe you had the bag open and some of the smell leaked out. He's going back to the car."

It looked like Vic was right. Rolf went around the corner and back toward the Charger. But at the last minute, he swerved again and nosed at the side service door. He snuffled at the gap at the base of the metal. Then he scratched at it and barked once.

Vic and Erin looked at one another.

"You owe my dog an apology," she said.

"Only if Randolph's inside," Vic said. Then, as she kept glaring at him, he added, "Okay, okay. We find the guy, the first round's on me. What's Rolf's drink?"

Erin smiled. "Just water. Can't have him getting hammered on duty, and Rolf's always on duty. How come you keep trying to get my dog drunk?"

"I just think it'd do him some good to loosen up." Vic looked around. "I don't see Randolph's car."

"He probably ditched it somewhere." Erin knelt beside her K-9 and examined the sliding door. She saw a ring for a padlock, but no lock. Taking hold of the bottom edge of the door, she pulled up. The door rattled up on its rails, revealing the dark space of a loading dock.

They were operating on shaky legal ground. If this had been a residence, it would have been flat-out illegal for Erin and Vic to enter without a warrant or the resident's permission. This was a place of business, so they had every right to be there—during open business hours. But this building appeared to be closed, though they hadn't fully verified that.

"What's the Patrol Guide say about this?" Erin quietly asked Vic.

"You kidding? I haven't got that damn thing memorized!"

The Patrol Guide was a good two thousand pages long. No cop knew the whole thing by heart, and every active-duty officer had violated proper procedure more than once, often by accident. The only hope was not to screw up too badly on something too important.

"Well," she said slowly, "I didn't actually see a sign that said the theater was closed. And we're within their normal posted hours."

"I like how you think," Vic said with a grin. Erin knew he'd back her up.

She looked at Rolf. "You sure about this, kiddo?"

Rolf cocked his head. Then he lowered his nose and went forward, into the darkened building.

Erin followed. Vic shrugged, brought his rifle up to his shoulder, and trailed them in.

"You want backup?" he asked in a whisper.

"Not yet." If they were wrong, bringing in more cops would only make for an uglier incident if they caused any trouble for the building's owner.

Erin pulled out her flashlight and flicked it on, holding it in her leash hand. Vic had a tactical light clipped to the muzzle of his M4. He turned that on, too. They saw an ordinary loading area strewn with cardboard boxes, a few forklift palettes, and some litter. A door at the far side of the room looked to be the only other exit.

Rolf seemed more confident now, forging through the room to the door. He got there and scratched at it, whining eagerly.

Erin felt her own excitement rising. "He's here," she murmured. She nodded to the door. Vic, holding his rifle at his shoulder with his right hand, reached out and twisted the knob with his left. He pulled. The door swung open.

Erin sidestepped into the hallway beyond, pistol leveled. Rolf was already pulling to the left. They were in the public part of the theater now, carpet underfoot, movie posters on the walls. There were also signs of renovations in progress. They passed open ceiling panels, exposed wiring, a stepladder in the middle of the hall. Rolf ignored all of it, and Erin followed her partner. She trusted his nose in this situation.

He stopped at the door to Screen 3 and gave his alert, scratching and barking once. The sound was explosively loud in that deserted corridor. Erin and Vic both winced.

"He's sure," she said softly.

"Okay," Vic replied in a low voice. "It'll be a theater. You know, rows of seats. Decent concealment, but the chairs aren't bulletproof. He could be anywhere in there. Once you're through, get some space and grab whatever cover you can. I'll be right behind you, but spread out a little. Ready when you are."

The thought flitted through Erin's mind that she should call for backup now, but she brushed it aside. She and Vic had handled more dangerous situations than this. She reached for the door handle and paused.

Faint sounds were coming through the door. It sounded like a movie soundtrack, something maddeningly familiar that she couldn't quite place. Maybe it was some sort of kids' movie. At any rate, it made her think of her childhood.

The movie would be a good distraction. Maybe Randolph hadn't heard Rolf. Erin shoved the door open. She went in fast, knowing the most dangerous place during a room entry was the doorway.

She found herself at the bottom row of seats in a darkened theater. On the big screen in front of her was an image familiar to any American child; the brown, furry features of the Beast from the Disney movie. He looked upset. It appeared to be the part of the film where the angry townsfolk were storming the Beast's castle with torches and pitchforks.

Erin paid little attention to the screen. Rolf was lunging into the room, running up the aisle toward the back rows. Erin leveled her gun and flashlight, hoping the bright beam would dazzle her target.

"NYPD!" she shouted. "Hands where I can see them!"

She swept the beam of her flashlight across row upon row of empty seats. The room was deserted.

Vic rushed in behind her, fanning out to one side, rifle poised. "Clear!" he shouted.

"Clear!" Erin echoed, confused. If Randolph wasn't here, where the hell was he? In the bathroom, maybe?

Then she remembered what Smith and Monson had told her, and felt like an idiot. Toby Randolph hadn't just watched the movies in Iraq. He'd run the films himself. She looked up to the projection booth, but all she could see was the bright light of the projector. Just like her flashlight, it made it impossible to see whoever was behind it.

"He's up—" she started to say, just as a glass bottle flew through the air, trailing a tail of fire. It arced down like a shooting star and struck the floor of the theater almost at Erin's feet. The bottle shattered. For just a fraction of an instant, nothing happened. Then the world seemed to explode.

A rolling blast of heat and fire smacked Erin in the face. She'd been in a burning building before. This was worse. She squeezed her eyes closed and saw only the brilliant afterimage of flames. She felt like she was burning. Rolf gave a high-pitched yelp. Erin screamed. She couldn't help it. The sound just ripped itself out of her throat. She tumbled over backward, flinging her arms in front of her face. Somewhere, she heard the hard, flat crack of a rifle firing again and again. Another rifle answered it.

Something grabbed Erin's arm. She slid a short distance backward. Whoever it was, they were strong. She was conscious of a piercing pain in her forearm. Then she forced her eyes open, blinking through involuntary tears. She sat up.

The whole room seemed to be engulfed in fire. The suddenness of it was astonishing. Liquid flames clung to the seatbacks and the floor. Dense smoke rolled up from the fire, filling the air. Hollywood flames never produced enough smoke; in a real fire, it was almost impossible to see or breathe. Maybe that was a good thing in this situation; it meant Randolph probably hadn't hit anyone with his rifle.

"Erin!" Vic shouted somewhere to her right. "You okay?"

"I'm good!" she shouted back, hoping it was true. She was aware of pain, but it wasn't as bad as she'd expected. She looked down at herself and saw sticky globs of something, burning their way into her jacket and Kevlar vest. More rifle fire echoed in the room, tremendously loud.

If Vic was over there, who had dragged her out of the fire? She tried to wipe her streaming eyes, but one arm felt heavy. She glanced down and saw a black, furry face. Rolf's jaws were clamped on her arm, not breaking the flesh, but holding her firmly. He was actually smoldering where he'd caught a few drops of the homemade napalm, but if he was in any pain now, he gave no hint of it. He'd dragged her away from the flames, without orders.

"*Pust!*" she said, giving him his "release" command. He obediently let go of her arm. Erin saw the place she and Rolf had been standing. It was entirely ablaze.

"*Sei brav*," she said. Then, to Vic, "Did you get him?"

"I don't know! We've gotta get out of here! This whole building's gonna go!"

As if in answer, a fire alarm began a repetitive, obnoxious buzzing somewhere in the building. White emergency lights began strobing, showing the way to the exits. Insanely, the movie was still running in the background. The Disney music was syncopated by three more rifle shots.

Erin grabbed the armrest of the seat next to her, which fortunately was still intact, and pulled herself to her feet. Her legs worked fine. One of her shoes appeared to be on fire. She noticed it with a sort of detached interest; it was unusual, but didn't seem to have anything directly to do with her. The sprinkler system engaged and it was suddenly raining indoors. That only added to the feeling of unreality. She was in a gunfight set to a Disney soundtrack, she thought. She wanted to laugh, or maybe cry.

"Randolph!" she shouted. Her voice came out hoarsely. She'd gotten a lungful of smoke. "Come out! You'll die if you stay there!

Come out with your hands up!" Then she had to stop talking and start coughing.

Randolph's response came in the form of five rapid shots from his rifle. Vic cursed, but the gunman was firing blindly into the smoke. Erin didn't even see where the bullets went. Vic returned fire. One of his shots, either accidentally or on purpose, shattered the lens on the projector. The movie screen behind them went abruptly dark, but the soundtrack continued on its merry way.

"Erin!" Vic repeated. "We gotta go! Get out! Now! I'll cover you!"

She set her jaw and studied the burning room. She could see the door to the projectionist's booth, on the other side of what looked like a river of flames. The fire was spreading, in spite of the sprinklers. Their way out was still clear, but wouldn't be for long. The water seemed to be doing nothing to the fire but making more smoke. She knew napalm didn't go out easily.

It was the very last thing she wanted to do. But Erin knew it was the right thing, maybe the only thing.

"Rolf!" she ordered, unsnapping his leash. "*Voraus!*"

Rolf knew the command. It meant "go out" and was used when he was supposed to leave. He hesitated a moment. His training told him to obey, but his instincts and loyalty told him to stay. Ultimately, however, Rolf was a professional K-9. He started retracing their steps, running to the door.

"Cover me!" Erin called to Vic. "Then fall back!" She flipped up the hood of her jacket and pulled it as far over her face as she could. She grabbed her gloves out of her pockets and yanked them on. Then she ran, but not for the exit. She ran through the fire.

It hurt almost as much as she expected it to. Napalm wasn't like a wood fire. It clung to everything it touched. The soles of her shoes picked it up and she left fiery footprints. The smoke choked her. She was practically blind. Randolph fired, right in front of her, and Vic answered with several shots of his own. But she made it through, stumbling to the back of the theater, one arm in front of her face.

When she got to the door, she realized her hands were empty. She'd lost her Glock somewhere. She'd probably dropped it when the firebomb had gone off. Why hadn't she noticed before now? That was something to worry about later. She stooped and snatched out her backup gun, the snub-nosed revolver she kept in an ankle holster. Then she kicked the door in.

The booth was very small, with just room for the projector and a chair for the operator. That chair was tipped over on its back. A young man was crouched by the projector, aiming a rifle Vic's direction. In the lurid glow of the fire, his face looked ghastly. He appeared to be crying, but even as Erin saw him, he fired two more shots.

Erin could have shot him. She should have. He was an armed man who was actively trying to shoot a police officer, an officer who was one of her best friends. But Erin held her fire. She jumped on the guy and threw an arm around his neck.

Randolph wasn't a big man. He was thin and wiry, but he was also a soldier, in excellent physical condition, trained in hand-to-hand combat. He wriggled like a weasel, dropping his rifle and twisting around. One fist struck Erin in the cheek, but she hardly noticed the blow. She put a knee in his stomach, dropping all her weight on him.

He grunted as the air was forced out of his lungs. His whole body tried to curl into a ball, but he was still resisting. Erin felt more than saw him fumble at his belt, grabbing something hard and metallic. *Gun*, she thought. She got a hand on his wrist and gave it a hard counterclockwise twist. Randolph made a breathless sound of pain and let go. Erin smacked the weapon away. Then she was kneeling on the fallen man with the barrel of her snub-nose pressed up under his chin.

"Do it!" Randolph wheezed.

"Toby Randolph," Erin said, getting the words out with difficulty, "you're under arrest for the murder of Frank and Helen Carson."

"Just do it! Do it! Do it! Do it!"

He was sobbing under her, choking on his tears, half-smothered by her weight. He *wanted* her to kill him.

All the desperate anger and fear went out of Erin, like a snuffed-out candle. All that was left was pity for this man—this kid—who lay, broken and hopeless, underneath her. And she'd promised his mom to bring him in alive if she could. She reached to her belt with her free hand and got out her cuffs.

"Fucking do it!" Randolph gasped.

"No," she said. She stuck her revolver in her jacket pocket and, with the experience of more than a decade of Patrol work, flipped Randolph onto his stomach, forced his hands behind his back, and cuffed him. "You've got the right to remain silent, so shut up. We're getting out of here."

If she could only figure out how.

Chapter 13

Smoke went upward. That was one of the first things you learned about surviving a fire; hug the floor. Unfortunately, in this case, Erin was stuck at the top of a slanted room, with fire below her. The booth was rapidly filling with a choking cloud. She could try a quick dash back through the flames, but hardly while carrying a handcuffed suspect who wanted to die.

Erin looked around the tiny projectionist's booth again, as if something might have miraculously changed. All she saw was Randolph, the projector, the chair, Randolph's guns, and a couple of bottles that were probably full of his homemade napalm. Whatever happened, she didn't want to be in this booth when those overheated.

It was getting really hard to breathe. She wondered what the fire department's response time was. From her time as a first responder in Queens, she guessed they'd show up about five minutes after they got the alarm signal from the theater.

"Vic!" she hoarsely shouted. "I got him! Call it in!"

No answer.

Vic would never abandon one of his comrades, no matter what. Had Randolph hit him with one of those final bullets?

Was Vic injured, or even dead? If so, she'd have to take care of herself until the firefighters showed up.

Could she and Randolph last five minutes in this booth? Erin didn't think so. The heat and smoke were only getting worse. And where was Rolf? He wouldn't have been able to open the door without her or Vic to help him. He was probably trapped in the theater, too.

It was better to die doing something than die doing nothing. On her knees, she turned around and put her arms under Randolph's body. He was doing nothing to help, just lying there, but at least he wasn't making things harder. She braced herself, curled him over her shoulders, and staggered to her feet. She lurched awkwardly sideways through the narrow door, bonking Randolph's head and her knuckles on the doorframe.

The heat outside the booth was even worse. The sprinklers were still pouring water down, but napalm made one hell of a good accelerant, and the massive amount of water hitting the flames produced an unbelievable cloud of smoke.

Erin wasn't a very good Catholic, but the words of the Hail Mary popped into her head. *Pray for us sinners, now and at the hour of our death*, she thought. *Well, Mother Mary, I'm a sinner, so if you're watching, I could use all the help I can get.*

She took a step, then another. She felt a stickiness under her shoes, like she was walking on soft chewing gum. She realized the rubber soles were partially melted. She couldn't see the red exit sign. She could hardly see anything at all. She just kept going. Intense heat seared her face on her left front. She shied away and tried aiming a little to the right. She coughed, feeling a rough, tearing pain in her throat and lungs. Burns didn't kill most fire victims, she recalled from her first-responder training. Smoke inhalation was what got you.

"Erin! Over here!"

That sounded like Vic. But she couldn't see him. She tried to answer and only managed a wheeze.

A fan of what looked like white mist cut through the flames right at Erin's feet. It wasn't nearly enough to put out the fire, but it beat back the flames for a moment. The mist swept back and forth, clearing a narrow path.

Erin lunged for it, tumbling down the sloping path between burning theater seats, and saw Vic. He was standing by the exit row, a portable fire extinguisher in his hands, hosing the carpet, holding open a way for her. The moment he saw her, with Randolph on her back, he turned and ran for the exit. He flung the door open and they hurried out of the blazing room.

The sprinklers had gone off in the hallway as well. The carpet was a squelching, waterlogged swamp under their feet. Erin tried to remember which way led to the loading dock. It was hard to think, maybe because of lack of oxygen. Her vision was tunneling down, going black around the edges.

"Rolf," she gasped.

"Outside!" Vic shouted in her ear. "I got him! He's okay! Come on! Gimme the guy!"

He lifted Randolph from her shoulders with astonishing ease. Erin's head cleared a little. There was the door in front of them. Now that her hands were free, she grabbed for the doorknob. They ran through the door and saw the open rectangle of the open sliding door. A familiar bark caught Erin's ear. There was Rolf. Vic had dumped him into the loading bay, where he'd have an easy exit if the rest of the building caught fire. Now he took up his usual place at Erin's hip, looking at her for further instructions.

Flashing blue and red lights were visible on the street. The familiar, throaty bellow of a fire truck's horn punched through the wail of approaching sirens. Fresh night air was the sweetest taste Erin could imagine. Then they were outside the theater, sucking in huge breaths, both of them coughing and leaning on the wall. A couple of cops were running toward them, shouting questions.

"Is anyone else inside?"

"Are you okay?"

Vic lowered Randolph to the sidewalk. Still coughing, he fumbled out his shield and held it up. "We're the only ones," he said.

"Watch out," Erin gasped. "Explosives... in the booth... screen 3."

"Copy," one of the cops said. He got on his radio to relay the information to the firemen. His partner bent down to look Randolph over.

"Hey, this guy's in cuffs," the cop said.

Erin nodded wearily. She was starting to get her breathing a little under control, but didn't dare try to say anything else yet. She checked Rolf. The Shepherd's fur was scorched clean off in a couple of places and he looked to have some minor burns. The stench of burnt hair hung over him like a dark cloud. But he wagged his tail gamely, ready to get right back in the game if she needed him.

Erin sat down on the concrete, stripped off her charred gloves, and buried her face in her hands. She tasted smoke on her tongue and smelled benzene fumes on her clothes. God, but she was tired.

* * *

The paramedics pronounced Erin basically healthy. Her burns were all on the surface and minor, thanks to Rolf's quick action and some plain dumb luck. The EMTs took a blood test for her oxygen, carbon dioxide, and carbon monoxide levels and slapped an oxygen mask on her for a little while, then gave her a bag of cough drops and told her to take it easy for a couple of days.

That was easy for them to say. Erin still had a case to close.

Vic was in better shape. He hadn't gotten as close to the fire and hadn't breathed in as much smoke. He hovered around Erin with an uncharacteristic expression of worry on his face. She found it both endearing and annoying.

"I'm fine," she said.

"Nice rasp you got in your voice," he said. "You sound a little like that chick from the '80s, Kim Carnes."

"Thanks. I think."

"Seriously. We gotta go out for karaoke. You could do 'Bette Davis Eyes.' Bring the house down."

"Vic, I can't sing when I'm healthy. The way I sound now, you'd think a cat was being tortured."

They sat on the hood of Erin's Charger and watched the firefighters work. The FDNY had arrived in time to save the building, but Erin guessed she and Vic had set back the renovations on the place a good six months.

"Someone's going to sue the city," she predicted.

"Someone's always suing the city," he said. "Forget about it."

Randolph was in the back of an ambulance, handcuffed to a gurney. A uniform was watching him. They'd warned the cop he was a suicide risk. He'd escaped the fire almost uninjured, but like Erin, he'd sucked in some smoke. The EMTs were keeping an eye on him, just in case, but figured they'd release him into police custody once they made sure he was basically healthy.

"Thanks," Erin said.

"For what?" Vic looked surprised.

"Saving my life."

"Oh, that. Sorry for running out on you. I noticed the extinguisher in the hall when we were on the way in. But then you did your crazy kamikaze thing before I could tell you about it. So once you got into the booth, I figured I better grab the extinguisher and get your mutt out of the way. If you'd waited a few seconds, you could've done the same thing with no burns. You trying to get yourself killed, O'Reilly?"

"Yeah. I'm just bad at it. Vic, when I had him down, he told me to shoot him."

"Maybe you should've."

"You don't mean that."

"You're right, I don't. Guys do it, though. Suicide by cop. They don't even have the stones to pull the trigger themselves, so they make us do the dirty work. Talk about assholes. They're miserable, so they gotta unload the weight on us? Like carrying the shield isn't heavy enough already."

"I thought you liked being a cop."

"I do. That doesn't mean I like everything about it. But you did a good thing tonight, Erin."

She looked down at her hands. "I don't feel like it."

"What do you mean?" Vic grabbed her shoulder. "You got the guy. Nobody got killed. That's a win."

"He wasn't doing anything. He was just sitting alone watching kids' movies."

"With a rifle, a lot of ammo, and some Molotov cocktails," he retorted. "He wasn't doing anything? Tell that to the Carsons. We got two bodies in the morgue because of him."

"He didn't know what he was doing. He thought they were going to kill him. Vic, when we feel like our life's in danger, we're allowed to shoot people. How's what he did any different?"

"It's different and you damn well know it, Erin. For one thing, we're responsible for protecting everybody else. The City of New York trusts us to carry guns and know when to use them. For another, this guy was whacked out on drugs. Try getting hopped up and blowing someone away. How you think that's gonna fly with Internal Affairs? You'd be on the street so fast your head would spin, if you didn't land in jail. He knew what he was doing when he popped the pills. Besides, it's not our job to pass judgment. You a lawyer now? A judge? Jury? Hell no. You're a cop. We just arrest 'em. Society decides what to do with 'em."

She nodded. That was a good way to think about it, especially if she didn't want to burn out. Haul the bad guys in, hand them off to the DA, and call it a good day's work.

"Hey, Erin?"

"Yeah?"

"You saved that guy's life. He's not thanking you now, but someday he will."

"You believe that?"

Vic shrugged. "It don't matter what I believe. This isn't about me."

Chapter 14

By the time Vic, Erin, and Rolf got back to Precinct 8 with their prisoner, it was after ten. It had taken a while to sort things out with the FDNY at the theater, and then they'd had the drive back across the East River for what felt to Erin like the tenth time that day. Randolph rode in the back of the car, next to Rolf's compartment. The K-9 kept a wary eye on him. The soldier was completely silent the whole way.

After they finished booking Randolph, they took him to the interrogation room. Webb was waiting for them there. They left the prisoner in the room, hands cuffed in front of him, and stepped next door to the observation room to discuss the situation.

"You smell like a bad cookout," Webb said.

"Sorry, sir," Erin said. "We didn't have a chance to change."

"You look like you've been through it," he said. "Are all of you okay?"

"We're fine," Vic grunted. "It's not the first time I've been lit on fire."

"You weren't lit on fire," Erin said. "Wait a second. This has happened to you before?"

"A few years back. Fourth of July thing that got out of hand. This crazy guy popped me with a firecracker. Caught me in the vest. No big deal. The equipment guys thought I was making it up when I put in for a replacement."

"This is the guy?" Webb asked, jabbing his thumb at the one-way mirror.

"Yeah," Erin said. "FDNY put out the fire and recovered his rifle and handgun. The gun's a USP .45, according to Vic. Just like the one we found under the Carsons' bed. Military gun."

"Probably the one that was used to hit the Carsons," Vic agreed. "It has some fire damage, but may still be usable for ballistics testing to get a match."

"Okay," Webb said. "Speaking of guns, where's your sidearm, O'Reilly?"

"Huh?"

"When we brought your guy into lockup, you put away your ankle piece. Your waist holster's empty."

"Lost it at the theater, sir. It got napalmed. FDNY found what was left of it."

"At least it's been recovered." Both Webb and Erin knew that an officer's weapon could cause serious problems if it was lost or stolen, then used in a crime down the road. "You know what this means, though," he added.

"Paperwork, sir?"

"Paperwork," he agreed. "But for now, let's wrap this case up and put it to bed, so we can get some sleep. You can take care of the gun thing tomorrow."

"Yeah, rough day for you, wasn't it, sir?" Vic asked with an out-of-place expression of wide-eyed innocence. "All that office work?"

"If you didn't have such a good closure rate, Neshenko, your mouth would land you doing crowd control at Yankee Stadium until you hit retirement," Webb said.

"Maybe I could get you some autographs, sir," he said.

"Vic," Erin said. "I've noticed you only say 'sir' when you're being insubordinate."

"I'll chalk it up to you having been in a critical incident this evening," Webb said. "I won't give you a rip for back talk."

"That's very generous of you, sir."

"O'Reilly, why don't you go in there and get us a confession, or at least some sort of explanation?"

"Alone, sir?" Erin asked.

Webb nodded. "I get the feeling with this guy, it'll be best if he doesn't feel ganged up on. He might open up to one person, alone."

"Especially if it's the person who just hauled his sorry ass out of a burning building," Vic added. "I'll keep an eye on the furball."

"Rolf, *sitz*," Erin ordered, pointing next to Vic. "*Bleib*."

Rolf obeyed, giving his partner a look that suggested he'd be the one keeping an eye on Vic.

Erin cracked her stiff neck, stretched, and tried to loosen her tense muscles. Sarcasm aside, Vic was right. It had been one hell of a long, rough day. It was best not to think about all the things that had happened. Better to look ahead and take care of what still needed doing. She stepped into the interrogation room.

Randolph slumped in the steel chair on the far side of the table. He didn't look up when she came in. He didn't react to her in any way, even when she pulled up the other chair and sat down across from him.

"Hey, Toby," she said quietly.

He didn't respond.

"I need your help, kiddo," she said, keeping her tone soft and nonthreatening. "We've got a bunch of worried people here, trying to understand what happened. You're the only one who can help us do that. But I need you to talk to me. My name's Erin, Erin O'Reilly."

Randolph glanced up. His eyes were bloodshot, from tears and smoke. He didn't say anything.

"I talked to your mom last night," Erin went on. "She's worried about you. I know it'd mean a lot to her if we can let her know you're okay. I can call her as soon as we're done here. Would you like me to do that? Or you can call her. You get two phone calls."

Nothing. Randolph looked straight through Erin with eyes like empty subway tunnels.

She tried to think how to get through to this guy. What would connect with him in his current state?

"Jamal Smith and Chris Monson really appreciated what you did with the movies," she said. "In Iraq. It really made a difference to them, helped them keep their shit together."

She was rewarded with a flicker of recognition in his eyes. Slowly, he nodded.

"How'd you pick out the movies?" she asked. "How'd you know which ones to show?"

"It was whatever I could get," he said, his voice very low. "I knew a guy in Baghdad, he got these bootleg CDs, from China I think. I just bought whatever he had on hand."

It figured, Erin thought. A street vendor in Iraq selling bootleg movies imported from China. That was the twenty-first century for you right there.

"How come the cartoons?" she asked.

"I like cartoons."

"What about them?"

"They're not like the war. They're clean."

"How do you mean?"

"No blood." As he said it, he rubbed his fingers on his pants, as if he was trying to wipe something away.

"The doctors put you on some meds," she said. "After you got hit?"

"Yeah."

"Did they help? With the pain?"

"Yeah. But they made me feel kinda weird, too."

"You were having bad dreams," she suggested.

He nodded. "I didn't want to go to sleep. But I didn't want to wake up, either. I dunno which was worse."

"What did the pills do?"

"When I just took the pills, they made me see stuff. Weird shit. Monsters, for-real monsters sometimes. But I found out if I had a flashback right before taking them, it'd be okay."

"A flashback?" She didn't understand. "You mean, you'd remember something right when you were taking your meds?"

He blinked. "No, ma'am. It's a drink. Something one of the guys cooked up in the field. Forster, I think. He was a bartender before he joined up."

"What's in a flashback?"

"Gatorade, and vodka, and... ginger ale."

That explained the drinks they'd found at the Carson apartment, Erin thought. Only soldiers would think to mix vodka with Gatorade.

"What happened when you chased that with the pills?" she asked.

"Nothing. Just black. I'd take it and it was lights out. It'd give me a headache when I woke up, but that wasn't too bad. It beat the dreams."

"When you came back," Erin said, "it was hard fitting in here, wasn't it?"

"I got my discharge," he said. "I didn't know what to do. I couldn't relax, but there's nothing for me to do, either. And Mom just kept at me. She kept hovering around, asking was I okay, and what could she do for me, and I just couldn't take it. She was driving me crazy, you know?"

"She didn't understand," Erin said. "Because she hadn't been there."

"Yeah," Randolph said. "I just wanted her to leave me alone. So I got out of there, got my own place."

"Then you heard from your old sergeant," she prompted.

"Yeah. Sarge kept tabs on all his guys. He sent me this letter, invited me and some others to come over. I figured why not. Maybe it'd be like it was over there, except safer, you know? No one dropping mortar shells in the perimeter."

"So you went?"

"Yeah. Sarge was always talking about his wife, how great she was. She'd send him these letters, he'd never tell us what she said, but we could smell 'em. On account of her perfume. And he was right. She seemed real nice. And Sarge, I know his leg was all messed up, but he looked pretty good, too. We started talking, and we mixed some drinks, and I guess we got drunk. I got a little loopy, and I had to go to the bathroom."

"What happened in the bathroom?" Erin asked gently.

Randolph looked uncertain. "I dunno, exactly. I looked in the mirror, and I felt real weird. I was back in Iraq, you know? We started taking mortar fire. It blew out the window. I hit the dirt and yelled for Sarge, and then I knew it wasn't really happening, but I was still seeing it. And I didn't have my meds, but there was this bottle in the bathroom, and I remember opening it and I think I took a couple. Then I think I had to puke, so, you know, I did."

"Then what?" Erin asked.

Randolph shook his head. "I don't know, ma'am. It's just black after that."

"What's the next thing you remember?"

"The next thing I remember, I was at the theater. Where I met you." He was looking at the table, refusing to meet her eyes.

"Toby," she said in a soft voice.

"What?" He didn't look up.

"You remember something else," she said. "I know you do. Why did you throw that bottle at me? Why did you ask me to shoot you?"

"I have this one thing in my head," he said very quietly. "This one picture, and it won't go away. It's like a photo, except there's sound."

"What is it?"

"It's Sarge's wife. She's kneeling on the floor, and Sarge is lying there, shot, and she's... she's screaming. And then, I... I..."

Tears filled Randolph's eyes. He brought his cuffed hands up to his face, the chain clinking, and covered his eyes. "I don't even know why. I just watched it happen. I... I didn't want... I didn't mean... oh God."

Erin couldn't stand it. Not anymore. She had to get out of that room. She couldn't take sitting there with this young man, absorbing his pain and guilt. She got up so fast her chair tumbled over backward, clattering to the floor. She practically ran out of the interrogation room.

Vic caught her in the hallway, grabbing her by the shoulders. "Erin! What's up?"

She shook herself free. "Let go of me!" She looked past him at Webb, who was standing in the observation room doorway. "That enough for you? You get everything you needed?"

"Yeah," Webb said. "That should be fine. But what about you?"

"I'm fine!"

Webb and Vic were looking at her with identical expressions of concern. She found it infuriating.

"Erin," Vic said. "Maybe you should—"

"I said I'm fucking fine!"

The words hung in the air, echoing off the cinderblock walls. In the shocked silence that followed, she grabbed Rolf's leash and yanked him with her, down the hallway and away from the other two detectives.

Chapter 15

Erin slammed the door of her apartment and leaned against it. She was shaking and didn't even know why. Her heart was racing. She felt sweat running down the back of her neck in spite of the cold March night. The smell of burnt hair, smoke, and gas filled her nostrils.

She stripped off her charred, smoky clothes and flung them into the corner of her bedroom. She turned on the shower as hot as she could stand it, even though she knew it would be painful on her fresh-bandaged burns. Then she climbed in and let the water run over her, trying to calm down.

Rolf lay down on the bathroom floor and put his snout between his front paws, watching her with his serious brown eyes. She'd have to wash him, too, and try to get the stink of smoke out of his fur. But just then, she couldn't do anything but try to take care of herself.

And she couldn't even do that. Her heart wouldn't slow down. Was she having a heart attack? She ran over the symptoms in her first responder's brain. Uncomfortable pressure in her chest? Check, but that could just be stress. Pain in one or both arms, back, neck, jaw, stomach? Check, but maybe that was from picking up a full-size adult man and carrying him. Shortness of breath? Check, but she'd just been treated for smoke inhalation. Cold sweat? Lightheadedness? Check and check, but again, there were reasons.

Erin put her hands on the shower wall and lowered her head. What was the matter with her? She'd been a cop for twelve years. Nothing had ever gotten to her, not like this.

The water was too hot. A part of her welcomed the pain, but she couldn't stand it anymore. The steam was soothing, but also making it harder to breathe. She turned the valve and got out, toweling off. Rolf wagged his tail.

"You're next, kiddo," she promised. She got out the dog shampoo.

Rolf's tail stopped moving. He knew what was coming.

Fifteen minutes later, Rolf was clean, soaking wet, and unhappy. Erin took him into the bedroom, wrapped a fresh towel around him to keep him warm, and left him swaddled there on her bed, staring mournfully at her. She dressed mechanically, automatically. It was only as she was fastening her belt that she realized she'd put on real clothes, not pajamas. What had she been thinking? It was late and she was in no condition to go out.

Head spinning, she went into the kitchen and opened the liquor cabinet. She had the Glen D whiskey in her hand before she knew she was doing it. She took a slug straight from the bottle, something she never did. The burn of the hard liquor on her raw throat made her gag and brought tears to her eyes. She stumbled and went down on one knee, holding onto the counter with her free hand and almost dropping the bottle.

"Jesus," she whispered. She looked at the bottle and tried to remember how it had gotten into her hand.

When Erin had been a teenager, her father had sat her down for one of his serious talks. Sean O'Reilly wasn't good at emotional support, but he was great at advice. When she'd started getting interested in boys, he'd given her the straight skinny on teen pregnancy, STDs, rape, and abuse, based on his police experience, but had added that her choices were her own. He just wanted her to be informed. This talk had been about alcohol.

"Kiddo, you're going to drink. I know that. It's natural. I like a good glass of whiskey as much as the next Irishman, and I'm not going to sit here and tell you not to. I'm no hypocrite. But I'm going to tell you there's a right way and a wrong way to do it. You don't want to drink with the wrong crowd, and you don't want to drink alone. If you go out with people you can't trust, you have to keep your mind clear, or there's no telling what's going to happen to you. You get drunk in the wrong place, and you'll get hurt. Drink alone, and that's how you become a drunk. You need to find buddies, good friends you can trust, people who'll look after you, and drink with them. That way you'll be safe."

Erin pulled out her phone and dialed with trembling fingers. She tried the number of Carlyle's current burner phone.

It rang and rang. He hadn't set up a voicemail; he didn't want to leave any sort of electronic trail, just in case anyone else ever got access to it. She let it go ten rings, twelve, and gave up. He was probably in some sort of business meeting, talking with scary criminals, and couldn't take a call from his girlfriend.

She thought of Vic, but he'd still be at the precinct, taking care of the arrest paperwork. The paperwork she should be doing. He'd be pissed enough at her already for running out on him. No need to make things worse.

There was Kira Jones, her other friend from Major Crimes, but Kira was with Internal Affairs now. The very last thing she wanted was for anyone in IAB to know just how edgy she was. If Kira saw her like this, it'd be Kira's job to report it, and next thing Erin knew she'd be on administrative leave, or maybe writing parking tickets on Staten Island.

Who did that leave? Who could you call late at night, when you felt like the world was falling apart on you?

Erin dialed. The phone rang once, twice, three times, four.

"O'Reilly."

The voice on the other end of the line was groggy. She'd woken him up.

"Dad?"

"Erin?" Sean O'Reilly came instantly awake and worried. A man's children didn't call that close to midnight with good news, not even in cop families. "What's up, kiddo? You okay?"

"Dad, I... I don't know." With that admission, her last walls of self-control crumbled. She started crying, crying like she hadn't since she was a little girl. Tough-as-nails Erin O'Reilly just fell apart.

"Hey, hey, kiddo," Sean said. "It's okay. Where are you? Are you at the hospital?"

"Huh? No," she sniffled. "No, I'm home."

"Are you hurt? Your voice sounds funny."

"No... not really. A little, I guess."

"What happened?"

"There was a thing, at a movie theater. A guy, he... he set the place on fire. I got burned a little. It's not bad."

"You get checked out by the medics?"

"Yeah, Dad, I'm not hurt. Rolf's okay, too."

"That's good." Sean was a very practically-minded man. Erin could see him working his way down his mental checklist. "How about the rest of your team? All of them get out okay?"

"Yeah, Dad. Vic was the only one who was there and he's fine." She was starting to get the tears under control. She hiccupped slightly as she took a deep breath and steadied herself.

"Okay, good. So what is it?"

"I don't know."

That made Sean pause. He clearly hadn't expected that answer. There were a few seconds of dead air on the line.

"Well, kiddo, you called for a reason, right? Just think back. It'll come to you."

"I'm having nightmares." The sentence slipped right out, without a plan or intention.

"Oh." Her dad sounded a little out of his depth. She hadn't complained of nightmares since she'd been a very young girl, and then she'd gone to her mom, not to him. Mom was the one who made bad dreams go away; every kid knew that.

"About stuff that's happened," she said. "Close calls. Dad, I keep dreaming Rolf and Vic and Kira and everyone, they all keep getting killed. I can't sleep, and when I do, it just keeps happening. And this guy we just brought in, he came back from Iraq, and he totally cracked up and went crazy and killed a guy who was one of his best friends. And I looked at him in the interrogation room and I wondered, what if that's me?"

"Erin, slow down, kiddo. You're not making sense. It's just dreams. I get it, the Job is hard on people. I've seen some stuff over the years, too. But it's okay. You've just got to learn to live with it, keep moving forward. You're a tough girl, you've got this. You'll be fine."

He wasn't listening, or if he was, he wasn't understanding. Erin clenched her hand into a fist and pushed her knuckles against the Formica countertop until they hurt.

"Dad, I'm scared."

"What're you scared of, kiddo? Look, you can't let the fear get to you. Just stay strong. You'll see, you can get through this. Fear can kill you on the street, kiddo. You have to face it down."

"Dad, stop! Stop it!" She slammed her fist on the counter.

"What?" Sean sounded genuinely taken aback. "What'd I say?"

Erin hung up on him. She never did that, not since her teen years. But she couldn't get through to him. She glared at the phone, then back at the whiskey bottle.

The phone buzzed in her hand. It was her dad, calling her back. She thought about throwing it across the room. She angrily swiped the red button, refusing the call.

Erin's dad had brought her up to face her fears head-on, to fight them and beat them down. When she'd met bullies in school, he'd taught her how to fistfight.

"You meet one of those hair-pulling, nail-scratching cat-fighters, you just give her a hard right to the gut. See if that doesn't fold her right up. Even nowadays, girls don't expect each other to know how to throw a punch."

Later on, when she'd put on the shield, she'd started carrying a gun. Then she'd known, if everything went to hell, she could put her enemies down permanently. But how did you shoot an enemy that felt like it was inside you?

Then she saw the answer, and for just an instant, the escape route was crystal clear. She thought of her backup revolver, lying next to her shield. One trigger pull, that was all it would take.

"God," she said. What horrified her wasn't that she'd had the thought. What was scary was how much of a relief that thought had been.

Erin pulled on her shoes. She heard a dog shaking himself in the bedroom, wriggling loose of the towel. Rolf came trotting out. If Erin was going somewhere, he wanted in on it.

"*Bleib*," she ordered, yanking on her jacket. Rolf, confused but obedient, stayed put. He cocked his head comically at her, but she wasn't even looking. She was already leaving. For the first time in years, she left her apartment without a gun on her person. For the first time in years, carrying a gun felt more dangerous than being unarmed.

And that, considering where she was going, was insane.

Chapter 16

It was the middle of a Friday night, which meant the Barley Corner was full almost to capacity. An ice hockey tournament was playing on the big-screen TVs. Boisterous blue-collar guys mingled with low-level O'Malley associates. At a guess, half the guys in the pub had criminal records. Some of them were doubtless armed, and many of those were drunk. Most unattached women would feel pretty nervous in that sort of setting.

But Erin was the proprietor's girlfriend, and all the truly dangerous guys in the Corner knew it. Several of them favored her with friendly smiles and greetings, none of them disrespectful. A path cleared for her as she crossed the room to the bar. Danny, Carlyle's number-one bartender, was there, serving up drinks with a practiced rhythm.

"Evening, Erin," he said as he slid a pint of Guinness along the bar into the waiting hands of a large, tattooed man. "What can I get for you?"

"I'm not here to drink, Danny," she said. "Where's your boss?"

"In back."

"He going to be out soon?"

Danny shrugged. "He's meeting with Evan. Don't know how long it'll take."

"Oh." That explained why Carlyle hadn't answered his phone. A meeting with Evan O'Malley took priority over everything else, including emergencies. Going face-to-face with Evan was a life-threatening situation every time it happened.

"Sorry," Danny said. "Look, anything you want? On the house, same as always."

"You know what a flashback is?"

"Sure. Ginger ale, vodka, Gatorade?"

"That's the one."

"Coming right up. That's a new one for you, isn't it?"

"You got a great memory, Danny."

He grinned. "It's a bartender thing. People like it when you know their drinks." He set a startlingly green cocktail in front of her. "Enjoy."

The bar was crowded, so Erin took her drink and drifted toward the wall. She found a handy patch of brick and leaned against it. She took a small, cautious sip of the cocktail, being careful of her throat. It was surprisingly refreshing and smooth. She tried to breathe, tried to get back to some sense of normality.

Her neck hairs tingled. Someone was definitely watching her. She slowly turned her eyes to the right, trying not to be obvious about it.

Ian Thompson was standing a few feet away, leaning against the same wall she was, looking at her.

"Evening," she said.

"Evening, ma'am." His eyes roved around the room.

"You working tonight?" she asked.

"No, ma'am."

"Except you're still keeping your eyes open."

"Place like this, wouldn't you?"

"Yeah."

They stood in silence for a short while, watching the crowd. Erin found Ian's presence oddly calming. Maybe it was because, whatever she'd been through lately, he'd survived worse. Maybe it was that she knew he'd have her back if anything serious went down. He'd saved her life more than once.

"So you hang out in a bar, on your downtime, but don't drink?" she asked.

"Sometimes I do. Don't feel like it tonight."

"Everything okay with Carlyle? I heard about his meeting."

"Far as I know, ma'am."

"What do you drink?" she asked. "When you drink, I mean."

"Beer, mostly. Sometimes a shot. What've you got there, ma'am?"

Erin looked at the green thing in her hand. "It's called a flashback."

Now she had Ian's attention. He didn't quite smile, but then, Ian never really smiled. "Guy at my FOB used to make those."

"FOB?" She didn't recognize the term.

"Forward Operating Base, ma'am. In the 'Stan."

"They let you drink on a forward base?"

"Brass didn't know about it. One of the guys smuggled in the vodka. We had lots of Gatorade."

"Ian?"

"Yes, ma'am?"

She didn't make eye contact with him, just stood there beside him, eyes on the room. "I think I'm losing it."

"Losing what, ma'am?"

"My shit. Falling apart."

She risked a sidelong glance. He didn't seem alarmed, or even surprised. He just nodded.

"Everyone does, ma'am."

"That's not true."

Now he did look at her. "Affirmative, ma'am. It's mathematical. Doesn't matter how tough you are. Enough combat, everyone breaks."

"I haven't seen that much... combat," she said.

"Guess you've seen enough," he replied.

"So that's it?" she asked bitterly. "I'm broken now?"

"Everyone's broken, ma'am. You are, so am I."

"What do I do about it?"

"You looking for a fix, ma'am? Or a cure?"

"Aren't those the same thing?"

"Not even close."

"What's the difference?"

"It's like this, ma'am. You want a quick fix, you're looking to keep doing your job, but you're not thinking long-term. Happens a lot on deployment. A guy cracks up, you need him to stay combat effective, you give him a fix. Can be a little thing; pep-talk, hot meal, shower, drink, even just taking a shit indoors on a real toilet. Excuse me, ma'am. But you want a cure, you're trying to get over the whole thing, solve the root problem, get *better*. That's the whole problem in the 'Stan and the Sandbox."

"What is?"

"The brass keep going for the quick fix instead of the cure."

"I didn't know you were political, Ian."

"I'm not, ma'am. I'm a tactics guy. Just like to know what works. So which one you looking for?"

"I have to keep doing my job. But I want a cure."

"You might have to choose, one or the other. Hard to get cured when you keep exposing yourself to the disease."

"Are you cured?"

"Not even close."

Erin thought about that, considered what her future might look like. Then, surprising herself, she said, "I thought about it tonight."

"About what?"

"A permanent solution." She couldn't believe she was telling him this, even obliquely.

He nodded. "Me, too."

"You think about it often?" she asked quietly.

"Some nights."

"What stops you?"

"I don't have the right," he said. He studiously kept his eyes off her face, and Erin realized he was doing it on purpose, giving her space out of respect for her feelings. He didn't want her to feel scrutinized or embarrassed.

"Why not?"

"Got some things to do still. A guy counting on me."

"Carlyle?"

He nodded. "And I've got some things to pay back."

"Duty? That's all you've got?"

He seemed a little surprised. "That's not enough?"

"Not for everyone."

"What would be?"

Erin had to think about that, too. "Love," she said at last. "Family. Doing things that matter."

"What are you missing?" he asked.

"Nothing." That was the truth. She had her family. She thought of her mom, her dad, her brothers, her niece and nephew. She thought of Vic and Webb. And Rolf, of course. And Carlyle. She thought of the Job, of all the people she'd met, the cases she'd closed, the cases that were still out there waiting.

She looked at Ian, and now he was looking in her eyes. What she saw was an intense devotion, a fierce refusal to give up, no matter what, but she also saw the love he had for the man she loved too. To her, Carlyle was a lover. To Ian, he was a father, not the father he'd been born to but the one he'd chosen.

"You just have to remember," he said. "The bad shit, what happens out there, seems like the most important shit, because it's life or death. Being through it sets us apart. But it doesn't define us. What matters is why, and for who."

"And being thankful for what we've got," she added. "And who we've got."

"Affirmative, Erin."

She blinked. "You've never called me that before."

He didn't change expression. "Sorry, ma'am. Won't happen again."

"I liked it."

"No excuse, ma'am."

Now she thought he was joking, but wasn't sure. "Thanks, Ian," she said.

"Glad to help, ma'am."

Ian was always on, always alert, but Erin saw him become just a little more aware. She pivoted and saw Mickey Connor coming out of the back hallway. It would've been hard to see anyone else through the crowded room, but Mickey was head and shoulders taller than nearly everyone there. Six foot six, weighing better than three hundred pounds, Mickey didn't need to push his way through a crowd. People got out of his way. A path cleared for him.

It wasn't just his size. Mickey was Evan O'Malley's top enforcer, a retired heavyweight boxer with a reputation for sheer, unreasonable violence. Erin had only been in close proximity to him a few times, and every time he'd scared her. His eyes were a very pale, flat blue, with almost no expression in them. She'd seen corpses with more empathy in their gaze.

Ian, with his veteran's sense for sizing up the biggest threat in a room, locked onto Mickey at once. He stepped out from the wall to give himself some room, rolled his shoulders slightly to loosen himself up, and flicked open the single button that held his coat closed. Erin knew that was just in case he needed to draw down on Mickey. And these guys were supposed to be on the same side.

Then she saw Evan O'Malley and Carlyle behind Mickey. Ian saw them too, and relaxed a little. The meeting was over. Evan was going home, and Mickey was going with him as a bodyguard. Just a typical night.

Evan gave a careless, disinterested glance around the room. He saw Erin, but gave no hint of recognition. If Mickey's eyes were dead, Evan's were pure, arctic ice. Evan was an eminently practical man. If he didn't have immediate use for someone, they were of no interest to him, so he was ignoring her. The head of the O'Malleys followed his enforcer out the door into the night.

Ian watched them go and casually buttoned his coat again. Erin realized he'd been waiting to verify Carlyle was okay. If Carlyle hadn't come out of that room, it was quite possible Ian would've whipped out the Beretta she knew he carried, and there'd have been more bodies to pick up before the end of the night. It was a good reminder of the sudden violence that was always right under the surface of Carlyle's world.

Carlyle walked to the bar and raised a finger to Danny, who already had a shot of Glen D whiskey waiting. He went to his seat of honor, a barstool which was somehow always vacant when he needed it, and took a seat, resting his elbows on the polished wood. He nodded to Ian, then saw Erin. Old-school gentleman that he was, he immediately stood again to acknowledge her presence.

She went to meet him. The seats on either side of him were taken, but a glance from Carlyle was sufficient to convince the guy on his right to stand up and move. She slid onto the stool. He resumed his seat.

"Evening, darling," he said. "I hope you've not been waiting long. I saw you'd called, but was unavoidably detained."

"Everything okay?"

"Aye, just some business concerns. It needn't trouble you."

Erin translated that as meaning they'd been discussing criminal activities he couldn't tell her about, because then she'd be duty-bound to arrest him. Part of the careful truce at the heart of their relationship was that she wouldn't ask him about O'Malley activities, and in return he'd give her no specific cause to come after him personally.

"Mickey gives me the creeps," she said.

"I'd worry if he didn't," Carlyle replied. "I'll confess he makes me nervous at times." He looked more closely at her. "Are you all right, darling?"

"I'm fine," she said. "I was just having a chat with your driver."

"Has Ian been helpful?"

"Very."

"That's grand. I've made some inquiries, darling, but I fear I've nothing to offer on the subject of Mr. Carson."

"What? Oh, yeah." She'd completely forgotten about his promise to ask about Carson's possible smuggling contacts. "That's okay. We got the guy. It wasn't anything to do with gunrunners."

"That's grand," he said again. "However, if you're ever needing some military surplus from your government's arsenal, I can likely lay my hands on anything you might require."

"Some guys just get flowers for their lady friends. You think I'm more of a hand grenade girl?"

He smiled. "I'd not want you to think I was neglecting you. Will you be staying long?"

"I'm pretty tired. I think maybe I'll go home in a couple minutes. It's been a long day."

"Are you wanting to talk about it?"

"Maybe later. You don't want to hear it right now."

"Erin, darling, there's nothing you can't tell me."

She nodded, but there were things he couldn't tell her, and that was still a stumbling block for them. He loved her, she knew that, but he was still trying to straddle the two worlds they inhabited.

"It got a little messy," she said. "A guy threw a Molotov at us. Rolf and I got a little scorched."

"Is he all right, then?" Carlyle asked, suddenly concerned. "I'd noticed you'd come without him."

"He's home, and he'll be fine. Just lost some fur."

"Close shave, was it?"

"Yeah. Was that a pun?"

"Am I the sort of lad who'd make that sort of joke?"

"Apparently you are."

"If there's anything I can offer to ease your discomfort, you've only to ask."

"I know, thanks. But I'm ready to go home. I'll call you tomorrow."

"I'll look forward to it." He kissed her cheek and whispered, "I do love you, darling."

"Back at you," she replied, and as she looked in his eyes, she thought just maybe everything was going to be fine after all.

She did feel a little better. Better enough that she didn't take another drink before bed. She hoped, when she went to sleep, she might manage without the nightmares. Rolf wasn't quite dry, but she didn't mind the smell of wet dog. It was a comforting, familiar smell, one that didn't remind her of danger. Erin put her arm around her K-9 and let herself drift off to sleep.

Chapter 17

Erin found herself at the bottom row of seats in a darkened theater. On the big screen in front of her was an image familiar to any American child; the brown, furry features of the Beast from the Disney movie. It appeared to be the part of the film where the angry townsfolk were storming the Beast's castle with the usual torches and pitchforks.

Rolf lunged into the room, running up the aisle toward the back rows. Erin leveled her gun and flashlight, hoping the bright beam would dazzle her target.

"NYPD!" she shouted. "Hands where I can see them!"

She swept the beam of her flashlight across row upon row of empty seats.

Vic rushed in behind her, fanning out to one side, rifle poised. "Clear!" he shouted.

"Clear!" Erin echoed, confused.

A rifle shot rang out. Blood and bone fragments showered out the back of Vic's head. He went down in a heap.

Erin looked up to the projection booth, but all she could see there was the bright light of the projector. Just like her flashlight, it made it impossible to see whoever was behind it. She raised her gun and began squeezing the trigger, but her hands moved so slowly.

A glass bottle flew through the air, trailing a tail of fire. It arced down like a shooting star and struck the floor of the theater almost at Erin's feet. The bottle shattered. The world exploded.

A rolling blast of heat and fire engulfed Rolf. The Shepherd cried out, a puppy's yelp of terrified pain. Erin squeezed her eyes closed and saw only the brilliant afterimage of flames. She was burning.

Erin screamed. She couldn't help it.

* * *

She woke up gasping, the silhouettes of flames still dancing behind her eyes. She groped for her gun on the bedside table. It wasn't there. She was unarmed, helpless. The terror of that thought drove her fully awake.

She flicked on the lamp and waited for her breathing to return to normal. Her T-shirt stuck to her back, soaked with sweat. She remembered now. She'd lost her Glock last night and hadn't been issued a replacement yet. Her backup gun was hanging in her closet. She hadn't wanted to risk a repeat of her experience with Rolf, so she'd left it out of reach. She still wasn't sure whether that was the right call or not. It might prevent accidents, but she wasn't sure it was helping her sense of security.

Erin tried to piece together what had happened. She'd felt good when she'd gone to bed. Her talk with Ian had helped, damn it. Why wasn't she better?

She looked at the clock. The red digital numbers blinked 03:43.

Erin slumped back on her mattress. She was exhausted. Something cold and wet poked her hand. It was Rolf's snout. His anxious, furry face loomed over her.

"I can't do this," she told him.

He wagged his tail and nosed her again.

"I can't, you dumb mutt. Not alone."

Rolf watched her patiently. She wasn't alone and he wanted her to know it.

Erin lay there and tried to think. She was just so tired. Not physically, but emotionally. It wasn't supposed to work like this. She'd just been on vacation, for God's sake. She was supposed to come back energized, ready to get right back to work.

Ian had given her some useful thoughts, some tools that might help. But Ian didn't have his own shit together. For all she knew, he was hanging by an even more delicate thread than she was. Carlyle would help however he could. So would Rolf. Her dad had tried, he just wasn't very good at the whole emotional thing.

"You're right," she told Rolf, rubbing the base of his ears. "I'm not alone."

But she had to face the fact it might not be enough. What could she do?

They taught every officer, in a bad situation, you called for backup. And if the regular officers couldn't help you, you called in the specialists. ESU, HRT, K-9 units, CSU. It wasn't a sign of weakness. It was smart and it could keep you alive.

What was stopping her? Pride? Fear? Needing to be tough?

Erin O'Reilly had always known she was tough. What she needed to prove now was that she was smart.

There was no getting back to sleep. She got out of bed, put on her running clothes, and loaded Rolf into the Charger. She drove to Central Park, to the place she'd met Ian the last two times. She was early this morning and he wasn't there yet. That was okay.

She ran. She ran until her lungs burned and her legs ached. The cold air was rough on her smoke-damaged throat, but she didn't care. She ran through the pain and into the peace on the other side of exhaustion. She ran until her thoughts dwindled to nothing and she forgot everything but putting one foot in front of the other. Rolf ran beside her every step, keeping pace, watching over her.

When she was finally done, she got back in her car, drove to her apartment, and showered. Then she went in to the precinct.

It was a Saturday, which meant very little from the point of view of a police station. They were open twenty-four seven. Erin was early, but that was deliberate. She didn't go to Major Crimes right away. She walked past the Patrol officers, hookers, drunks, and other early-morning denizens of the precinct.

Doc Evans was in his office again. He answered her knock, seeming neither surprised nor upset at the interruption.

"Good morning, Erin," he said.

"Morning, Doc. Got a minute?"

"Always. Come on in."

Erin brought Rolf in and stood just inside the door, fidgeting a little. Evans made a couple of quick notes on his files and closed his cabinet.

"Did you find the guy you were looking for?" he asked.

"Yeah. You were a big help. Thanks." Erin grabbed the opportunity to talk about something else, to play for a little time. "Our guy is a veteran. He picked up a drug habit overseas, after being wounded, and was using oxy and alcohol to try to take the edge off his trauma issues. He had a combat flashback, exacerbated by the drugs, and killed a couple of people, thinking they were enemies."

"That's rough," Evans said. "How'd you find him?"

Erin smiled slightly. "Profiling."

Evans raised his eyebrows. "Really?"

"Yeah. I learned some things about his background, what made him feel safe, and it let me guess where he'd be. Then we got lucky and ran him down. Nobody else got hurt."

"You and your dog look a little roughed up to me."

"Not really hurt, I mean. Nothing permanent."

"What's going to happen to the guy?"

"I don't know," Erin said. "He's pretty screwed up. If his lawyer's any good, he'll plead some sort of insanity defense. That's not up to me. I just catch them, I don't punish them."

"What if it was up to you? What would you do?"

"Huh?" Erin was caught off guard. "I don't know. I mean, I'm in Major Crimes. The guys we chase down, they're pretty bad guys, most of them. They ought to be in jail, and I'm glad to put them there for as long as possible. But this kid? He's not bad. He didn't want to do what he did. I don't think there's anything we can do to him through the legal system that's any worse than he's already doing to himself. He doesn't need to be punished. He needs help."

Evans nodded. "Sounds like it. I hope he gets what he needs."

Erin returned the nod. "Yeah." She stood there, uncomfortable, hesitant.

"But you didn't come here to tell me about your case," Evans said quietly.

She shook her head.

"Something on your mind, Erin?"

She took a deep breath. "Doc, I think I need some help. For me. I've been having these dreams. Flashbacks, maybe, I don't know. I don't want to be a wimp about it, but I'm... I'm a little bit scared. I thought maybe if we could... I mean, you and me...

talk it over a little, I could figure out what to do. Maybe find a fix, or a cure."

Evans smiled. "I think that's a great idea, Erin. Why don't you take a seat, and tell me what's on your mind."

Keep reading after the sneak peek to enjoy a special bonus.

Dehydration

An Ian Thompson Story

Here's a sneak peek from Book 10: First Love

Coming 2020

"Would you care for a glass of champagne, darling?"

"You've got champagne in there?"

Erin O'Reilly raised an eyebrow at the picnic basket. It looked like the full romantic deal. The wicker basket sat on a checkered cloth under a couple of parasols. There were even a pair of comfy-looking pillows to sit on and a single red rose.

"I believe it's part of the package, aye," Morton Carlyle said. "The fine folks who provide the service offered a carriage ride into the bargain, but I thought you'd consider that a bit much."

"I don't know," she said. "No one's ever bought me a carriage ride before."

They were in Central Park, on Cherry Hill, overlooking Bow Bridge. It was the sort of spot that made Erin think of fairy tales and rom-com movies. This wasn't a side of Manhattan she was accustomed to seeing. But she had to admit, as Carlyle opened the picnic basket and started laying out food, it had been a good idea.

Her only real concern was that someone might recognize them. After all, New York had eight million people in it, so of course they'd be bound to run into someone familiar. The probability might be low, but the stakes were high. Erin was a cop, a Major Crimes detective, and Carlyle was a mid-level organized crime associate. If they got spotted by the wrong person, Erin's career could be over. If they got spotted by an even worse person, both of them could get killed.

That was why Erin had brought two guns and her partner along on their romantic picnic lunch. Her primary sidearm, a Glock nine-millimeter, was holstered on her hip. Her backup piece, a snub-nosed .38 revolver, nestled in an ankle clip under her slacks. And her partner was flopped on his belly on the grass, tongue hanging out, grinning at her.

"What're you looking at?" she asked Rolf. The K-9 cocked his head in the endlessly endearing German Shepherd style.

"He's looking well," Carlyle said.

"Yeah. His hair's growing back."

"And the burns?"

"It's been a month. He's fine." Rolf and Erin were both carrying some scars from their last big case, which had culminated in a struggle in a burning movie theater. They'd gotten out of it okay, but not without a few mementos.

"And yourself, darling? How are you?"

"Hungry." She settled herself on one of the cushions. "What've we got here?"

"We've all manner of fine meats and cheeses, and what looks to be olives, nuts, and a grand loaf of fresh bread. Not to mention fruit and chocolate. What more could a lass be wanting?"

"Got any whiskey?"

He laughed. "Only the champagne, sad to say. But if you're wanting a wee nip, we could always slip back to the Corner after."

"I have to get back to work," she said. "This is just a long lunch, remember."

"This city's criminals have no sense of romance," he sighed. "Present company excepted, naturally."

Erin helped herself to some of the food, assembling a sandwich. Rolf watched with interest. There was always the possibility the humans might not want all the cold cuts.

"I'm sorry I've been so busy," she said. "It's all this petty bureaucratic bullshit. We haven't had a real takedown in a while."

"Are you bored, darling?"

"Yeah, a little. You know me. I live for the action." She took a bite. "You've got to try this pastrami. It's fantastic."

Carlyle sampled it. "Ah, that's grand. Are you well mended, yourself?"

She held up a hand and wiggled her fingers. "Everything's where it's supposed to be."

"You've hit it off well with my lad Ian. He tells me you and he are still running together most mornings."

"You're not jealous, are you?" she teased.

"Ought I to be?"

"You tell me. He's a handsome former Marine with a body a lot of guys would kill for. He's got that whole strong, silent thing going. He's polite. And the tattoos give him that exotic appeal."

Carlyle laughed. "A fine effort, lass, but I know both of you better than that."

"Ian's a good guy," she said, and meant it. Ian was Carlyle's driver and occasional bodyguard, a combat veteran who'd been a sniper in Iraq and Afghanistan. Carlyle had once called him the most dangerous man in New York, but Erin had come to feel safe around him.

A lot of that could be traced to the shared experience of trauma. One thing Erin hadn't told Carlyle was that she'd been wrestling with some bad memories lately. She'd started seeing the Precinct 8 police psychologist, Doc Evans, when the nightmares had gotten to be too much to handle. She knew Ian dealt with some of the same things from his war experiences, and knowing that had built a bridge of respect and trust between them. He'd protected her a couple of times in the past, and she trusted him as much as she did any fellow officer at her precinct.

The thought crossed her mind that she hadn't trusted Carlyle himself with the knowledge of her post-traumatic stress. But she pushed that to the back of her mind. There were all sorts of things he wasn't telling her, about his criminal associates and activities, because disclosure would do more harm than good to their relationship. Erin and Carlyle lived in a world where knowledge was both powerful and dangerous, and therefore needed to be guarded. They didn't subscribe to twenty-first century pop-psychology ideas of full openness between romantic partners. If they had, they wouldn't have gotten as far as they had.

"I'm glad you like him," Carlyle said. "He's rather fond of you, I'm thinking."

"How can you tell?"

"If he wasn't, he'd hardly keep going for morning runs with you. He'd have varied his route and you'd be unable to find him. If the lad wants to go unnoticed, I doubt even your partner would be able to track him."

"So you're not even a little jealous?" she prodded with a smile.

"Some lads might think this line of questioning indicated a bit of insecurity," he shot back. "Nay, darling. I love you. When a lad truly loves a lass, jealousy doesn't even enter his mind. Jealousy is for people who are afraid of losing someone. I know you're mine."

"I'm yours, huh? We'll see about that."

"The picnic lad offered me a surprise photographer as well," he commented. "But I thought that mightn't be the best idea. I told him if a lad sprang out of the bushes with something in his hands, you'd likely shoot him dead on the spot. He laughed."

"He probably thought you were joking," she said. "That's what I love about you."

"My sense of humor?"

"You understand me. They say only cops understand other cops, but we found a loophole."

"I'm good at loopholes," he said, smiling. "Believe me, darling, if there's any way out of a tangle, I'll thread my way through it."

"What if there isn't?" she asked. "What if we come to a dead end?"

"A lad's got to die sometime. In that case, the best we can hope is to make it mean something, and perhaps leave something worth remembering behind us. We're none of us getting out of this world alive."

"But we're alive here and now," she said. "How about cracking open that champagne and giving this girl a drink?"

* * *

Erin walked back into the Eightball, the Precinct 8 station, feeling pretty good. Her life was more or less back on track. The nightmares weren't as frequent as they had been. She was doing good work. While what she'd told Carlyle was true, they'd still closed some cases, busted some perps. However, as Vic Neshenko had pointed out, the bad guys hadn't quite fit the strict definition of "Major Crimes."

"Look who's back," Vic said. The big Russian was finishing his own lunch, chow mein takeout, washed down with a gigantic cup of Mountain Dew.

"Miss me?" she asked, sitting down at her desk.

"Yeah, but after I put in some time on the firing range, next time I won't."

"Promises," she said with a smile. "Anything happen while I was out?"

"We got a flag from Interpol," Vic said.

"Really? What about?"

"Remember that Finneran chick?"

The bottom dropped out of Erin's stomach. She wasn't likely to forget Siobhan Finneran. Siobhan's father had been a friend and comrade of Carlyle's, back when he'd been in the IRA in the early '90s. When Mr. Finneran had been killed, Carlyle had become her de facto father. Siobhan and Erin had disliked one another at first sight, and further association had only made things worse. Siobhan saw Erin as a rival for Carlyle's attention. She was a natural killer who'd learned from the best IRA assassins. The last time they'd met, Erin had been with an ESU team that had tried to arrest the other woman, only for Siobhan to vanish from New York for the second time.

"Yeah, I remember her," Erin said as offhandedly as she could. "Is she back in town?"

"No. The British Interpol office sent this," Vic said. "Since we've got a warrant outstanding for her, they let us know if anything pops on their side. Looks like she shot some guys in Belfast last week."

"Really? What guys?"

"Three suspected UVF terrorists," he said, referring to the Ulster Volunteer Front, an anti-IRA paramilitary group.

"How do they know it was her?"

"According to what I got from the Brits, she walked right into the pub where these three mopes were drinking, no mask, no disguise, that long red hair of hers hanging right down her back, pulled a pistol, said something to get their attention, wasted all three of them, dropped a ten-pound note on the table to pay for their beer, and walked out again."

"Witnesses?"

"Plenty. Half a dozen statements, all pretty much agreeing. Plus, they got the banknote; they'll be able to get DNA off it. She didn't care they knew it was her."

"Sounds like an IRA job," she said.

Vic shook his head. "If it was, they had buyer's remorse. Sinn Fein, the IRA political boys, immediately denied responsibility. They've disavowed her. You know, like in *Mission: Impossible*?"

"You saying Siobhan's a secret agent now?"

"No, I'm saying she's gone off the reservation. She's a crazy free agent. The IRA must be shitting bricks right now."

"I'll say," Erin said quietly. An uneasy peace had held in Northern Ireland ever since the Good Friday Accords had ostensibly put an end to the decades-long low-grade civil war the Irish just called The Troubles. A rogue operative knocking off members of the other side would be just the thing that could restart the cycle of killings, bombings, and terrorism.

"Not that we can do anything about that," Vic added. "Hell, the Irish want her worse than we do now. They'll be looking to scoop her up. If we want her, we'll have to wait till they're done with her, and she's looking at life, so I wouldn't hold my breath. That's if the IRA or the UVF don't get her first, in which case she'll just plain disappear."

"But they don't have her in custody?"

"You kidding? That girl's pure Teflon. We almost had her twice, but she keeps slipping through."

"Not our problem now," Erin agreed. "Nice of them to let us know. I wonder why she decided to knock off those losers?"

"Who knows? Probably one of them killed somebody on her side, who killed somebody on theirs. Isn't that how that whole thing worked for about five hundred years?"

"Pretty much," she sighed.

"Tell you what," he said. "I'll send you the Interpol file, just for giggles."

"What's funny?" asked a familiar voice from the stairwell.

"Nothing, sir," Erin said as Lieutenant Webb walked in. Rolf's nostrils twitched as Erin's commanding officer walked past her desk. She could smell the fresh cigarette smoke off his old trench coat. Apparently he'd been grabbing a smoke break outside.

"Good," Webb said. "You two look bored. Want some excitement?"

Vic perked up visibly. "We catch a body?"

"That's right," Webb said. "Normally this one would go to Homicide, but those boys have three detectives down with some stomach bug, so I told Lieutenant Peterson we'd pick up the slack. Sounds like one of the Homicide guys had a bachelor party and he and his buddies got a bad batch of oysters."

"Serves 'em right," Vic said. "It's a little late in the season for oysters."

"So we've got a garden-variety homicide?" Erin asked.

"One victim, apparent assault and murder. Duane Street, upstairs apartment. Just happened this morning. The scene's at least three hours old. Let's not let it get any colder than it already is."

Erin and Vic got up. Rolf sprang up from his snoozing spot next to Erin's desk, ready for action.

"We got a dead person," Vic said. "The day's only getting better."

"Not for her, it isn't," Erin said.

"Killjoy," he said. "You know you like chasing down bad guys, admit it."

"Gladly," she said, and they got back to work.

* * *

Webb was right. The crime scene wasn't fresh. A bored-looking Patrol officer was standing guard at the apartment, but the paramedics had come and gone. The site of the crime was a second-floor unit in a four-story apartment with the ironic name of the Hope Building.

"I guess this is the place," Vic said, cocking his head at the door of Unit 202. "If I had to, I'd guess there's signs of foul play."

The uniformed officer gave him a lopsided smile. "You could say that." The door stood open. Even a quick glance showed splintered wood around the doorframe. Bits of broken wood were strewn on the carpet.

"Where's the victim?" Webb asked.

"Hospital morgue," the cop said. "The responding officer thought there might be a chance to save her. The EMTs took her to Bellevue, but I heard she was DOA."

"I'll call the hospital," Erin said. Her brother was a trauma surgeon at Bellevue and would be glad to tell her what was going on.

"No rush on that," Webb said. "The body will keep. Let's take a look around."

"The scene will be contaminated," Vic predicted.

"Of course it will," Webb said. "That's what happens when the medics get there first. Deal with it."

"Where's CSU?" Erin asked.

"They'll be here soon," he replied.

"Who was she?" Vic asked.

"Amelia Bledsoe," Webb said.

Erin pulled on a pair of disposable gloves and peered into the apartment. Just inside, a claw hammer lay on the floor. She knelt beside it and looked closely, but didn't touch it.

"No blood," she reported. "Looks like it was used to pry open the door, but the perp dropped it once he got inside."

"Wonder why," Vic said. "A hammer's a pretty handy weapon. What killed her?" he asked the uniform.

"EMTs said it was strangulation. She had something wrapped around her neck."

Erin, Vic, and Webb shared a look. All of them were thinking the same thing. Vic was the one who said it.

"Sounds like a sex crime."

Erin nodded. Strangling someone was a tricky business, and a robber wouldn't have bothered when he could just bash the victim's head in with a hammer. Strangling the victim was a personal, intimate gesture.

"Any signs of sexual assault?" Webb asked.

The cop shrugged. "Dunno."

"We'll know that at the autopsy," Erin said. "Can we get Levine on it?"

Sarah Levine was Precinct 8's Medical Examiner. She was a little strange, but very good at her job.

"Sure thing," Webb said. "It's our case, so our people. I'll let her know, have her go to the hospital to pick up the body."

"Where was she found?" Erin asked the cop.

"Bedroom."

"Of course," Vic muttered. "I'm telling you, sex crime."

The detectives made their way through the apartment. It was comfortably furnished, but didn't look like a particularly wealthy residence. They passed the living room, where the bookshelves had been swept clean. Books, mostly trade paperbacks, were scattered everywhere. A lamp had been knocked over and lay across the detritus.

"Someone looking for something?" Vic guessed.

"Maybe," Webb said doubtfully. "Not much of a ransacking."

"Who else lives here?" Erin asked.

"I saw a pair of men's dress shoes by the front door," Vic said. "A guy lives here for sure. I don't think kids."

Erin nodded. Her brother Sean had two children, aged eight and six, which was immediately obvious upon entering their house.

"Small mercies," Webb said, poking open the bathroom door. "Nothing out of place in here."

"Not junkies, then," Erin said. Addicts looking for a fix always went for the medicine cabinets.

"It'll be a pervert," Vic predicted. "Some rapist asshole who just graduated to murder."

"It better not be," Erin said, and Webb nodded agreement. All of them knew sex crimes were some of the most likely violent crimes to be repeated. If their perp got a taste for it, they could be looking at a budding serial killer.

Webb got to the bedroom door first. He stopped in the doorway.

"Well?" Vic said, craning his neck to peer over his boss's shoulder.

"I'd say we've got signs of a struggle," Webb said dryly, stepping gingerly into the room.

It wasn't a very large room, but it looked like a tornado had torn through the place. There were two dressers. One appeared intact, but every drawer had been pulled out of the other one and its contents upended across the carpet. The bedclothes were pulled and torn, sheets and comforter in a crumpled mass. A few framed photos, which Erin guessed had been on top of the dresser, were lying next to it in a sparkling pile of broken glass.

It was impossible to tell what had happened. The EMTs, in their well-intentioned attempt to save the victim's life, had hopelessly contaminated the scene, as Vic had predicted.

"Hey!" Vic called back to the uniformed cop, who had taken up his old position at the entrance.

"Yeah?"

"Was she on the bed, or what?"

"Yeah, she was lying there, right in the middle of the bed, arms and legs all spread out."

"What was she wearing?" Erin asked.

"One of them, you know, robe things."

"A bathrobe?"

"Yeah, the fuzzy kind. Pink. The belt was pulled off it. That was the thing around her neck."

"Choked her with her own bathrobe," Webb said.

"That's a bad way to go," Vic said.

"Was the robe open or closed?" Erin asked.

The cop didn't answer. He cleared his throat and looked uncomfortable.

"I asked you a question, Officer," Erin said sharply.

"It was open," he said quietly.

"Was she wearing anything else? Under it?"

"Yeah. Underwear."

"Bra and panties, both?"

"No, just the bottom part."

"If she was still wearing her underwear, she may not have been raped," Webb said thoughtfully. "That may make it harder to get DNA."

Erin swallowed an angry response. She hoped the victim hadn't been raped as well as murdered, for reasons of common humanity. But Webb did have a point. If the attacker had left any body fluids on his victim, it would make a conviction a slam-dunk if they could catch the guy.

She looked around the room, looking for patterns, for anything that would make sense. Rolf stood at her side, waiting for instructions. Unfortunately, there wasn't much for him to do right now. His specialties were tracking and suspect apprehension, and there was no need for either of those at the moment.

"It's the woman's dresser," she said.

"What's that?" Webb asked.

"The clothes," she said, gesturing to the heaps around the room. "The attacker dumped all her drawers. He didn't touch the other one."

Vic went to the other dresser and opened one of the drawers. "You're right," he said. "This one's full of men's clothing. Untouched. Maybe our guy's got a thing for women's underwear. You know, gets off on going through their stuff."

"Or taking trophies," she said. Her skin was crawling. This was looking more and more like a serial killer. It wouldn't be the first one for her; she'd taken down a serial murderer last year. It hadn't been a pleasant experience, especially once he'd picked her for his next victim.

"That's speculation," Webb said. "I don't know what else we can see here, but Neshenko and I will keep looking. I want you at the hospital, O'Reilly. Connect with Levine, see what you can find out about the manner of death. We'll see what more we can learn about her."

"And her husband, or boyfriend, or whatever," Vic added. "Hell, he probably doesn't even know she's dead yet."

"Copy that," Erin said. She twitched the leash and gave her K-9 a command in his native German. "Rolf, *komm!* We're going to see my brother."

Ready for more?

Join Steven Henry's author email list
for the latest on new releases, upcoming books and
series, behind-the-scenes details, events, and more.

Be the first to know about new releases in the Erin O'Reilly Mysteries by signing up at tinyurl.com/StevenHenryEmail

Now keep reading to enjoy

Dehydration

An Ian Thompson Story

Dehydration

An Ian Thompson Story

Steven Henry

Clickworks Press • Baltimore, MD

First publication: Clickworks Press, 2020
Release: CWP-EORIT1-INT-P.IS-1.0

"We've got God on our side
And we're just trying to survive.
What if what you do to survive kills the thing you love?
Fear's a powerful thing.
It can turn your heart black, you can trust.
It'll take your God-filled soul,
Fill it with devils and dust."

— *Bruce Springsteen*

Dehydration

What happened?

Head hurting. Dizzy. Ears ringing. Can't hear.

Where are you?

Try to say something. Gritty feeling in mouth. Try to spit. Mouth too dry. Tasting metal. Blood.

Situational awareness.

Sound, now, coming back. Faint, far away. Someone talking.

"Mama? Mama?"

What the hell?

Dark. Stars overhead. Silver stars on black sky.

Of course it's dark, idiot. Night op. 0200, give or take. How long were you out?

Wristwatch. Broken. Arm still working fine. Skinned knuckles, no big deal.

"Mama?"

Sounds like Valchek. He's hurt, bad. Needs a corpsman.

"Corpsman!"

Okay, voice works. Croaking like a frog. Play through it, Marine. Self-evaluation. Wounds?

Sore head, disoriented. Concussion, maybe. Better stay still, in case of spinal damage. Road rash on hands, knees too.

You were riding a Blackhawk. Chopper crash. Has to be.

Flicker of memory. Blast of fire overhead, engine casing. A single image, door gunner tossed out of the chopper. Can't remember his name. Strange.

Navarro.

Right, Navarro. Why wasn't he wearing his safety strap?

And where's the damn corpsman?

"Mama...?" Valchek not shutting up.

Think fast and think sharp, Marine. That crash was from ground fire. Shoulder-launch missile, probably. Maybe RPG, if the Talibs got lucky. They'll be coming for the crash site. Goddamn Blackhawk Down. Remember what happened to those guys?

Saw the movie a couple times. Don't remember what happened.

Naked bodies crowd-surfing.

Shit. Have to move. Never mind the back. Don't know if a distress call went out. No time to wait and find out. Head clearing a little. Arms and legs working fine. Helmet gone. Raw spot under the chin, strap must've snapped.

A little light away to the right. Burning wreckage. Fifteen meters?

Damn, Marine, how'd you get way over here?

Thrown clear. Landed on sandy ground. Lucky. Big rocks all over the place.

Okay, stand up. Move to the crash site, check on the others. Then get the hell out of here.

First Night

His brain was coming back on line. Like a computer rebooting. One subsystem at a time. There were gaps, though. Ian couldn't remember the mission briefing. They'd been at the base, prepping. The last thing he remembered for sure was loading his rifle. He always checked his bullets, one at a time, made sure they were clean. They gave him a lot of shit about that. But his gun never jammed in a firefight.

He started to walk toward the crashed Blackhawk. Did a quick equipment check. Rifle was gone. Still had his pistol, useless in open terrain. Two grenades. Body armor. No night-vision goggles. Torn off along with the helmet. Head really hurting. Stumbled on a rock he hadn't seen, nearly fell. Inner ear was off.

A body about three meters from the crash, face down. Valchek? He knelt and started to check for a pulse, then paused. A piece of jagged metal as long as his arm was rammed straight through the guy's chest. Felt for the pulse anyway. You never knew. People survived some crazy shit.

No pulse. Skin already going cool. Cold out here. He turned the body a little, saw the face.

Stanhope.

He got one of Stanhope's tags, put it in a pocket. Left the other one with the body. Stood up, went on to the crash.

Valchek was next. He'd been strapped in tight and hadn't been thrown loose. The chopper had gone straight into the side of one of those goddamn Afghan mountains. Blackhawks were tough, but they'd come in hot and fast. Valchek was pinned in place, legs crushed by a piece of fuselage. He wasn't crying for Mama anymore. Blood coming out of his mouth. Too much to just come from biting his tongue. Internal damage.

Can't move him without killing him.

"Hey, Valchek," Ian croaked. "You with me, man?" Almost hoping he was already gone.

Valchek opened his eyes a little, couldn't focus. "Thompson? That you?"

"Yeah. Hang tough. We're gonna get you out of here."

You're a goddamn liar. He's got minutes left, tops. Even if the medevac gets here right now, he won't make it back to an aid station. And you have to bounce. The Talibs are coming.

"Thompson?"

"Yeah?" Trying to think. It was hard. Head still fuzzy.

"Tell my mom..."

Ian clenched his fists and squeezed his eyes shut. Couldn't lose it now. Had to stay sharp. "You stay right there, man," he said to Valchek. "Hang tough." No time to hold a dying man's hand. Looked around the wreck for the others. Cockpit was smashed in. Not much chance for the pilot and copilot, but had to check. Plus, the radio was up there. If he could make a call, just maybe there'd be another bird in the area, could scoop them up.

Radio shot all to shit. Not even in one piece. The copilot, Norman, looked okay, basically. Ian did a pulse check. Nothing.

Look at the way his head's hanging, dumbass. That's a broken neck.

The pilot. Couldn't remember his name. Nickname... Firefly. Because of that time his engine casing overheated and his chopper glowed in the dark. Why couldn't he remember? Head still hurting. Didn't matter, anyway. Half the pilot's head gone. Ian reached around, got both guys' tags, didn't bother trying to read the name off them.

Valchek was passed out, maybe dead. Just as well. Not a damn thing Ian could do. Took another pulse check anyway. Nothing. Valchek was gone.

You're on a clock, Marine. Prioritize.

First priority, survivors. How many guys on the chopper? Couldn't remember. Stanhope, Valchek, Norman, Firefly...

Colby.

Right, Colby. Colby was Firefly's name. Plus Navarro. Not a chance of finding him. That was five, plus himself made six. Anyone else?

Robbins and Barton.

Ian pushed his knuckles into the side of his head, felt his pulse pounding there. Blood on his hand. Hadn't known his head was bleeding.

He found Barton by the smell. Worst barbecue in the world. Hoped he'd been killed on impact, before the fire got him. Flames still burning. Couldn't get at Barton's dogtags. Tried again, burned his fingers, got them.

One more. Robbins.

Ian scanned the Blackhawk's interior. Didn't see anyone.

Take a breath, Marine. Do it fast, but do it right.

Looked again. Saw a boot, sticking out behind the fuselage. Climbed out of the chopper, saw Robbins. Leg pinned by the wreck. Out cold, but alive. Strong pulse, breathing well.

Ian considered. Couldn't move the chopper. Tons of metal. Lots of blood on Robbins's leg. Might kill him to take the pressure off the leg. Bleed right out.

Tourniquet.

What was the point? He couldn't shift the Blackhawk.

Can't go over, go under.

Right. Ian's E-tool wasn't on him. Left it at the FOB, maybe. But Robbins still had his. Ian pulled out the folding shovel. Before digging, he tied a tourniquet around the thigh of the injured leg.

Make it tight. Loosen it later, once you check the damage.

He started digging. The shovel's blade was loud when it glanced off rocks. Couldn't help that. He was surprised the muj weren't already here. Maybe they'd taken their shot from another valley. It took time to navigate in the 'Stan. Up one hill, down the other side, walking those goddamn goat trails. Could take them an hour, maybe two, from the next valley over. How long since the crash?

Don't sweat it, Marine. Work the problem.

Okay. The leg was loose enough to move. Looked pretty bad, but still in one piece. Ian put a quick field dressing on the open wound.

Robbins moaned.

Ian worked faster. Robbins's gear was tangled in broken metal. Ian pulled his K-bar, cut through the straps, got him free.

Voices. Other side of the chopper, still high up, but coming. Excited, calling each other in Pashto. Poor noise discipline. Amateurs.

Amateurs with AKs and shoulder-launch missiles, Marine. Too many amateurs. A whole lot of muj are about to come down on you.

Robbins's eyes flew open. His moan started turning into a scream.

Ian's hand moved without thinking. Had it over Robbins's mouth before the scream got loose.

"Quiet!" he hissed. "Hajjis inbound!"

Comprehension in Robbins's eyes, thank God. Robbins nodded. Ian felt the muscles in the other man's jaw set hard, teeth gritting against the pain. He took his hand from Robbins's mouth. Robbins flinched. Pain had to be tremendous, but Robbins didn't make a sound. Damn good man.

Ian risked a quick glance around the side of the fuselage. Parts of it still on fire. The Talibs shouldn't be able to pick him out in the dark. They'd be looking at the flames, wrecking their night vision. Glint of moonlight on metal, halfway up the hillside. They were maybe five minutes' climb away.

No time for a long search for supplies. Couldn't hold them off by himself. Robbins couldn't fight. Prioritize. Survivors, check. Second priority, weapons and ammo. Third priority, water and food.

Move.

Keeping low, he scooted back into the wreck. No idea what had happened to his rifle. To his surprise, he saw it, wedged in the corner. First piece of good luck.

Not so lucky after all. Fine, expensive piece of precision sniper equipment. Nothing but fine, expensive scrap metal now. Optics smashed, barrel bent.

Quick scan. Valchek's M4 looked okay. Grabbed it, with a spare mag from Valchek. Thermite grenade. That'd be useful. No time for more. Valchek's canteen was punctured. Ian's own was dented, but still full. Maybe Robbins still had his.

Time to get out of here, Marine.

Food. Didn't need much, just emergency rations. Always kept a couple MREs in his BDUs. The other guys gave him shit about that, too. They packed extra ammo instead. Ian knew better. An army travels on its stomach. Who'd said that? Couldn't remember.

No comm gear, couldn't call for help. Unless relief found them, they'd need to walk to the nearest FOB. Didn't even know which direction that was. They'd need more supplies.

Wasn't Norman big on snacks? He always brought candy bars along, every op. Guys called him Candyman.

Hell of a thing, risking his life for a couple chocolate bars. Found two Snickers in Norman's side pocket. Put them in one of his ammo pouches, replacing a useless mag for his broken sniper rifle. His rifle took 7.62 rounds, Valchek's M4 used 5.56. Had a full load of incompatible goddamn ammo.

He checked the action on the M4, chambered a round. Seemed to be working. Felt better.

Voices, closer. Laughter. More Pashto words, a few he knew. Really close. Could get five, six of them easy, before they could drop him. Wouldn't do him or Robbins any good. Had to be at least a dozen from the sound. Probably more. Too many.

He went out the far side. Paused in the doorway, pulled one of his frags. Eased the pin out, careful to keep the lever depressed. Slipped it behind Valchek's body. Added the thermite grenade next to it. Next person to move him would get a surprise. Serve the fucker right. Talibs always wanted to capture American dead. They'd pay for this one.

Robbins was waiting. Had lost his own M4, was holding his pistol. His hands shaking. In shock, probably.

Ian went under him, braced, lifted. Laid Robbins across his shoulders. Couldn't shoot while carrying, but this wasn't going to be a fight. Scanned for an exit with good defilade.

Dry stream bed, a few meters out. Ian made his move, quick, quiet. Expected a shout of warning, burst from an AK maybe.

Nothing.

Amateurs.

Into the stream bed. Caught his breath with every rattle of stones, but the Talibs were talking too loud to hear him. Ian kept moving, head low. Damn, but Robbins was heavy. Ian was the smallest man in the unit, except maybe Navarro. Robbins outweighed him by twenty pounds, easy.

You could leave him.

"Shut up."

"Sorry," Robbins whispered, teeth gritted.

Hadn't meant to say it out loud. Ian felt like shit. Poor guy was doing the best he could, getting bounced around with a broken leg, and he thought Ian was pissed at him. Apologize later.

Excited shouting behind him. Muj were at the chopper. Ian moved faster. Sweating now, breathing hard. Head really pounding. Had to lie down, rest.

No time. Sleep when you're dead.

An explosion. Frag grenade. Bright light from the thermite. Burned at something like three thousand degrees. Shouts cut off, a few seconds' silence. Then a man screaming, high-pitched. Hadn't gotten them all, the others were yelling now, and damn did they sound pissed. But he'd gotten at least one.

For the first time since he'd come to, Ian smiled.

Half a klick, maybe more, carrying Robbins. Stream bed twisted and turned, so they weren't making much forward progress, but there wasn't any other cover. Lots of rocks and scrub brush, nothing tall or thick enough. Valley curved, taking them out of sight of the crash. Not running any longer. Couldn't. Breath short. Walked as fast as he could. Thought he was out of juice. Dug deep, found more. Kept going.

Finally saw a good spot, hollow place at the foot of a hill. Big stone had rolled partway out, left a cave behind it. Good visual cover. Twenty meters of open ground to cross. Last gasp, stumbled behind the rock. Laid Robbins down as gently as possible. Shoulders aching. Legs trembling. Went down, flat on his back.

Rest for a bit, but you can't sleep. Not yet. You're not out of this, Marine. Not by a long fucking shot.

* * *

Couldn't rest. Had to check Robbins's wound.

You don't loosen the tourniquet, he loses the leg.

Loosen the tourniquet, Robbins might bleed out. Ian rolled over, took a look. Loosened it just a little, ready to clamp it down again.

Bleeding, but not bad. Steady flow, not arterial pulse. Field dressing should hold.

"Thompson?"

"Yeah?" Keeping his voice quiet.

"Where are the other guys?"

"We're the only ones that made it."

"You sure?"

"Yeah."

"Shit."

"Yeah."

"You know where the fuck we are?"

"I don't even remember the briefing."

"No shit?"

"Got clocked on the head."

Robbins thought about that.

"How about you?" Ian asked. "Any idea where we are?"

"Sure."

"Where?"

"Afghanistan."

Ian didn't laugh, but Robbins did, a little.

"Okay, we're in Kandahar," Robbins said. "I think we were on bearing 135 when we got hit."

"So we go reciprocal, 315 to get back," Ian said. Rubbed his head. Still hurt like hell.

"You okay, man?"

"Yeah. How long were we flying, before the crash?"

"Shit, I don't know. Maybe forty minutes?"

Christ, could be a hundred and eighty klicks.

"We got anything closer?" Ian asked.

Robbins shrugged, regretted it, flinched and lay back. "I don't know, man. We got evac on the way?"

"Only if Firefly got a call out," Ian said. "Radio was wrecked."

"Stanhope had a cell phone."

Hadn't thought of that. Damn. Too late now.

"We can't wait at the crash site," Ian said. "Muj all over it. Our guys'll find it eventually, but might take a couple days. Hajjis have to know at least one of us got out. They'll be looking."

"What are we gonna do, man?"

You're a sergeant, Marine. Robbins is a PFC. You're in command.

"I'm gonna get you back to the FOB," Ian said.

A hundred eighty klicks? On foot? Carrying a wounded guy? Like hell. You won't even make it halfway.

Fuck it. Got to try.

"We'll rest here for a bit," Ian told him. "Not long, though. Have to use the dark, while we've got it. You know what time it is?"

Robbins looked down. "No, man, my watch is gone. I think maybe the band caught on something, snapped it off."

"Don't worry about it. Get some sleep."

"You gonna sleep, man?"

"I'll stand watch."

Had some things to do. Shouldn't sleep after a head injury anyway. Couldn't remember why, just knew it was a bad idea.

"Hey Thompson?"

"Yeah?"

"You got an Aspirin or something?"

"No, sorry. How bad is it?"

"Not too bad."

He's almost as shitty a liar as you are. He's toughing it out.

In spite of the pain, Robbins dropped off. It'd been a long night.

Ian used the time to lay out his gear, set aside what they wouldn't need. Ian was wearing his scalable plate carrier body armor, middle-weight ballistic plates. Ditched the plates. Be fucked if he got hit, but they'd be traveling light, and those plates were too heavy. Otherwise, he had on his BDUs, all-terrain boots on his feet, and his ILBE over the top, all the pouches and straps for carrying his shit.

Went through all the pockets. Ditched his useless 7.62 ammo. Kept the last grenade. Two MREs, too dark to see what they were. Pair of Snickers bars. Canteen; still whole, still full; kept it. Earplugs; didn't weigh much, but couldn't see the point right now. Flashlight; shook it gently, heard pieces rattle around. Lens was cracked. Put his hand over the lens, tried the switch. Nothing. Busted. Robbins's E-tool; kept it. K-bar knife; definite keeper. First-aid kit; QuikClot hemostat agent, water-purification tablets, bandages, burn ointment; kept all of it. Used the burn ointment on his fingers where they'd been scorched in the chopper fire. Robbins had his pistol, canteen, and knife. No ammo on him, dammit. He'd cut Robbins's ILBE off at the crash.

Robbins was still out. Ian could hardly see anything in the cave. Checked the rifle by feel. Used to wonder why the instructors made them strip down and assemble the guns blindfolded.

So when the shit really hits the fan, it comes back to you. Like riding a bike. Through the Afghan mountains in the dark. Your shit has well and truly hit the fan, Marine.

Field-stripped the M4. Checked the gun carefully, one piece at a time, put it back together. Unloaded the mags, counted bullets, reloaded. Sixty rounds. Set the selector switch to semi-auto.

Went through the same routine with the pistol, blind, slow, careful. Felt better. Calmer.

Sat in the dark. Waited. Tried not to think.

* * *

That was long enough. Time to move, while there was still darkness. Ian went to Robbins, woke him gently.

"Ah! Jesus!" Robbins hissed. Leg still hurting him.

"Sorry," Ian whispered. "We have to move. Use the night."

"SAR didn't come?"

"Nope." Hadn't heard a single chopper.

"Okay."

"Can you walk?"

"Fuck no. But I can hop like hell."

Ian helped him strip off his body armor and gave him an arm. Slung the M4 so he could fire from the hip on the other side. They went, keeping to the valley floor. Ian didn't like it. No mobility. Ground wasn't too rough, but they were going slow, on a predictable route. Head was clearer, though. Night vision had recovered from the fire, too.

Not much moon. That was good. Sky was clear. Stars all over the night, silver, bright, cold. More than he'd ever seen growing up.

He thought of home. Other side of the goddamn world. Queens, New York. Sky was never full dark there. Best you could see was a couple of the brightest stars, on account of all the city lights. He used to look out his window at them. He liked the night. Lots of kids were scared of the dark. Not Ian. The dark was his friend. In the dark he was safe.

But he was used to hiding on his own. Healthy. Able to move fast. Robbins was useless deadweight.

Cut him loose. Leave him.

No, damn it. Marines didn't leave their brothers behind. No matter what.

He'll slow you down. He'll kill you. He's killing you right now.

Fuck that. We're getting back to the FOB. Both of us.

Voices behind. Speaking Pashto. The muj were still chasing them. Bad luck? Or had they left tracks? If any Talib could follow footprints in the dark on this stony ground, they ought to take his eyeballs and reverse-engineer them, use them to steer drones.

It was going to be a slow-motion race. Robbins couldn't go faster than a hopping walk on his broken leg. But the Talibs had to check for hiding places along the way, in case Ian was laying for them. On the other hand, they knew the ground and he didn't.

Slow-motion race, hide-and-seek thrown in.

Every Marine ought to be issued a drunken asshole father before they let him into boot camp. It made SERE training practically redundant. Ian had learned how to hide practically as soon as he'd learned how to walk.

They were making shitty time. Robbins was hurting, but didn't complain. Gutting it out.

The voices behind them were getting closer. Calls and answers. Ian looked back. Hard to see in the starlight. That was good. They couldn't see him either. But they were spreading out. They knew he'd gone this way.

Without him you can get away clean.

Shut up.

How good were these muj? Could he go to ground, let them roll past him? Or could he pin them? Snipe a couple, let the rest hug dirt while he got the hell away. Alone, unhurt, he'd have tried it. But Robbins couldn't move fast enough.

Leave him with half the supplies, have him duck and cover. Then pick off some muj, get them after you. Lead them away.

Shitty idea. Robbins would die whether the Talibs found him or not. Exposure was a bitch.

He couldn't outrun them, couldn't stand and fight, not on this ground. So he'd have to hide, let them go past. Ian started looking for a spot. Not a true cave; they'd check those.

Something that didn't look like much. It just had to keep them hidden overnight.

There. A patch of scrub brush, right out in the open, middle of the valley.

Tactically terrible. No exfil route, just concealment, no cover. That place is a deathtrap.

No soldier worth his training would even think about it. Which was why it might work.

Ian hustled Robbins over, made a quick check. They could just fit underneath. "Okay, man," Ian said. "You got to stay quiet. No matter what."

Robbins nodded.

They went down, scrambled under the brush. Had to lie real quiet, make sure the branches didn't move. Tried to hunch his shape down, make it less human. Lay on his stomach, on top of his M4. Then the hard part. The waiting.

* * *

It wasn't more than five or ten minutes, but the time really crawled. Ian was used to waiting in a sniper hide, but that was different. Then, he was the hunter. Being the prey was a lot more nerve-wracking.

Half a dozen shapes in the dark, moving down the valley, spread out. Holding rifles; AK-74s, probably. Looking behind rocks, checking hiding places, but moving pretty fast. No lights; they'd be worried about air recon.

One of the Muj walked right up to the bush. Started to go past, paused.

Ian reminded himself not to hold his breath. Just slow and easy, in and out. Watched out of half-closed eyes. The Talib wasn't sure. If he knew, he'd already be shooting, or calling his buddies over. Let him see what he expected to see, just rocks and brush in the dark.

Rustle of robes. The guy squatting down.

This is it.

Ian got ready to move. He could get this guy if he was quick enough, maybe another one or two.

A shower of hot liquid splashed him in the face.

He almost gave the game away, almost moved. But Ian was a guy who froze when he startled. Good survival skill. Closed his eyes tight, but stayed still and just let it happen. Twenty, thirty seconds, and the asshole was done. The Talib moved off to rejoin his buddies.

There might be more of them. He couldn't move, not yet. Ian stayed put, felt the liquid soak through his collar. That was gonna chafe something nasty.

Gave it half an hour, then an hour. Long enough. He eased out from under the brush, came up to a crouch, scanned for targets. Nothing. They'd lost them.

"Thompson?"

"Yeah."

"They gone?"

"Yeah."

"Shit, that dude *pissed* on you."

"Really? I just thought it was raining."

And it was worth it, because Robbins laughed. Not much, and it hurt him while it happened, but Ian was glad he could still see the funny side of it. Hunger, thirst, exposure, wounds, those would kill you, but despair killed quicker than any of them. How likely are you to live? The SERE guys said, "It depends. How bad do you want to live?"

I'm gonna live. Gonna get the fuck back to New York City.

He considered going back toward the crash site. Couldn't risk it. Talibs that way, too.

"You good to go, Robbins?"

"Hell yes. Let's get out of here."

* * *

They covered some more ground, a couple klicks, before Robbins gave out. Ian found a hollow spot against the hillside, decent cover. Robbins went down, asleep almost before he hit the rocks.

You need to sleep, too.

Not yet. Too many bad guys, too close. Ian stayed up and watched. The sun was coming up soon.

"Die tomorrow," he said quietly. "Live today."

First Day

The cover didn't look as good by daylight. Not even a real cave, a little scrub brush. Partial concealment, the best they could do. The weather bright and sunny, colder than it looked. As soon as he saw the valley, Ian gave up any hope of moving to a better spot.

Talibs everywhere. Little groups, single guys, moving around. Looking for something.

Looking for you, Marine. Where's the goddamn Air Force? Get a couple A-10s, do a gun run right down this alley, even up the scorecard a little.

Way too many of them. Ian counted thirty, and that was just the ones he could see.

He settled down to wait. Snipers were supposed to be good at that, and Ian was patient. He had a little water, half a Snickers bar. Saved the other half for Robbins. Passed the time setting up shots on the Muj on the other side of the valley. Centered the sights just below the throat. Bang, you're dead, buddy. Enjoy your forty virgins. Gave him a little sense of power.

Sun moved slowly, up into the sky. Goddamn Talibs kept searching. They just didn't want to quit.

Could be worse. They could have dogs.

Robbins woke up around noon, hurting. Ian heard him groan, quick got a hand over his mouth.

"You good?" Ian whispered.

Robbins nodded.

Ian gave him the rest of the candy bar and a drink. Robbins didn't look good, like he might throw it right back up.

"No puking, man," Ian whispered. "In my after-action report, I gotta account for every calorie. Don't waste Corps resources. I mean it. I will write you the fuck up."

Robbins managed a shaky grin, gave him a thumbs-up.

Ian checked the bandage. Blood soaking into it. He should change it, but only had one spare. Better save it. He'd change it in another day.

If you're still alive.

* * *

Time passed. Slowly.

Ninety-nine percent boredom, one percent terror. That's what they said about being a soldier. Damn right. Ian played games with his mind, waiting for nightfall. Took trips through his memory. Thought about the old neighborhood.

Queens, New York. Running the streets with the rest of the gang. Billy, Fred, Tom, the rest. Staying as far from home as he could, wondering if he could maybe just run away, find somewhere else. Getting in trouble, tagging underpasses, swiping candy from gas stations, dodging the NYPD. Trying to get close to where the real wiseguys hung out. The Italians were losing the war with the cops, Giuliani had locked most of the Mafia guys up. Other gangs moving in. Irish, Mexican, Colombian. Lots of young tough guys with tattoos on their faces and scary eyes.

He wanted to be one of them. Hell, why not? They were badass. They didn't give a shit about anything, they did what they wanted, they had lots of money. They didn't let their dads beat on them. Ian wanted to be tough. Picked fights, gave better than he got. He wasn't big for his age, wasn't too strong, but he was quick and he didn't panic. A guy in basic, his unarmed-combat instructor, liked to quote Mike Tyson: "Everyone has a plan till they get punched in the mouth." Ian was good at that. He'd pick his moment, hit the other kid right in the face, and he'd see it in their eyes. Pain and anger made them stupid. They'd come at him, some of them growling, actually *growling*, like junkyard dogs, and he'd know he'd win. Because Ian didn't get stupid. He got hit in the face, it just made him feel cold. They'd see it in him, and some, the ones who weren't total morons, would back away.

One day, one of the Irish mob guys, a big bruiser named Ryan, watched Ian fight two other boys, both bigger than him, in the parking lot by the funeral home. Ian was maybe twelve. Ryan leaned on the chain-link fence, not saying anything. Two on one, Ian had to be careful. If they got hold of him, he was in trouble, so he kept moving, waiting for his moment. He took a couple hits, a bruise on his cheek. Then he saw his chance. Kid on the right was moving in too confidently. Ian let him get close, let him take his swing, took it on the shoulder. Hit him with a hard jab right in the nose. Kid went back on his ass, howling. Blood squirting through his fingers.

Other kid hesitated. Ian turned and put a fist in his face, mashed his lip into his teeth, split it right open. Saw the kid go wild, those crazy animal eyes, knew he had him. Kid came at him, swinging, no control. Ian took a couple punches, gave him a knee in the stomach, doubled him over. Grabbed him by the hair, put the knee into his eye. Kid went down, not even screaming.

First kid was back on his feet. Quicker than Ian had thought. Ian turned right into his fist, got it just over his nose, knocked him flat.

Had to get up, couldn't just lie there and get kicked. Ian rolled, got a sneaker in the ribs, but kept his breath and got up. Squared off, made eye contact.

The kid saw the look in Ian's eyes. His own eyes got wide. He backed up, fists coming down, making motions like he wanted to calm him down. *Holy shit*, Ian thought. *He thinks I'm gonna kill him*. Liked the thought.

Ian took a step forward. Kid turned, almost tripped over his own feet, ran like hell. Other kid, the one he'd given the knee, was stumbling away, too. No point chasing him. Fight was over.

Sound of slow, rhythmic clapping. Ryan, over at the fence, giving him a one-man ovation.

"Damn, kid," Ryan said. "You one cold motherfucker." He laughed, but Ian didn't mind. That laugh wasn't mocking. It was *respect*.

* * *

Midafternoon. A few Talibs still in sight, but moving further away. Ian breathed easy. Robbins was hurting worse, though. Ian gave him a little more water. Didn't take any for himself. Had to go easy on it.

"How you doing, man?"

Robbins grimaced. "Second worst I've ever been hurting."

Ian gave it a beat, asked. "What's the worst?"

"Third day of boot camp."

"Why's that?"

"Missed my home, man. Missed Mom, you believe that."

Ian nodded.

"She didn't want me in the Corps," Robbins said. "She cried when I left. I felt like a real dick, but hey, I was gonna do good. Gonna be a hero."

"The few, the proud," Ian said, grinning at him.

"You think this is funny?"

"Getting fewer all the time."

"Fuck you, Thompson."

"Fuck you, Robbins."

"What about you? You miss your mom?"

"I guess. Haven't seen her in a while."

"What happened? She leave?"

"Sort of."

The smile fell off Robbins's face. "Aw shit. She's dead, huh?"

"Yeah."

"When?"

"I was eight. Car crash."

"I'm sorry, man."

"Me too."

"Hey. Get some sleep, Thompson."

He shook his head. "Can't. Not yet. They're still over the other side of the valley. I can see 'em, moving around in the rocks."

"How many?"

"Enough."

"How many you think you could get from here?"

"Six or seven, before they mark our location."

"And kill us?"

"Yeah."

"So that's Plan B."

"Yeah."

"What's Plan A?"

"We wait for dark and keep moving. Make it to the FOB."

"Says the guy with two good legs."

"I'll carry you if I have to."

"You gonna give me a nice reach-around while you do it?"

"It's easier than listening to you bitch."

"Fuck you."

"I see your lips moving, but all I hear is whine, whine, whine."

"Read these lips. Fuck. You." But Robbins was grinning. Good. He hadn't given up yet.

Second Night

They ate before heading out. Ian opened one of the MREs. It was goddamn ham and lima beans, of course. Side dish of canned corn. M&Ms for dessert.

Robbins groaned. "Jesus. That's all we got?"

"I could ask the locals, see if they've got some nice goat."

He groaned again. "You *trying* to make me puke?"

"Tell you what, we'll go through the McDonald's drive-thru on the way."

"Big Mac for me. Large fries, Coke."

Ian gave him the MRE. "Take as much as you want, man. I'll have what's left."

Robbins didn't have a lot of appetite. Not that it meant much. No one had an appetite for ham and beans MREs. But he did eat some before handing it over. Ian made himself eat the rest. Chose not to taste it. Food was fuel.

Goddamn lima beans.

* * *

Robbins did what he could, but it was up to Ian. No idea how fast they were going. It wasn't even an easy walking pace. Night air was cold. Breath misting the air in front of them. Ian worried about exposure. Keeping moving would help.

No sign of the Talibs. Even the muj had to sleep sometimes. Ian kept a steady course toward the FOB. Tried not to think how many klicks still to go.

Head was still hurting, but not too bad. Thoughts were a little fuzzy, but that was probably mostly sleep deprivation. How long had he been awake? Since the crash. Zero-dark hundred hours.

Being unconscious doesn't count, asshole.

Okay, the morning before the op, then. 0430? Thirty-eight hours, give or take. He'd done better than that plenty of times.

They covered a couple of klicks, taking it slow. Didn't see anyone. Talibs were under cover. Heard a jet overhead, echo of sound after it'd already gone over. Probably the Bone, B-1 bomber making an airstrike.

Smelled something.

That's goat shit, Marine.

Fresh. Goats nearby meant people, civilians. Maybe talk to them, get help?

Fat chance. This part of Kandahar wasn't friendly. They'd take him in, all right. Then Al Jazeera could show a double feature, two Marines getting their heads sliced off. No thanks.

Maybe supplies, though.

Water. You're almost out.

There, on the hillside. Small village, built right into the stone, rooftop of one house making a patio for the one above. Typical Afghan place. Everything quiet.

Ian saw the well. Midway up, old-school stone.

"Hey, man," he whispered to Robbins.

"Yeah?"

"Gonna go get some water. You good here?"

"Got my pistol." He tried to take it out, but his hands were shaky.

Ian set him behind a big rock, pulled Robbins's M9 for him, gave it to him. "Loaded, one chambered. Just don't shoot me, okay?"

"Copy that." Robbins gave Ian his canteen.

Ian went carefully, watching his footwork. Didn't like the situation, but they needed water. Their supply was already mostly gone. M4 at his shoulder, checking his corners. Village looked deserted. Take away electricity, people didn't move around much at night.

Made it to the well. Heavy metal cover. Slung his rifle, took hold of the lid. Steel scraped stone. Ian winced, but no point in stopping. Slid it open. Got his rifle up, took a knee behind the well, waited.

Gave it five minutes. No movement.

Turned the crank, bringing up the bucket. Squeaking, rusted metal. Nothing he could do about that. Kept going, got the bucket up. Ian took out his canteen, drank the whole thing, and filled it from the bucket. Filled Robbins's, too. Popped a purification tablet into each canteen. Getting diarrhea in the middle of Kandahar wouldn't help their situation.

He almost left the well uncovered, but remembered his SERE training. When possible, leave no sign. Lowered the bucket, foot by foot. Picked up the lid and replaced it. Another slight scraping sound.

Time to get the hell out. Ian started his exfil. He'd taken about four steps when a door swung open two meters left of him. A guy came out. Not much light, but Ian could see the AK in his hands.

Ian froze. Waited. Light spilled out the doorway. Other guy wouldn't have good night vision. If he turned away, Ian could get out of sight.

The man turned toward him.

Shit.

Maybe he was muj, maybe not. Didn't matter. The Afghan had a gun and was raising it to point at him.

Ian's M4 was already pointed. He put two into the guy, center mass. The target went down.

Rifle shots were loud, echoing off the walls. Ian saw movement in the open doorway, heard men shouting in Pashto. Sounds of weapons being cocked.

Shit. Shit. Shit.

Training kicked in. Ian dropped his rifle on its sling, grabbed his one grenade, yanked the pin, tossed it through the door as he ran past. Had the M4 back in hand by the time the explosion came, tremendous blast, smoke and noise pouring through the doorway.

Lots of shouting. Another door opened on the right. Talib standing there. Ian aimed, fired, hit him. Guy went down squeezing his trigger, wild spray of AK rounds chewing the air.

More fire behind him. Ian grabbed cover at the corner of the building, planted his feet, swung back around. Fixed his targets by muzzle flash. Two riflemen on a rooftop. Gave three shots to the one on the left, five to the one on the right. Saw men stumbling into the square from the door he'd grenaded. Traversed the M4, kept shooting. Dropped two of them, sent the rest scrambling for cover.

Someone running at him from the side, screaming "Allahu akbar!" Foreign fighter, maybe. Holding a knife, for God's sake. Ian put three rounds through his chest, range less than ten meters. Crazy bastard kept coming. Shifted his aim, put two through his face. That knocked him over.

Aimed back into the square. Bullets blasted stone dust in his face. He blinked, fired twice blind, stupid, wasting bullets. M4 clicked empty. Ejected the empty mag on reflex, grabbed his spare, slapped it home, smacked the side, chambered a round.

Someone shooting from the roof again. New guy, or maybe he'd missed one of them. Ian felt something graze his shoulder, ignored it, shot the guy. The muj fell off the roof, arms spinning, just like in the movies.

Two more, out of the dark, running right at him. He dropped the first one with three shots. Goddamn 5.56 rounds didn't have any stopping power. Second guy firing from the hip, spraying AK rounds. Couldn't shoot for shit. Ian hit him twice in the belly. Man kept coming. He shifted higher, put three more through the chest. Crazy fucker wouldn't go down. Was practically on top of him now. Ian fired high, aimed for the head, took off the guy's ear. Knocked the bastard sideways but he kept right on coming. Heard screaming, didn't know whether it was him or his target. Fired three, four, five times, punching holes through the man's stomach, groin, thighs. Hit bone with the last shot, shattered the femur. The target went down, finally, still twitching.

Jesus Christ. What's that asshole made of?

Ian was taking more fire. How many of these bastards were there?

Shit, this must be where the search party bedded down. You dropped what, nine? Plus whatever the grenade got. There were thirty bad guys, maybe more. Time to go, Marine.

The only reason they hadn't outflanked him and put him down yet was that he'd caught them by surprise. They didn't know he was just one guy. Ian fired a few more shots, just to give them something to think about, ducked back, and started running.

He heard more shooting, but none came close. They didn't know where he was. He angled sideways, kept moving, went up the hill. Stopped, stooped, grabbed for loose stones. Threw them as far as he could, uphill and away.

Ian went to ground. Waited. Lots of running and screaming in the village, but the Talibs were getting organized. He chucked a couple more rocks. Sure enough, some of them started off that way.

He gave it a few minutes. Circled back, closing on Robbins's position.

"Robbins?"

"Thompson?"

He slid around the rock. "You good?"

"Yeah, man. The hell happened?"

"Pissed off the locals."

"Sounded like World War Three up there."

"Yeah, I stirred 'em up."

"We moving?"

"No, we chill here for a few. They think we bushwhacked 'em. They'll assume we evac'd. We stay here, let 'em go running off. Then we move."

Ian gave it half an hour. While they waited, he unloaded his mag and counted bullets by feel. Six. Six goddamn rounds left. He didn't think he'd fired that much.

You gotta think like a sniper, not an infantryman, Marine. Count those bullets.

Yeah, great advice now. Ian reloaded the magazine and got the M4 back up and ready. They still had their M9s, if it came to that. Fifteen nine-millimeter rounds in each. If things really went to shit, all they'd need was two bullets. Talibs weren't getting them alive.

The muj weren't coming this way. Time to go. Ian helped Robbins up again. They moved.

* * *

The rest of the night was short moves, long pauses, watching and listening. The muj were awake now, that was for sure. He could hear them calling to each other. One party came within about thirty meters of them while they hunkered behind some scrub. Ian started looking for a good sniper hide. When the sky started getting light, he found it. An overhanging rock with a ledge under it, most of the way up a ridge. It'd be a bit of a climb to get there, but they'd be safe from observation unless one of the muj was right there with them.

Robbins had trouble with the slope. His leg was really getting to him. Ian had to pretty much carry him the last few meters. Finally rolled him onto the ledge and pulled up alongside. Lay down to catch his breath just as the sun peeked over the ridgeline.

"Another glorious day in the Corps," Robbins muttered.

Ian smiled tightly. "Damn right. Die tomorrow. Live today."

Second Day

Ian changed Robbins's bandage. The blood had dried and it was stuck to his leg. Ian had to cut it away with his K-bar. Robbins put his own knife between his teeth so he wouldn't scream.

The smell told Ian what he'd find before he even saw the wound. Infection had set in. The leg was swollen and red, oozing pus and blood. He told himself not to pay attention to it, just do the job, and got the fresh bandage on. Robbins's skin was hot to the touch. Fever, probably.

That's it, Marine. He's toast. You did what you could, but he's gone.

He didn't listen to the voice in his head, didn't even bother telling it to shut up. He'd gotten Robbins this far.

How far? Ten klicks? Five?

More than that. Way more. Had to be. They must've covered forty klicks, at least.

Just keep telling yourself that.

Ian got the new bandage on. No antibiotics. Had to hope for the best.

Then more waiting. Ian told himself to get some sleep, but he couldn't. Didn't matter how long he'd been up. Every time he started to nod off, he'd think of something from the firefight, see a Talib down in the valley, hear a distant gunshot. He was edgy, still keyed up on adrenaline.

He tried to think about New York, about home. Wasn't easy at first, but his mind started wandering. Coming unglued. Third day he hadn't slept. How long could a guy go without sleeping? He'd heard somewhere that after five days you went crazy and died. Something to look forward to. Wondered what going crazy would feel like. Probably kind of like being in Afghanistan.

* * *

He started doing jobs for Irish mob guys, running messages, carrying stuff, when he was thirteen. Ryan spoke for him, said he was a good kid, stand-up. Ian didn't know what that meant, but it sounded cool. Guys would give him something to take somewhere else, a little bundle, a shoebox, that sort of thing. When he got there, another guy would give him a twenty-dollar bill. Easy money.

The best thing was, word got around the neighborhood that Ian was working for connected guys. *Serious* guys. The other kids gave him respect. He hardly even needed to fight anymore.

And he met Mr. Carlyle.

He had a message from Ryan one day, early September. He was supposed to take it to Mr. Carlyle at the Barley Corner. That was pretty cool. The Corner was in downtown Manhattan. Ian wasn't used to going there by himself. He was skipping school. Eighth grade was boring compared to the street. He was learning more with these mob guys than he ever did in the classroom. He'd have to watch out for cops, since he didn't look old enough to be out of school, but he knew the tricks to stay clear of them. He hopped a subway turnstile and took the train downtown.

"Hey, kid," the waitress called as he stepped inside. "Gotta see some ID."

Ian showed her his finger and scurried sideways through the crowd. He was small for his age, so it was no problem easing between the big bodies of the lunchtime crowd. He found Mr. Carlyle where he'd been told he would, at the bar.

"Hey, Mr. Carlyle?" he called.

The pre-puberty little-boy voice caught Mr. Carlyle's attention. He turned to look at the kid. "Hello, lad," he said in a thick Irish accent. "And what brings you here?"

"Got a message for you," Ian said.

Mr. Carlyle moved only a little, but Ian noticed the same loosening of the joints he did before a fistfight. The man was tensed, ready for anything. Ian suddenly realized Mr. Carlyle might think he was a threat. That idea pleased him.

"It's nothing much," Ian went on. "Ryan told me to tell you he can't make it Friday, on account of the heat."

"Aye, thank you, lad," Mr. Carlyle said, smiling gently at him.

At that moment, a hand fell on Ian' shoulder. He twisted and sprang sideways, tearing himself loose from the waitress's grasp. He took a second to check his exits, getting ready to make a run for it.

"Easy, lad," Mr. Carlyle said. "It's all right, Marian," he added to the red-faced, angry-looking woman. "He's with me."

Ian gave her his best saucy wink. She didn't seem impressed. As if she'd suddenly forgotten him, she turned away.

"Is an answer expected immediately?" Mr. Carlyle asked Ian.

"No."

"Then you'll share a drink with me, by way of thanks."

"Really? Sweet!"

Mr. Carlyle waved to the bartender. "Ned, a Coca-Cola for my young mate here, and one for myself as well."

Ian's face fell. For a magical moment, he'd imagined sipping whiskey with this cool old Irishman. Not that he was *that* old; probably not even forty. But to Ian, that was pretty old.

"Now then, lad," Mr. Carlyle said, when their drinks were in front of them. "What do they call you?"

"Ian."

"Ian what?"

Ian hesitated. Mr. Carlyle saw the indecision on his face.

"There's no shame in being where you're from, lad," he said quietly. "No matter where that may be."

"Ian Thompson."

"And is there a reason you're not in school today, Mr. Thompson?"

"No one calls me that."

"Ian, then," Mr. Carlyle said. "I see you're already good at evading questions you've no wish to answer. That's a fine skill, but I'd not overdo it."

"I don't like school."

Mr. Carlyle didn't do what grownups usually did when he said something like that. He didn't get mad, or try to tell Ian school was all the things it wasn't. He just nodded thoughtfully. "And why is that?"

Ian took a sip of his Coke. Even though it was the same drink he'd swiped from gas stations, it tasted different here. More grown-up. Here he was, talking to an important man in the O'Malley organization, like just another guy.

"It's boring," he said at last. "And I'm not learning anything."

"If you're learning nothing, I'm not surprised you're bored," Mr. Carlyle said. "I imagine they're telling you all manner of things you already know."

"That's right."

"And are there things you don't yet know?"

"Well, yeah. Sure."

"Such as?"

"I dunno. I haven't learned them yet."

Mr. Carlyle laughed. "That's a fine answer, lad. I can tell you've a grand mind working behind those eyes. Your mum must be very proud of you."

Ian felt his face freeze up. He was very aware of Mr. Carlyle watching him, reading his expression. He tried to give nothing away.

But Mr. Carlyle nodded to himself, as if Ian had explained the whole thing. "I'm sorry, lad," he said softly, putting a hand on Ian's shoulder.

Suddenly, Ian was fighting back tears. He knew he shouldn't cry, not in front of this tough mob guy, but he couldn't help it. He swallowed hard, and made the mistake of taking a gulp of Coke at the same time. He choked and felt it fizz up into the back of his nose. He bent forward, coughing and spluttering, leaving a mess of snot and Coca-Cola on the countertop.

Mr. Carlyle patted him on the back, letting him work it out of his system. When it was over, Ian couldn't look at the man's face. He was so ashamed of himself.

"Some napkins, I think, Ned," was all Mr. Carlyle said on the subject.

They sat there in silence. Mr. Carlyle and Ian both worked on their drinks, eventually slurping them down to the ice cubes. Then Ian got up to go.

"Ian," Mr. Carlyle said softly. "Look at me, lad."

Ian stopped and turned reluctantly. He didn't see pity, not exactly.

"You're a tough lad," Mr. Carlyle said. "So you needn't be so concerned about proving it to everyone. The true hard men? Are they the ones who are always getting in fights, bloodying noses?"

Ian thought it over. "I guess not."

"Do you see me starting fistfights, getting in pissing contests with these lads?"

Ian glanced around. "No."

"Why not? Practically all of them are bigger than I, and most can handle themselves."

"I dunno." Ian shrugged.

"That's never a good enough answer," Mr. Carlyle said, his eyes going a little harder. "It's not good enough for me, but more to the point, it's not nearly good enough for you."

Ian thought about it, hard. "You're their boss," he said at last.

"Aye, some of them," Mr. Carlyle said. "But why am I the boss?"

"'Cause you're the toughest," Ian said defiantly.

Mr. Carlyle grinned at him. "Perhaps I am, lad. But then why am I not proving it? Why do they know it already, without the testing?"

Ian thought some more. "Because you already know," he said, thinking of the look in the eyes of those two boys he'd beaten up. In that moment, Ian had known he was the toughest son of a bitch in Queens. They'd seen it, and it'd scared the hell out of them. That was when the fight had ended. If Ian could've put that look in his eyes, that swagger in his walk, there wouldn't have been a fight in the first place.

"That's right, lad," Mr. Carlyle said. "There, you've learned something worth knowing today. Perhaps you've spent it better than in a classroom."

Ian grinned at him.

"On the other hand," Mr. Carlyle said, "there's no knowing what you'd have learned had you been at school. So we can't say for certain you've come out ahead of the game."

Ian's smile faltered.

"Well, Ian," Mr. Carlyle said, standing up from his own stool and actually extending his hand. "I'm very pleased to have met you."

Ian reached out and shook hands with the man. His hand almost got lost in Mr. Carlyle's big, grown-up palm. He started trying to outsqueeze the man, prove how tough he was, but then he remembered. The point wasn't to prove it to the other guy. He relaxed his grip to what he hoped was an ordinary, firm handshake.

"Perhaps I'll be seeing you again, lad," Mr. Carlyle said.

* * *

It's not about proving how tough you are to the other guy. It's about knowing it yourself.

Damn right. Ian was still awake, but he'd been daydreaming, remembering. It'd been a long time since he'd wondered whether he was tough enough, but now, the thought was on his mind. How far to the FOB? A hundred fifty klicks? No, less than that. Maybe a hundred thirty.

Too far.

Maybe, maybe not. He checked Robbins again. Poor bastard was out, either asleep or passed out. Best thing for him. That leg was infected for sure. He already might lose it, even if they got scooped up by medevac in the next five minutes.

Leave him. Just walk away. He's out, he won't even know, and neither will anyone else.

Bullshit.

Leave him. You proved you wouldn't abandon him. You carried him practically on your back, two solid nights. You got nothing left to prove.

But that wasn't true. Because if Ian left him, he'd know himself. He'd know he hadn't been able to cut it, when the shit really went down. He'd know he'd failed not just Robbins, but himself. And knowing that, how could he even save himself?

"Fuck that," he muttered, checking the sky. Getting on late afternoon. He was hungry, but ignored the thought of the last MRE. Better save it. He took a little water, rolled over, unbuttoned, urinated lying on his side. It was dark yellow, smelly.

You're dehydrated.

Couldn't be helped. They couldn't count on more water. Had to save what they had. It'd be dark soon. Time to get moving again.

"Die tomorrow," Ian repeated to himself. "Live today."

Third Night

Robbins couldn't walk anymore. Ian got him into the support carry, what he'd been using, but Robbins's good leg buckled.

"Sorry, man," Robbins slurred. He tried to get up again, but just scrabbled on the dirt.

"Don't sweat it," Ian said. He shifted to the Hawes carry. It'd be harder on him, but it was all he had. He got Robbins's left arm up over his shoulder, put his back against Robbins's chest so they were basically spooning, and stood up. It was awkward, but he still had one hand free to hold his M4.

"We see any muj, you gotta hold on to me," Ian told him. "I'm gonna need both hands."

"Okay, man. Whatever."

Ian wasn't sure the other man had even heard him. He'd given the wounded guy water, probably more than he should, but he could tell Robbins was sweating from the fever. He was dehydrating faster than Ian was, and that might kill him quicker than the wound itself.

He took his bearings and started moving. He was still trying to keep to cover, but it didn't seem as important now. Maybe it was the knowledge that he was running out of time, and they'd die out here whether the Talibs found them or not. But it was probably the sleep deprivation.

Ian felt drunk. Not good, happy, cheerful drunk, like dancing on a table in a bar. This was mean, ugly, sad drunk, the kind where you got hung-over before you'd even worked through the booze. Little snatches of sentences wandered through his mind. He snatched at them pretty much at random. There were song lyrics, old conversations, movie quotes.

"Got my finger on the trigger, but I don't know who to trust. I look into your eyes, there's just devils and dust..."

"This gun will be pointed at your heart the whole time."

"That is my least vulnerable spot."

"Hey, Thompson?"

"They say there's a place where dreams have all gone, they never said where, but I think I know..."

"We're a long long way from home, Bobby. Home's a long long way from us..."

"It's about the man beside you. That's all there is."

"You're one microscopic cog in his catastrophic plan, designed and directed by his red right hand..."

"Hey, Thompson?"

"It's not about proving you're tough..."

Looked up at the night sky, got a direction fix from those cold, silver stars. They were still pretty much on course.

"Thompson, man?"

Realized Robbins was talking to him. Wondered how long he'd been doing it.

"What?"

"Don't mind the singing, but maybe a little quieter?"

Hadn't known he was singing. Ian let his M4 fall on its sling for a minute, slapped himself on both cheeks, hard. Woke up a little. Picked up the gun again, kept going.

Don't think about the end of the march, they'd told him in boot camp. Convince yourself it's never gonna end. This is life, this is all there is, this moment. The future doesn't exist, so it doesn't matter. What matters is right here, right now. Can you take it?

"Course I can," Ian muttered.

Then you can do it forever. Pain's just a feeling, feelings are supposed to be enjoyed. Enjoy the pain.

Walked for a while, couldn't say how long. After a while, the cold didn't bother him. Must've gone a little numb. Couldn't tell where his feet were, stumbled a few times but didn't go down.

Stopped a few times to catch his breath, but didn't let himself get comfy. Knew if he stopped on the march, he might not get going again. Had some water, gave some to Robbins. Shared the last Snickers bar. Probably a bad idea. Just woke up his appetite. Couldn't think about anything but food.

Remember that Irish stew at the Corner?

God, did he ever. Didn't know exactly what was in that, but it sure as shit wasn't goat meat. Thought he'd heard they used Guinness to make the gravy.

Shepherd's pie. Baked potatoes. Marian said once you hadn't had a mom, so she'd have to stand in. Remember?

"Yeah, I remember."

And this was after you flipped her off the first time you met, right? You were such a little shit.

"Mr. Carlyle took care of that."

"Who's that?" Robbins asked.

"Just a guy I knew stateside. Good at solving problems."

"We could use him here," Robbins said. Laughed a little shakily.

"No shit."

"You tired, man?"

"Hell no."

"You're a shitty liar, Thompson."

"That's what my ex-wife said."

"Didn't know you were married."

"I wasn't. But I'm a better liar than you thought."

* * *

Didn't see any sign of the Talibs that night, for a change. Did see a plane. Either that or a shooting star, fast-moving fire across the sky. Not that it did him any good. Even if they were looking the right way, it'd be hard to pick them out. They hardly looked like Marines, even by daylight. BDUs filthy, no helmets, blood and dust all over. He'd need to remember that.

Remember... remember... remember what?

Didn't look like Marines. Right. Don't get shot by the retrieval patrol.

What retrieval patrol?

That was a silly question. Of course there was a retrieval. They didn't just leave Marines out here in the 'Stan all by themselves. That'd be ridiculous. Ian chuckled a little.

Holy shit. I'm going crazy.

Damn right. How do you like it?

Don't know. Ask me in a hundred years, see if anyone knows the difference.

Ha ha.

Sky getting light again. What'd that mean?

Time to find a place to lay up. Under cover, Marine.

"Looking for a lover who will come on in and cover me," Ian sang softly.

The Boss sure knew how to write catchy songs. He even seemed to understand the way soldiers thought, which was weird for a draft-dodger. Ian had always liked Springsteen. The rest of the squad liked heavy metal... excuse me, *used* to like. These days they weren't listening to many tunes. Unless those boys at the pearly gates issued you an iPod along with your wings and halo. What'd they listen to in heaven, anyway? Harps, wasn't it? How about in hell?

"Boy bands, mostly."

"Thompson? You good, man?"

Oh, shit. Said that out loud. "Yeah, I'm good."

There was a decent spot. Actual, honest-to-God cave. Maybe they could get some sleep.

Didn't have a light. Ian felt his way in, saw some lumps of something. Nudged one with his foot.

It was soft.

Didn't understand at first. Too tired.

Bedroll.

Oh, shit. Someone lived here. Time to go. Ian started to move Robbins toward the exit.

Too late. Voices, outside. A lot of voices. Coming closer.

Sudden panic cleared his brain, a little. Maybe thirty seconds to figure what to do. Six bullets in the M4, fifteen more in the pistol. Another fifteen in Robbins's sidearm. He could hold them, for a while.

Until you kill the first two and the others toss in a grenade, dumbass. There's no back door. Where you gonna go?

There were a couple crates at the back of the cave, not quite against the wall. A little space back there. Tight fit. He got Robbins squeezed in.

"Stay quiet, man," he hissed in the smallest whisper he dared. "No matter what."

Robbins didn't answer. Might be passed out.

Ian tumbled in beside him, lying on top of his rifle, couldn't use it. Fumbled for his M9, got the pistol in his hand, thank God. Voices coming into the goddamn cave. Men, tired, pissed off from the sound of it.

How many? Couldn't tell. They were moving around, getting out food. A light came on, oil lamp probably. Must have a curtain over the entrance. Ian pulled his feet just a little further in, curled half fetal. Waited.

Times like this, he really, really wished he believed in God. It'd be nice to have someone to talk to in his head who wasn't going crazy and about to die.

Third Day

Maybe he'd already gone totally bonkers. It was a comforting thought. Because this situation was insane. Ian was in a Taliban hideout. A Taliban hideout that was, by the way, *full of fucking Taliban*. Taliban who'd probably just been out all night looking for him. And here they all were, one big happy family. Except he was the crazy uncle in the attic that no one talked about.

Because no one knows you're here, remember?

Right. But the cave had something like a dozen guys in it. So he was warm, relatively speaking, from all the bodies, and out of the wind. He was more comfortable than he'd been the last few days. And as long as no one saw or heard him, he was actually kind of safe. But he couldn't go to sleep, for fear one of them would wander around the backside of these crates, see him, and cut his head off with a fucking butcher knife. So he lay quiet, holding a pistol, trying not to go to sleep while he waited to blow a man's head off.

Insane.

Good thing he wasn't a cocky, impatient teenager anymore. That dumb kid wouldn't have lasted an hour. Ian knew how to be patient now. Scout Sniper training had finished what Mr. Carlyle had begun.

* * *

He didn't really know how Mr. Carlyle had done it. He'd broken through to Ian. Maybe it was just that he took the time and trouble. It wasn't like anyone else had. Even the rest of the gang, the kids Ian hung out with, never bothered to find out what was really going on with him. Talking to Mr. Carlyle, though, that was different. That man always made Ian feel like he was a real person, like he mattered.

It didn't come fast, but that was what was beautiful. It happened over the summer between eighth and ninth grade. He'd somehow made it to high school, despite a whole lot of unexcused absences. Later, Ian would suspect Mr. Carlyle had something to do with that, but he'd never be able to prove it. Mr. Carlyle had started showing up around the neighborhood, spending time with Ian, taking an interest.

It might've been a little creepy. They warned kids about people like that in school; older guys who liked to hang out with young boys. But it was never like that. Mr. Carlyle never touched him the way they talked about in health class, no way. They talked, and the man listened to what he had to say.

Ian figured it was because Mr. Carlyle worked for Evan O'Malley, that he was being a talent scout. Sooner or later, they'd have a real conversation about something really important. That was what Ian wanted; to be a wiseguy, one of the guys who got *respect*, who got things done, made money, kicked ass.

But when the conversation happened, at the Corner around the end of August, it didn't go like Ian thought it would.

"So, lad," Mr. Carlyle said. "I suppose we'll be seeing a bit less of you now."

"Why?" Ian took a pull on his straw. He knew Mr. Carlyle was a whiskey man, from asking around, but he always drank whatever Ian was drinking, so he wouldn't feel left out.

"School's starting up again."

"Oh, yeah. That. Forget about it. It won't be a problem."

"What do you mean?"

"Whatever you need me for, I can still make it happen."

Mr. Carlyle sat back and gave Ian a long, thoughtful look.

Here it comes, Ian thought. He squared his shoulders and tried to look as much like a grownup as a kid pushing thirteen can.

"I lasted two years longer than you," Mr. Carlyle finally said.

Ian blinked. "At what?"

"School. I was fifteen when I left. I couldn't wait to get into the fight."

Ian nodded. He got that. "I heard about you. That's why everyone calls you 'Cars.' It's 'cause of the car bom—"

Mr. Carlyle cut him off with a small, decisive movement of one hand. "I know what they call me, and I know why. Take it from me, lad, I'd have done better to stay in until graduation."

"What for?"

"You want to do what you want, don't you?"

"Well, yeah."

Mr. Carlyle smiled. "That's something only your education can give you, lad. Freedom. Else you'll find yourself living a life that's been decided by mistakes you made a long time before."

"What do you want me to do?"

"That's my point, lad," Mr. Carlyle said. He was still smiling, but there was something sad behind the smile. "I want you to figure out what it is you want. And I've a thought it isn't working for Mr. O'Malley."

"I don't want to work for O'Malley," Ian said. "I want to work for you."

"Then I want you to think things over," Mr. Carlyle said. "I've a position in mind for you, though."

Ian sat forward. "I can do it," he said eagerly.

"There's just one thing," Mr. Carlyle said. "When you interview for a job, lad, there's qualifications you must present. This particular position requires a high school degree."

Ian deflated. "Seriously?"

"Aye, lad. But not to worry, I'll hold it for you. You've my word of honor. If you still want it, the job's yours the day you show your diploma to me."

"What if I want to work for someone else?"

"Now lad, why are you asking me questions you'd better be asking yourself?"

And that was the end of that conversation.

So Ian got through high school. He took it as a personal challenge. Part of him did it because he thought Mr. Carlyle didn't think he'd go through with it, and the other part did it because he thought Mr. Carlyle believed in him. It was a paradox, for sure, but it worked. His GPA climbed from the low 2s in his junior high years up to a solid A-minus average by senior year. At Mr. Carlyle's suggestion, he went out for sports and found out he was good at those, too. When he couldn't afford the activity fees, Mr. Carlyle put up the cash for him. He ran track and played soccer, and senior year he was captain of both teams.

Somewhere along the line, he started shaving and girls started paying attention to him. He wasn't any good at dating. The weird thing was, the way he was awkward just seemed to make them more interested. He asked Mr. Carlyle about that, and was told that was just one of those things.

At graduation, his dad didn't come to the ceremony. Ian didn't even know where his father was that day. But Mr. Carlyle was there, applauding when he walked across the auditorium stage and shook the principal's hand. And afterward, he went to a little graduation party in the private back room of the Barley Corner. How cool was that? None of the other kids had a party at a Manhattan pub.

Not that there was any underage drinking going on. Not that Ian knew. The funny thing was, ever since Mr. Carlyle had started taking a particular interest in Ian, he'd been trying pretty hard to keep Ian away from anything illegal. Now, taking a drink of Coca-Cola, it suddenly struck Ian that he hadn't been in a fistfight in better than two years.

"So, lad," Mr. Carlyle said. "Now you can do what you want. Have you made up your mind what it is?"

And he had. "Thanks," he said. "For everything. And I know you've got that job for me."

"If you want it, aye."

Ian nodded. "I think I do."

Mr. Carlyle nodded, like he'd expected that answer but had hoped it wouldn't be coming.

"But not yet," Ian went on.

Mr. Carlyle raised an eyebrow. "And what is it you're needing first?"

"I think... I think I'm better than I thought," Ian said. "Does that make sense?"

"Aye."

"But I gotta make sure. I have to know. It's like I've been taking all these tests, and I'm passing them, but I don't really know who I am. I maybe didn't get started right on being me, so I need a little more time to figure it out."

Mr. Carlyle nodded. "So?

"I'm joining the Marines," Ian blurted out. He hadn't said that to anyone else, not to any of his teammates, not even to Amanda, the girl he'd been seeing off-and-on most of senior year. After he said it, he stared at his mentor, the only true friend he'd ever had, and wondered what he'd say. Would he try to talk him out of it? Or tell him how proud he was? There were a hundred things a guy said at a time like this, all of them wrong.

What Mr. Carlyle did was step toward him, look him straight in the eye, and give him a firm handshake. While still holding their grip, he said, "You take care of yourself, Ian. You're going looking for yourself. Don't get lost out there."

* * *

In a cave in Afghanistan, Scout Sniper Sergeant Ian Thompson, USMC, lay hunkered behind a box full of Russian-made automatic rifles. He waited for an endless day to run out of hours.

I'm trying, Mr. Carlyle, he thought. I'm trying.

Fourth Night

If he'd been alone, Ian would've tried to take out the guys in the cave. Most of them were asleep. He'd get the drop on them, kill the ones who were awake first. He might even get all of them. But there was Robbins to consider. And he was too worn down. Now he was wondering if he could even hold his gun steady enough to shoot straight.

It got dark, really dark. Ian wondered why. Realized the Talibs had turned out the lamp. Careless of them. Or maybe they were out of oil. Listened, couldn't hear anything.

That's because they've left, dumbass.

Made sense. Must be nighttime again. The Afghans had all gone outside to do... something. What? Looking for someone. Wonder who. Poor bastard.

You.

Right. Damn, but he was tired. He could just sleep right there.

No, you can't.

"Course I can't," Ian slurred. "Got things... things to do. C'mon, Robbins. Semper fi."

Robbins didn't answer.

"Hey, Robbins. Up and at 'em. Semper fi."

Still nothing.

Ian fumbled around in the dark, found Robbins's leg. Worked his way up it, felt something wet. Sticky. Like half-dried soda pop. Couldn't remember what it was. Not important. Worked his way higher, found Robbins's face.

Wet. Clammy. Man shivering.

Tried to think what to do. Remembered Mom, long time ago, before she left.

"Feed a cold, starve a fever."

Laughed a little. That'd be easy.

Hungry. Got out his last MRE. No point saving it. Opened it up. Knew it by smell. Spaghetti and meat sauce.

Got the flameless heater out, made supper. Breakfast. Whatever.

No point in saving it. No point in feeding Robbins, even if he was able to eat. Ian would need the strength to carry the poor bastard.

Like hell you can carry him. You'll keel over before you get half a klick.

"Fuck..."

Ate everything in the MRE. Oreos, energy-drink mix in the canteen, corn on the side. Tasted good. Thought of that Italian place down in Queens. They wouldn't be caught dead serving this shit, but damned if it wasn't the finest pasta he'd ever had.

"I'm not Italian anyway," he told Robbins. "Fuck 'em."

The candy made him pause. Someone had told him, when he first got to the Sandbox, that Skittles were bad luck. You got Skittles in your MRE, man, you were screwed.

Ian laughed quietly. How much more screwed could he get? He checked the package, to make sure it hadn't torn open and the bad luck had leaked out. Would've explained some things.

Ate the Skittles. Drank the last of his water.

Time to get moving. Remembered why Robbins's leg was sticky. Didn't bother checking the wound. Nothing he could do for him anyway. Only one way to carry him now. Stood up, crouched, got the man over his shoulders, stood again.

Almost fell down. Legs weak. Not enough food, not enough sleep.

Took a step toward the cave entrance. Didn't fall down. Took another.

Out in the night again. Clear night. Stars overhead. Blurry when he looked at them. Eyes having trouble focusing.

You don't lie down and sleep, Marine, you're gonna fall down.

Can't sleep. Muj.

"Muj..." Ian muttered. "Muj... muj... gotta muj... Scaramouche... Scaramouche... will you do the fandango?"

Bohemian Rhapsody? Really, Marine? You are way over the edge.

"Here... there be... monsters."

Down the slope, into another of those goddamn Afghan valleys. Maybe he was following the Talibs who thought they were following him. Crazy thought. Someone had shown him a cartoon once, from Big Two, said it was everything he needed to know about being a foot soldier.

Image: two dirty GIs, unshaven, plodding through the rain. One with a big nose, one with a little nose. One says to the other, "Hell. When they run, we try to ketch 'em. When we ketch 'em, we try and make 'em run."

Was still funny. Ian smiled.

He was still smiling when he went around a big rock and practically ran smack into the Talibs.

They were taking a break, hunkered down, sitting on their heels, maybe ten meters in front of him. Plain as day under the stars. For what seemed like a really long time, Ian and the Talibs just stared at each other. One of them had been eating. Crumbs in his beard. His mouth hung open, half-chewed bread on his tongue.

Almost comical. Awkward moment, like climbing in your girlfriend's window and finding her dad in there. Except dad was a crazy fundamentalist with an AK in his hands, murder in his heart.

Ian's mind went totally clear, just for a moment, from the shot of adrenaline. He dropped Robbins. Couldn't help it, no time to put him down. If the Talibs had been less startled, the two of them would already be dead.

Close quarters, and he had just six rounds in his rifle. Ian pulled his M9 from the cross-draw holster on his chest instead. The Talibs were moving now, raising their guns. Ian started shooting, working his way left to right. Three of them went down. The other three were shooting, but they were panicky, letting go full auto when they should've used short bursts or single shots.

Ian shifted to the fourth guy, put three rounds in his chest. Aimed at the fifth one, pistol slide locked back. Click.

Shit.

A bullet hit him in the shoulder, spun him halfway around. Ian fell next to Robbins, behind the big stone. Fumbled for his M4, got it up. The Talib who'd gotten lucky came around the rock, ready to finish him off.

Ian punched his ticket with three shots, point blank, center mass.

He came up on one knee, leaned around the rock. Sixth guy was running up the slope, totally freaked. Ian fired, missed.

Damn. Vision blurry. Hard to hit a moving target.

You're a sniper, Marine. Act like it.

He snugged the M4 up to his shoulder, took careful aim, squeezed the trigger.

Missed again.

How many rounds left? Couldn't remember. Talib was almost out of sight, over the ridgeline. Couldn't let him get away. He'd be back with ten, twenty more.

Ian tracked the man, forced himself to breathe, took his time. Found the stillness inside himself.

His shot almost surprised him.

The Talib lurched, fell, slid back down the slope. Wasn't moving.

Heard groans from the others. Hadn't killed them all. Didn't matter. They wouldn't be after him, not anytime soon. Ian got Robbins up, started moving back the way he'd come.

He'd gotten about a hundred meters before thinking he really should've grabbed one of the Afghan AKs. Couldn't go back for it now. Others might've heard the gunfire, maybe the survivors had cell phones, too many variables.

At two hundred meters, his shoulder started hurting like a son of a bitch.

You've been shot, Marine.

Stumbled on a little further, grabbed some cover on the slope. Checked the arm. Bullet had gone clean through the meat, just under the joint. Didn't look too bad. Got the QuikClot out of his aid kit, slapped it on the wound. Slowed the bleeding. Out of bandages. Took off his undershirt, cut it up with his K-bar, wrapped the holes. Best he could do.

Robbins was semiconscious now, mumbling, raving. Not making any damn sense. Talking to people who weren't there. Ian tried to get him on his feet, but it wasn't happening. Wondered if he could carry the man with one good arm.

Found out he could.

Didn't remember much of the rest of the night. Kept moving. Like wading through quicksand. Saw faces in the night, people he knew. Valchek. Mr. Carlyle. Dad. Valchek's mother, even though Ian had never met her, didn't know what she looked like, which was crazy because she was standing right there. Stanhope. Some of them talked, but Ian didn't remember what they said. Saw fireworks on the horizon, like the Fourth of July at Coney Island. Could be an airstrike. Could be he was out of his damn mind. Music in his head. Some Springsteen, some movie soundtrack, some Britney Spears of all things.

"Hit me... baby... one more time," Ian mumbled in a cracked, crazy voice.

He caught his foot on a rock and went down, hard. Face-planted. Kandahar punched him right in the nose. Typical.

Ian had nothing left. Just lay there, hurting, tired. Breathing was all he could do.

Breathed.

* * *

An hour, maybe a year later, the sun came up.

Fourth Day

Ian rolled onto his back and looked up at the sun. "Die tomorrow," he croaked. "Live today."

He got his canteen out. Empty. Looked at Robbins.

Robbins looked like shit. Pasty face, not sweating anymore. Eyes half open, looking at nothing. Looked dead.

Ian looked closer. Saw a little movement. Got the man's head back, put Robbins's canteen to his lips. Made him drink everything that was left.

Ian was on his knees, BDU shirt open, no undershirt. Couldn't remember what'd happened to it. Shoulder hurt. Face hurt, too. Dried blood crusted under his nose.

Force of habit and training. Ian checked his weapons. M4 was in good working order. He popped the mag and saw it was empty. Didn't have his pistol. Must've dropped it last night. Stripped the M4, smashed the firing pin with a nearby rock. Threw the useless gun away.

Tried to stand up. Couldn't.

Tried again. Managed it, a little shaky. Legs trembling.

Looked at Robbins. There was just no way.

Robbins looked back. His eyes were open, and he looked at least a little alert. The man's lips moving. He was saying something, whispering.

"We... there... yet?"

"Just about, man."

"You... shitting... me?"

"No. Just... gonna go over that hill... get help."

"Don't... leave me here, man."

Ian swallowed. His throat made a clicking sound. "Not... gonna leave you, man. Just gonna... get help. I'll... be back. Promise."

"Don't go, man." Robbins looked scared. "I'm hurt. Don't leave me."

Ian nodded. Then he turned away and started walking. He couldn't make a straight line. He zigzagged his way between the stones, working his way down the valley in broad daylight. Didn't even care anymore. Just had to put as many steps behind him as he could.

Fuzzed out a little. Probably kept walking.

* * *

Time passed. Or maybe it didn't.

* * *

"Hey, man! Hey!"

Ian smiled to himself. More voices in his head. Without them, this would've been a really lonely op.

"Hey, you good, buddy?"

"Jesus Christ, he's all fucked up."

Someone grabbed him. That was a new one. Hallucinations weren't supposed to be able to do that. Ian tried to grab him back. His fingers didn't listen, scrabbled at the front of someone's body armor. He went down, onto his knees. The image of four guys in helmets and full battle rattle swam in front of his eyes. There was a Humvee behind them, another Humvee moving toward them.

"Shit, man," one of the mirages said. "Where'd you come from?"

That was funny. "Queens," Ian said. He tried to laugh but started crying instead. No tears; too dehydrated. Just dry, wracking sobs. Sounded like a coughing fit. He fell over and lay on the floor of that Afghan valley, curled into a ball, sobbing.

Someone was next to him, a young-faced guy, talking quietly to him. Yellow stick of butter on his collar.

Lieutenant.

"Hey, man. Are you alone out here?"

Ian shook his head. Raised one hand, extended a shaking finger.

"One guy? Is he okay?"

Shook his head.

"Where is he?"

Shook his head again. Waved his arm vaguely.

"Back where you came from?"

Nodded.

"Okay, squad," the young-looking guy said, standing up. "Let's do a sweep. Might be muj around. I want eyes on that ridge."

Another guy's face filled Ian's field of view. Army medic, looked like.

"You're gonna be okay, buddy," the medic said. "Shit, didn't even know there were Marines in our sector. It's fine, man. We're gonna get you out of here, get you home."

Home. The word echoed. The sun went black. Then nothing.

Later

What happened?

Head hurting. Dizzy.

Where are you?

Try to say something. Mouth dry. Thirsty.

Situational awareness.

Sound. Rhythmic beeping. Faint, far away. Someone talking.

"Blood pressure is still 125 over 80, but he's bouncing back well. I think in another twelve to twenty-four..."

Doctors.

"Corpsman!"

Okay, voice works. Croaking like a frog. Play through it, Marine. Self-evaluation. Wounds?

Eyelids working. Bright light. Fluorescents. White ceiling, white walls. Sterile smell, like disinfectant. Shoulder hurting, not too bad. Clean white bandage on it. Tubes coming out of damn near everywhere.

"Doctor! He's awake!"

Female voice. Face in his field of view. Brunette, young, pretty. Tired, though. Lines under her eyes.

When's the last time you saw a woman who wasn't wearing a burka? Looks good to me, Marine.

Try a smile. Shaky.

A man coming into the room. Tall, thin, older guy. Gray hair. Captain's bars on his coat.

Try to come to attention. Salute.

"As you were, Marine." Doc coming over, smiling. "How you feeling?"

"Thirsty."

"Drink this."

Plastic cup filled with God only knows what. Tastes all right. Not very much of it.

"More, sir?"

"All right, but just a little. We don't want you to get sick. Severe dehydration cases will throw fluids right back up if they drink too much at a time."

"Yes, sir."

"How's the shoulder?"

"A little sore, but I'm good, sir. Where should I report?"

A smile. "You Marines. You're not going anywhere, unless it's stateside."

"Where am I?"

"Landstuhl Regional Medical Center, just south of Ramstein."

"Ramstein?"

"Germany."

I know where Ramstein is, damn it.

"How long, sir?" Can't remember getting here.

"They brought you in two nights ago."

"Unconscious?"

A laugh. "Asleep. Apparently you'd been on your feet a while. You didn't even wake up while we were treating your arm. How long were you on the go, anyway?"

Think it over. Count back.

"Four days, sir. No, five. Got knocked out for a few minutes, after the first day. Four days after that."

"Oh my God." The nurse, a hand at her mouth. Eyes wide. Nice eyes, green with flecks of gold in them.

Another laugh. "You must have slept sometime during that."

"No, sir."

Not laughing anymore, is he?

A smile, but a little bit forced. "Okay, Marine. You just get your rest. You've earned it."

Something else. "Sir?"

"Yes?"

"There was a guy with me. Do you know what happened to him?"

"There'll be a Marine in to talk to you soon. Take it easy. He'll let you know the score."

* * *

The nurse lingered a moment, staring at him. Ian stared back. It was fine with him. She gave him a nicer view than most of the things he'd been looking at over the past week.

"You can't have been awake that long," she said at last.

Ian shrugged.

"It's impossible," she went on. "You'd go crazy, probably die."

"Maybe I did, a little."

"Which one?"

"Both, I guess."

Something in his eyes spooked her. She left.

* * *

A Marine full-bird colonel came in to talk to him. Ian was always a little uncomfortable with any brass higher than captain, but Colonel Jacoby seemed all right. Hard, leathery face, bright blue eyes, gray hair. Those eyes had seen combat, so they understood each other.

"As you were," Jacoby said, interrupting Ian's salute.

Ian lay there, waited.

"You saw some action out there."

"Yes, sir."

"Doc says you're good for a short talk. You up for a little debrief?"

"Yes, sir."

The colonel got out a map, came around to the bedside. Ian recognized those goddamn hills. Kandahar.

"Your chopper went down here, six nights ago." Pointed to a spot on the map. You were picked up by an Army patrol here, day before yesterday." Pointed again. "You went a hundred and five kilometers, through hostile country, carrying a wounded man."

"Permission to speak, sir?"

"Absolutely, Sergeant."

"What happened to Robbins, sir?"

The colonel cracked a smile. "He's here, in Recovery."

"How is he, sir?"

"He'll make it. Afraid he lost the leg, but you saved the rest of him."

"Yes, sir."

The colonel saw something on his face. "What is it, Sergeant?"

Suddenly Ian was fighting off tears. In front of a Marine colonel, damn it. Swallowed, tried to hold them back. Looked in the older man's eyes, saw something there he'd seen in Mr.

Carlyle's face, too. The thing he'd always wanted to see in his dad's eyes, never had.

"Sir, I left him there."

"Bullshit, Marine. You saved his life. The patrol picked him up two hundred meters from where they found you."

Ian shook his head. "I told him I'd go get help."

"And you did."

"No, sir." Looked hard into his face, tried to make him understand. "I lied. I couldn't... couldn't carry him any farther. Tried to save myself. I'm sorry. Jesus Christ, I'm sorry." Losing the battle with the tears.

The colonel put a hand on his shoulder. "Son, you went through hell out there. And you came back. You're a hero, Thompson. Private Robbins told us all about you, when we talked to him yesterday. They've put you in for a Silver Star. You'll get it, too."

A medal? They were giving him a goddamn medal? For what?

Ian stared at Colonel Jacoby. "I don't want it."

The colonel smiled again, but there was sadness in it. "I've got one," he said quietly.

Ian didn't say anything.

"Iraq," Jacoby went on. "The first time around. Back in '91. Every time I look at it, I see a day I'd like to forget."

Ian didn't ask what had happened, and Jacoby didn't tell him.

"You'll take the medals," Jacoby said. "The Silver Star, the Purple Heart, and anything else they throw at you. You'll say 'Thank you, sir,' when they pin them on you. Because you're in the Corps, son."

"When can I go back, sir?"

Again the sadness. "Son, you're not going anywhere but home."

"I've still got six weeks on deployment."

"Time's up, Marine. Your kit will be flown up here, should be here in another day or two. You've done nearly two full combat tours, one in Iraq, one in the 'Stan. You've done your part."

Ian shook his head. "I don't want this, sir."

"You didn't want the chopper crash either, I expect," Jacoby said. He stood up. "I think you need a little more time to process, Marine. I'll be back tomorrow morning for your full report. Any intel you can give us on enemy positions and movements will be helpful." In the doorway, he turned, smiled again. "Good work, Marine."

* * *

Good work.

Didn't feel like it. Felt like shit.

Could still remember Robbins, could still hear him calling, begging Ian not to leave him. The Army guys had saved him? Okay, great. For them. Ian had left him to die. And for that, they were making him a hero. Pinning a fucking medal on him.

He wasn't crying anymore. Couldn't. Too tense. Remembered flashes of what had happened. Gunfire. Flames. Screams. Pain. Thirst. Darkness. Those cold, silver stars overhead. Being so completely alone.

Ian Thompson lay in his hospital bed and wondered if he'd ever feel different. If he'd ever feel like he wasn't alone.

Glossary

5.56	Caliber of rifle round (in millimeters). Caliber for M4, M-16, AR-15, and many other US Military rifles.
7.62	Caliber of rifle round (in millimeters). Caliber for some high-powered rifles, including Marine M40 sniper rifles.
A-10	US military ground-attack aircraft. Official name: A-10 Thunderbolt II. Affectionate nickname: "Warthog." The ugliest US military aircraft, and most beloved by foot soldiers. Excellent close-support aircraft, armed with a very large 30mm cannon and lots of missiles and bombs.
AK	Russian assault rifle. Usually short for "AK-74," descendant of the original AK-47.
AK-74	Russian assault rifle. 5.45mm caliber.
Allahu Akbar	Arabic for "God is great." Popular battle cry among Islamic militants.

Ballistic Plates Metal or ceramic armor plates, inserted into **Scalable Plate Carrier** for additional protection. Will stop most projectiles up to and including military rifle rounds.

BDU Short for "battle dress uniform." Standard US military field uniform, emphasizing camouflage and utility.

Blackhawk US military transport helicopter.

Bone US military slang for the B1 (B-ONE) bomber, a high-altitude heavy bomber. Descendant of the Vietnam-era B52.

Boot Camp US military basic training. An unpleasant time in every recruit's life.

Burka Traditional female garb worn in the Middle East. Full-body dress and veil which leaves the wearer completely concealed from view.

Corpsman Naval medical personnel, attached to a Marine unit as a medic.

E-tool Short for "excavation tool." US military folding shovel.

Exfil Short for "exfiltration." Sneaking away from an area. The opposite of infiltration.

FOB Short for "forward operating base." US military forward outpost.

Frag Short for "fragmentation grenade." Hand-held anti-personnel explosive meant to be thrown.

Full-bird US military slang term for a Colonel. Reference to their eagle insignia.

GI Short for "general issue." US military slang term for an infantryman.

Hajji US military slang term for Islamic militant. Referencing the hajj, the pilgrimage to Mecca which every Muslim is supposed to undertake at least once.

Humvee Phonetic spelling of HMMV (High Mobility Military Vehicle). Four-wheeled military transport and scout vehicle. Descendant of the Jeep.

ILBE Short for "improved load bearing equipment." External harness for US Marine uniform, with an array of straps and pouches for carrying gear. Worn over **BDUs**.

Kandahar Province of Afghanistan, noted for strong anti-American sentiment and strong Taliban presence.

K-Bar	Marine combat knife.
Klick	US military slang for "kilometer."
Landstuhl	Landstuhl Regional Medical Center, in Ramstein, Germany. Main destination for those significantly wounded in the US Military while serving in Afghanistan or Iraq.
Mag	Short for "magazine." A removable spring-loaded box holding ammunition for a gun.
M4	US military standard-issue assault rifle. **5.56mm** caliber. Descendant of the M-16. Has a capacity of 30 rounds.
M9	US military standard-issue pistol. 9mm caliber. Has a capacity of 15 rounds.
Medevac	Short for "medical evacuation." Medical helicopter removing wounded personnel.
MRE	Short for "meal ready to eat." US military field ration, including a main course, side dish, dessert, and drink mix powder. The joke goes that the name is three lies in one.
Muj	Short for "mujaheddin." Afghan word meaning "freedom fighter." Derogatory slang used by US Military to refer to Afghan militants.

Op	Operation.
Pashto	The native language of Afghanistan.
PFC	Short for "private, first class." The second-lowest combat rank in the **USMC** or US Army, above Private and below Corporal.
Purple Heart	US military medal bestowed on personnel wounded in action. A purple heart-shaped medal with gold trim and a gold bust of George Washington. Ribbon is purple with white vertical stripes on either side. Originally a purple heart-shaped piece of velvet given to wounded members of George Washington's Continental Army during the American Revolution.
Quikclot	Hemostatic (hemostat) treatment for wounds. Aids in blood coagulation. Standard equipment in military and police first-aid kits.
RPG	Rocket-propelled grenade. Shoulder-launched explosive weapon.
Sandbox, The	US military slang for Iraq, or the Middle East in general.
SAR	Short for "search and rescue." Units sent to find and retrieve missing or wounded personnel.

Semper Fi Short for "semper fideles." Latin for "always faithful." The official motto of the **USMC.**

SERE Short for "survival, evasion, resistance, escape." US military survival training, including living in the wilderness, avoiding enemies, resisting interrogation, and escaping from prison facilities.

Scalable Plate Carrier US military Kevlar-weave body armor with pouches for inserting metal or ceramic plates for additional protection.

Semi-auto Short for "semi-automatic." A firearm that fires one bullet each time the trigger is pulled, until the gun is empty.

Silver Star Third-highest US military award for valor (after the Medal of Honor and Distinguished Service Cross). Awarded for gallantry in action against an enemy of the United States. A gold five-pointed star, 1.5" across, with a laurel wreath in the center around a 3/16" silver star. Inscribed on the reverse side FOR GALLANTRY IN ACTION. Ribbon is red, white, and blue vertical stripes (4 alternating blue and white stripes on either side of a red central stripe).

'Stan, The Short for Afghanistan. US military slang.

Stick of Butter US military slang for the gold-bar insignia of a First Lieutenant.

Talib US military slang for Taliban, Afghan militant. Interchangeable with **muj.**

Thermite Metal-powder explosive charge which burns extremely hot.

USMC Short for United States Marine Corps. The few, the proud.

Zero-Dark Hundred US military slang for "really, really early." From the military 24-hour clock, which refers to 3AM, for example, as "zero-three hundred" (0300).

About the Author

Steven Henry learned how to read almost before he learned how to walk. Ever since he began reading stories, he wanted to put his own on the page. He lives a very quiet and ordinary life in Minnesota with his wife and dog.

Also by Steven Henry

Ember of Dreams

The Clarion Chronicles, Book One

When magic awakens a long-forgotten folk, a noble lady, a young apprentice, and a solitary blacksmith band together to prevent war and seek understanding between humans and elves.

Lady Kristyn Tremayne – An otherwise unremarkable young lady's open heart and inquisitive mind reveal a hidden world of magic.

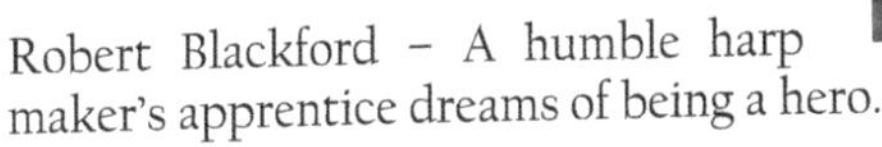

Robert Blackford – A humble harp maker's apprentice dreams of being a hero.

Master Gabriel Zane – A master blacksmith's pursuit of perfection leads him to craft an enchanted sword, drawing him out of his isolation and far from his cozy home.

Lord Luthor Carnarvon – A lonely nobleman with a dark past has won the heart of Kristyn's mother, but at what cost?

Readers love *Ember of Dreams*

"The more I got to know the characters, the more I liked them. The female lead in particular is a treat to accompany on her journey from ordinary to extraordinary."

"The author's deep understanding of his protagonists' motivations and keen eye for psychological detail make Robert and his companions a likable and memorable cast."

Learn more at tinyurl.com/emberofdreams.

More great titles from Clickworks Press

www.clickworkspress.com

The Altered Wake

Megan Morgan

Amid growing unrest, a family secret and an ancient laboratory unleash long-hidden superhuman abilities. Now newly-promoted Sentinel Cameron Kardell must chase down a rogue superhuman who holds the key to the powers' origin: the greatest threat Cotarion has seen in centuries – and Cam's best friend.

"Incredible. Starts out gripping and keeps getting better."

Learn more at clickworkspress.com/sentinel1.

Hubris Towers: The Complete First Season

Ben Y. Faroe & Bill Hoard

Comedy of manners meets comedy of errors in a new series for fans of Fawlty Towers and P. G. Wodehouse.

"So funny and endearing"

"Had me laughing so hard that I had to put it down to catch my breath"

"Astoundingly, outrageously funny!"

Learn more at clickworkspress.com/hts01.

Death's Dream Kingdom

Gabriel Blanchard

A young woman of Victorian London has been transformed into a vampire. Can she survive the world of the immortal dead—or perhaps, escape it?

"The wit and humor are as Victorian as the setting... a winsomely vulnerable and tremendously crafted work of art."

"A dramatic, engaging novel which explores themes of death, love, damnation, and redemption."

Learn more at clickworkspress.com/ddk.

Share the love!

Join our microlending team at
kiva.org/team/clickworkspress.

Keep in touch!

Join the Clickworks Press email list
and get freebies, production updates, special deals,
behind-the-scenes sneak peeks, and more.

Sign up today at clickworkspress.com/join.

Printed in the USA
CPSIA information can be obtained
at www.ICGtesting.com
LVHW041729170923
758449LV00044B/768